# Tides of Fate

Stephen Donoghue

AOS Publishing, 2025

Copyright © 2025



ISBN: 978-1-998662-96-8

Cover Design: Meredith Lindsay

Visit AOS Publishing's website:
www.aospublishing.com

Death is softer by far than tyranny.
- Aeschylus

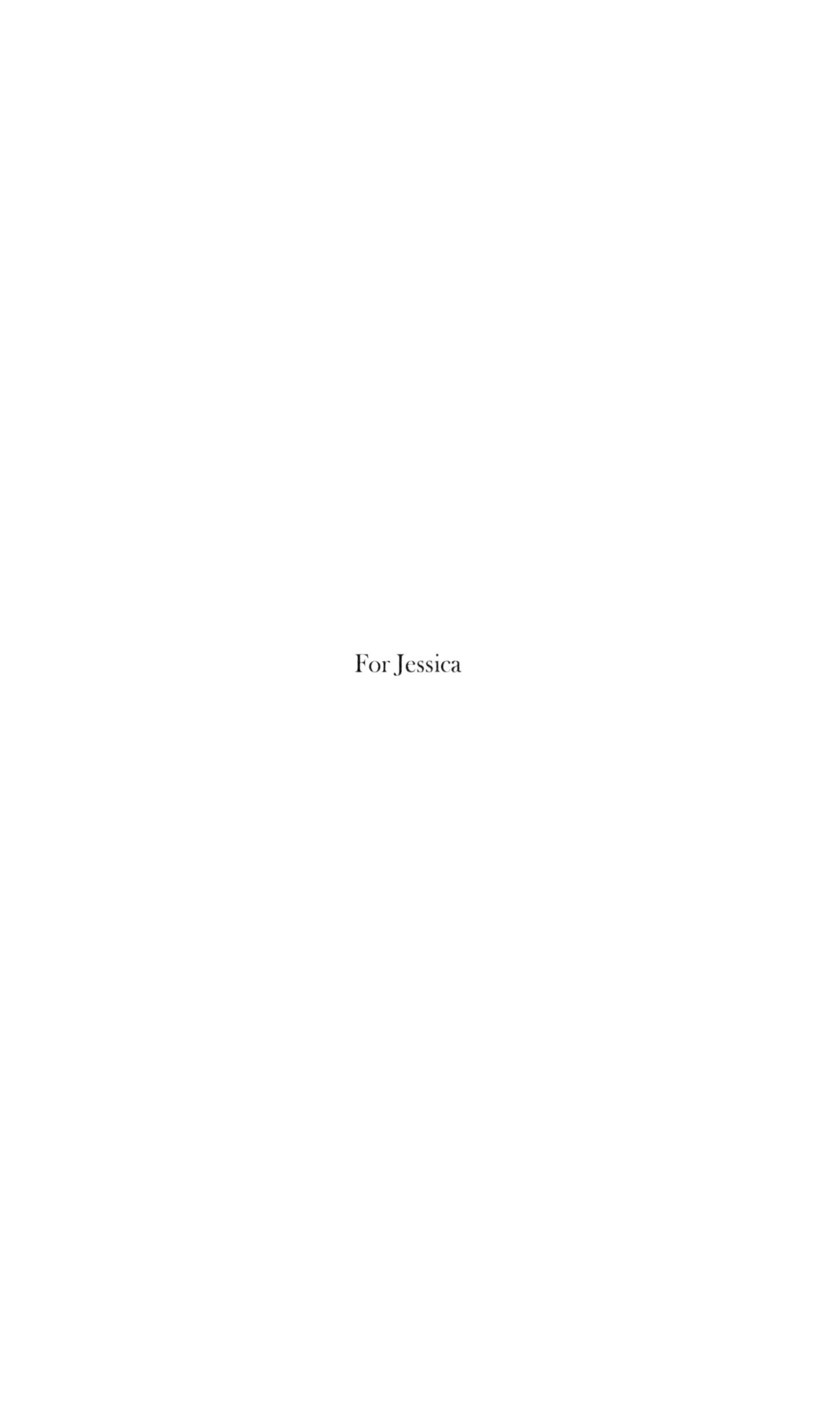

For Jessica

# London, May 1941

Rafe sensed light at the surface and pulled hard, clawing his path skyward through the freezing sea. Again and again he surged up, only to be pulled further into the darkness. Something vast and heavy was snagged on him, dragging him down into the abyss. Rafe's lungs spasmed in outrage. His body would betray him at this point, he felt it coming; his face surely would soon gape open, and in a great convulsion, would suck the deathly cold saltwater into his chest. Oblivion beckoned, and Rafe was near the final surrender. With a final, desperate frenzy, he forced himself upward into the light.

Gasping, Rafe sat bolt upright, half-pitching himself off the bed. His lungs greedily drank in the stale air while his body shivered, despite the warmth in the room (the lights and gas fire had been left on overnight and the air was fervid). The sensation of drowning subsided as the terror melted away. Wearily, he took in the scene around him: the weak dawn light played tricks with his eyes . . . he saw strange hunched shapes scattered around the floor.

At first, he thought he was in his childhood bedroom, the shapes his scattered toys and books, and gradually his frantic mind began to make sense of the scene: his own dinner jacket discarded on the parquet floor, a women's undergarments next to it, the lingering odour of stale cigar smoke and gin. A warm body rolled over and pushed him further still across the rumpled bed towards the floor.

"Molly," he groaned, "you wicked child." Rafe swung his legs off the mattress and stood gingerly. Despite a rather stuffy head and dry mouth, the nightmare was forgotten, replaced with a surge of excitement.

Unsteadily, he tiptoed around the discarded ashtrays and wine bottles to the bathroom, where he relieved himself noisily into the pan. There was another casualty in the bath, in full RAF dress uniform and empty Seagers bottle clutched to his chest. Rafe set out his shaving kit and daubed a steaming hot washcloth over his face. There was a long feminine groan from the bedroom.

"Rafe, dear," Molly's voice was raw and a few octaves lower than usual. "Could you please shoot me? It would be a mercy killing."

"Not today, duckie," he said, painting shaving soap over his chin. "I'm back on flight duty today, remember?"

"Oh, yes, I recall now"-she paused to light a cigarette. "that little celebration got out of hand quickly."

From the look of the dining room, it had, indeed: broken crystal glasses and piles of gramophone discs littered the wool carpets. Molly's cat, Henry, licked the last of the salmon mousse from a silver dish on the windowsill. The well-appointed Cambridge apartment this morning smelled like a dockyard tavern.

Rafe set out his wash cloth and shaving kit, combed out his luxurious black moustache and winked at himself in the mirror. His shiner from last weekend's brawl had faded to a pale yellow smudge under his eye. He hoped his CO wouldn't notice it.

Freshly shaven, Rafe Padded barefoot into the kitchenette. He threw together a morning-after cocktail of two raw eggs, tomato juice, and a generous lashing of Worcestershire sauce. He downed half in one go as he weaved back into the bedroom. Molly looked a fright: her styled hair was a rat's nest and her bright red lipstick was smeared across her chin. She took the glass off him and gulped it down in three rings. His long-time friend always amazed him with her stamina and capacity for drink. She could put most of his service chums under the table . . . case in point: Second Lieutenant Mitchell in the bath.

"Oh, Rafe, my dearest ... don't go back, please." She pouted theatrically but there was  real concern in her eyes. "You could get yourself killed for nothing. Papa says the Americans will be here next year, then the shits will all fuck off back to Berlin with their tails between their legs." Her plummy school-girl tongue made the curses obscene.

Rafe threw her his best charming grin. "You know I can't pass this up, duckie. I'm bored shitless at Hatfield and Old Beckett is going to reinstate me as  Flight Officer for sure." Rafe shrugged on his uniform jacket and assessed his profile in the dress mirror.

"Yes, I know, Rafy, but we will miss you so." Molly sulked out the window at the rain soaked street. "At least let me have Taylor take you in the Rolls. It's raining stair rods out there."

"Nonsense, just a light sprinkle," he said, stepping into his riding boots. "Anyway, I need a blast of fresh air . . . helps clear my head." He bent and kissed her forehead. She looked up at him with that poor little rich girl face that drove most men into fits of penitence. "Look, duckie, if I make it through the war with my jewels intact, I shall come home and make you my wife."

Her pale pixie face crinkled into disgust. "Ew. Papa would never let me marry an Irishman."


Rafe thundered down the stairs and into the courtyard. Taylor was there to meet him with his shirtsleeves rolled up, wiping his greasy hands on an equally greasy rag.

"She's all shipshape, sir. I've adjusted the carburettor and she should run out to the ton now."

Rafe gazed lovingly at his machine. She was a $21^{st}$ birthday present from his father last year and he rode it at the slightest excuse. A brand new BSA Gold Star 500 motorcycle, her sculpted brightwork twinkled merrily in the morning sunshine. Taylor was obviously taken with her, too, since he had polished the steel tank to a mirror finish and the chain gleamed with fresh oil.

"Good man, Taylor!" Rafe dropped to a conspiratorial whisper as he put an arm around his shoulder. "See here, my good man—after I leave here, I want you to take Molly straight back to her mother's in Shropshire."

They both looked up to the window, where she stood in the frame with Henry in her arms and waved. Rafe spoke behind his cheerful grin. "Don't want any of those young London hounds sniffing around our spring lambs do we?"

"Not a bit of it, sir." Taylor puffed up and his head tilted back. "There will be none of that carry on around here."

"Good, good, glad to hear it." Rafe swung his leg over the bike and settled himself into the soft leather saddle. The big single-cylinder engine burst into life on the second kick, emitting a sharp bark and settling into a steady baritone beat.

Taylor shouted over the noise, "You give those Hun bastards a good biffing for us, sir!"

"I shall do my best, Taylor!" Rafe shouted back, fitting his goggles over his face. He twisted around to see Molly leaning out the window waving a handkerchief up and down like a lady offering her favour to a joust. Rafe spun the bike around and caught it as it floated down. He held it up with a flourish, tucked it into his collar, and gunned out the gates at speed.

The city was sleepily coming to life around him as he motored through the damp streets. Gangs of volunteer workers still laboured over piles of masonry and the charred carcasses of timber roof frames, and the people went about their usual business with something of a weight lifted off their weary shoulders. The crisis was over, for the moment. Although there were occasional air raid sirens, the Luftwaffe had mostly turned its back on England and looked eastwards. People in the street who noticed Rafe's uniform smiled warmly. A traffic conductor stopped a line of ash lorries for him and waved him through with a nod and a wink. Rafe had missed the attention the tailored blue woollen suit had afforded him. The nation had narrowly avoided invasion, largely thanks to the RAF, and the prime minister had even given a rousing sermon saying as much.

The foetid funk of war still haunted the East End, especially on days like this when the wind drifted across the river, bringing with it acrid odours of scorched timber and sulphurous High Explosive residue.

Rafe was spared the worst of it in the cockpit of a Hurricane hunting the Luftwaffe. Wave after wave of bombers and their fighter escorts crossed the Channel to pound the nation into submission. For Rafe and his brethren it seemed like great sport, and in the beginning it was, with swarms of heavy bombers flying slow and level, easy prey for the fighter squadrons. As the attacks intensified, the sport soon became a desperate fight for survival, as the Luftwaffe attacked airfields to destroy RAF fighter command. In the last week of September, forty pilots were flying thirty-hour shifts (many falling to sheer exhaustion) and hastily-trained recruits took their place, adding to the butcher's bill. Only when Hitler and Göring changed the focus down to London were the pilots of fighter command given reprieve.

Coming out of the city traffic, the roads opened up and Rafe had time to think. Apparitions from the past had been unwelcome companions lately, and being idle had brought out the worst of Rafe's vices: the drinking, cards, and women he took up to chase the ghosts away. Now, he looked forward to putting these aside and focusing on flying again. His thoughts turned to what lay ahead, savouring the prospect of a new breed of offensive machinery, perhaps a Spitfire squadron, bringing the fight to the enemy this time. He had heard stories in the club about attack sorties across the channel, real aggression! The thought made him giddy with excitement. He could redeem himself, regain the esteem of his friends and his father.

Rafe suddenly realised he had been riding for over an hour. He shook himself as though waking from a reverie; the ghost had him under its spell, and Rafe knew one sure to break it.

He was well familiar with this route from London to the airfield, and he knew a good mile stretch of new seal lay ahead. He reached down to the brass lever by his knee and turned it to full rich. The motor sputtered and fired into a new ferocity, twisting the throttle wide open, and the machine surged forward and pitched up, lifting its front wheel clear off the road. Rafe snapped the throttle closed, and there was a fearsome crackle and series of pistol cracks as a footlong flame burst out of the pipes.

The overnight rain had left the surface slick and treacherously greasy. A long left-hand curve led to the straight as the road turned to join the railway line. Rafe knew he would have no chance of hitting the magic ton of one hundred miles per hour if he didn't exit this bend better than forty. He sat up in the saddle and carefully controlled the lean of the bike around the gently-cambered curve. At the apex, he slowly opened the taps, and the rear wheel spun and fishtailed wildly under his hips. Rafe straightened up and tucked in behind the bars, and he let her have her head. The speed rose steadily as he kicked her through the gears with a flick of his left boot; the wind blast rose to a deafening howl around his ears and a tall rooster tail of spray flew high in his wake.

Rafe glanced down to the violently oscillating smiths instrument as the needle swept around to eighty. His head was buffeted mercilessly and his vision blurred; the machine skipped and danced over the uneven surface as it kicked into the fourth and final gear. Rafe tucked in even lower, hugging the tank with his elbows and knees until only his eyes and the top of his head peeked over the handlebars. The end of the straight was looming. He realised with horror that he had just flashed past the phone box on his left—his self-imposed braking marker to slow down in time to take the turn.

Rafe cursed ruefully and sat bolt upright to apply his body as an air brake; immediately the rear wheel began to slide, and he modulated between front and rear brakes. He knew by experience that if he locked the front wheel, he would lose control. He began shunting down the gears, desperately trying to control the sliding bike as it weaved around on the wet tarmac. The stone wall grew to fill his entire range of vision, time seemed to slow to a crawl, and he could see every tiny detail of the solid black mass as he charged helplessly to what could only mean a certain death. His only chance was to ditch the bike in a low side slide and friction with the road surface to slow him enough to survive the impact. He grimaced as he locked the rear tyre and leaned into the slide, kicking the bike away from his body with all his strength. He landed on his backside; the slick road saved him from most of the pain of wicked abrasion.

He instinctively spread his arms wide and came up on his heavy leather gauntlets, sliding on gloves and boots to preserve his largely unprotected posterior, while ahead of him the doomed machine caught the edge of its foot peg and launched into a savage series of spins and cartwheels. It bounced and spun down the roadway, flinging sprays of oil, shards of twisted and tortured steel, and bright orange sparks, with a tremendous crash like a eight-pounder gun. The bike exploded in a cloud of white-hot gas and fuel. Rafe was not far behind, and he slammed into the stone wall, feet first, using his legs as a levered spring to absorb the worst of the collision. Still, the breath was bashed out of him, and a great shuddering blow ran up his spine and to his skull. There was a flash of white light in his head and he came to a stop.

Rafe was dimly aware of the heat on his sleeve. His vision cleared enough to see the  blue sky above through flashing points of light. As the world came back into sharp focus, it occurred to Rafe that he was on fire and he would be best to do something about it. He rolled lazily over and over across the wet turf until the flames were out, then did a quick check of all his vital equipment. Despite a nasty rash on his backside and a cracked tooth, it seemed he had come out alive. He sighed and fished for a cigarette in his jacket pocket.

"Jesus Christ, man!" a thickly Yorkshire-accented voice said. "You're one lucky bastard." A broad, swarthy face appeared above him. Rafe held up his hand and the shepherd helped him to his feet. Rafe gazed sadly towards the flaming wreck of his beloved machine.

"I thought the bloody Nazi were attacking—the rate O knot you come down that hill."

He saw the shepherd was driving a sulky, half full of milk kegs.

"I don't suppose you could give me a lift to the airfield, could you?"

Rafe walked the last quarter of a mile to the huddle of barrel buildings and hangars that housed 11 Squadron. There was an eerie quiet surrounding the place. Last time he was here, the field was humming with the nervous energy of an air force at war. The guardsman at the gate barely looked up from his copy of *Punch* to wave him though.

Rafe limped to the officers' mess and peeked in the door. It was deserted, bar a single pilot officer snoring in a wooden rocking chair. Just twelve months ago, this room would have accommodated an unruly mob of British, Canadian, Australian, and Polish fighter pilots on combat duty: jazz blasting on the wireless, a noisy poker game in one corner, an equally raucous game of gin rummy in the other, blue haze of cigarette smoke so thick one could scarcely make out the ceiling. "Where the blazes is everyone?" Rafe thought aloud. Nobody answered.

Walking over to the OPS building, he was met at the door by a fresh-faced young adjunct in a well-tailored women's auxiliary uniform.

"Flight Officer Rafael O'Rourke reporting for briefing," he said, handing over his rather tatty order sheet.

Before she could read it over, a familiar booming voice sounded from across the hangar bay. "You are late, Rourke." The voice's owner was obscured by the corner of the building. There was a swoosh and sharp whack of a driving iron and a golf ball shot out across the field almost to the horizon. It was followed immediately by a flash of white as a speeding Jack Russell raced to fetch it. Squadron Commander Beckett strode out from his tee spot. He was a good two heads taller than Rafe and thin as a whip. His braces held his uniform slacks almost up to Rafe's eyeline. Rafe set his face solid and looked straight ahead as he saluted stiffly.

"Apologies, sir. Slight problem with my transport, sir."

"Yes, indeed." Beckett circled Rafe like a cruising shark to appraise his scorched jacket and shredded trousers.

"Did you slide over from London on your backside, O'Rourke?"

"Just some of the way, sir."

The female officer stifled a giggle.

"Don't try to be funny, O'Rourke. You're on thin ice as it is." Beckett obviously held Rafe in low esteem since his fall from grace last summer. He narrowed his icy blue eyes and pursed his lips. He had a tall face and a long hooked nose that resembled the beak of a bird of prey, and his stature allowed him to hover over his men like a hunting falcon, peering down his long face with paternal disapproval.

"You may have noticed things have changed around here. No. 145 Squadron are down in Plymouth, embarking for Cairo. You won't be joining them." Rafe felt a plunging slide of disappointment in his guts.

"Sir, I have arranged to meet old George, my batman, here tomorrow. He's bringing all my–".

"No time for all that bloody rot, Rourke," Beckett interrupted. "You'll be in operations tonight. We have a special assignment for you, something we couldn't spare our regulars for."

Beckett pulled a battered hunter watch out of his trouser pocket. "Get yourself cleaned up and meet me at the ops room in ten minutes. Kate here will escort you to the quartermaster to get you fitted out."

Rafe sat outside Beckett's office trying to make out muffled telephone conversations behind the door. His mind was turning over the possibilities: *Why was the airfield all but deserted?* That was obvious, really: the threat of invasion was gone, so the real battles were being fought elsewhere, but what was he doing here? Now he realised what a fool he'd been: the war had moved on, and the strategic situation had changed. He realised he was wringing his gloves in his fists like an old maid.

Abruptly, the phone slammed down on its receiver and Beckett's booming voice rang out from behind the door. "Come in, Rourke!" Rafe jumped out of his seat and his pulse thudded in his ears as he poked his head around the door. Beckett was sitting behind his desk, packing his pipe. "Come in, come in, sit down, we haven't got all bloody afternoon." He gestured to the small wooden chair with his chin. Rafe sat on the little chair and quite suddenly felt like a schoolboy in the headmaster's office. The room was sparsely furnished in a very masculine manner. A portrait of the King hung on the far wall, glowering malevolently between Beckett's golfing trophies, while a grandfather clock ticked in the corner, and the air was pungent with tobacco and dog hair.

Beckett was framed by a large bay window that looked over the hangar block; the afternoon sunlight silhouetted him so his face was hard to read. He struck a match with his thumb and regarded Rafe over his pipe. He seemed to be building himself up to do something repugnant. "You're a fair pilot, Rourke, and a good shot," Beckett paused and drew on his pipe until it burned evenly. "But you're an awful shit. If it wasn't for your father's influence at fighter command, you'd have been court-martialled and shot for that little performance last year."

A warm flush of blood rose to Rafe's face as he recalled the incident. It was New Year's Eve 1940; he and a group of his friends had become overly *refreshed* on the regimental 'special punch' served at the officer's mess, and thought it would be a grand lark to take a staff car on a ride around the perimeter fence. Rafe was driving and pushing the little Austin to her top speed when she hit a drain ditch and rolled. Poor old 'Chalky' Davis was hanging out the back window at the time and crushed his shoulder. Chalky joked about it afterwards and credited Rafe with excusing him from the rest of the war, but he never regained full use of his arm and never flew again.

Beckett sighed and his face softened a little as he gazed out the window, "Look here, Rourke, we are all sorry about that rotten bloody business with your wife." Rafe stiffened at the mention of his wife and felt his hackles rise uncomfortably. "We are at war, Rourke, and we simply must put our personal feelings aside and act responsibly." He picked up the phone receiver and dialled out. "Kate...Bring me the operation file and tea, please...and ah, send Thompson in when he arrives, will you? Good girl." He hung up and stood facing out towards the field, clasping his hands behind his back and rolling on the balls of his feet. "All our current personnel are tied up in Malta for the foreseeable, and what little we do have we need for defence in case Göring decides to have another poke. I understand you have been flying with De Havilland over the winter."

"Yes, sir. Ferry and speed test mostly." Rafe had spent time test-flying up at Herefordshire, mostly the experimental DH.98 prototype for speed trials.

"Well, you must have impressed somebody there, because you have been recommended for operations." Rafe smiled inwardly. *Good old Young Dee-Ache!* he thought.

"We need a steady hand here, and with your night vision score and your hours on the Mossie, you're it." Rafe frowned at the carpet. "Sorry, sir... Mossie?" At that moment, Kate walked in carrying a tray with a steaming pot of tea and a few grey-looking scones. She set a thick Manila folder down in front of Beckett and poured tea into chipped tin mugs.

"The DH.98, Rourke... it's been operational since March," Beckett explained. Things were beginning to make sense now. With all hands on pumps down in the Mediterranean, they hadn't time to rate pilots for the new aircraft, so this sortie had come up and Young D.H. had fingered Rafe. He was astounded that high command had chosen to fly the 98; it was a radical design, a completely unarmed bomber that relied on outright speed to escape fighters with a lightweight construction using bonded pine and spruce laminates in place of scarce aluminium. Despite jokes about wings snapping off and furniture polish, the test pilots quickly realised that the airframe had far more potential than that of just a bomber. Rafe himself had cracked three hundred and seventy knots in level flight.

Beckett moved the tray aside and spread a technical drawing of the new configuration over the desk. Rafe nodded approvingly. The design always made him think of two Spitfires in a freak Siamese birth. She had a standard single boom tail arrangement and shoulder mounted wings with two enormous Merlin engines mounted close to the fuselage; things had changed considerably since his last encounter. She was a fighter now, and one with a heavy punch. The drawing showed four Hispano 30mm cannons under the cabin and four Browning .50 calibre guns in the nose, ordinance enough to shred any enemy aircraft to flaming confetti. The forward windscreen had been replaced by an armoured unit, and more armour plating had been added to the aft bulkhead. The twin Merlin engines were fitted with the latest dual stage superchargers. She should have been good for four hundred knots now, maybe even more. Most of the bomb compartment had been filled with ammunition, but there were some puzzling structures that Rafe had never seen before: a projecting instrument that looked like the skeleton of a fish on the nose and a bank of rectangular objects under the cockpit. "This, Rourke..." Beckett tapped the blueprints with his pipe. "Is the DH.98 NF Mk II; the apparatus you see is an Aircraft Interception array, the first of its kind, in fact." He thrust his chin out proudly. "It is designed to allow us to operate in total darkness, to track down and destroy the enemy under the cover of night."

"Good lord, how in the dickens does it do that?" Rafe was doubtful.

"I have no idea," Beckett admitted. "Some of our boffin friends across the Atlantic came up with it."

As if on a stage cue, there was a crash of dropped objects followed by a string of expletives and apologies. A small, flustered man backed hurriedly in through the doorway, bowing under a pile of scientific equipment and boxes of documentation. "We've got the battery packs working again. If we keep them dry, we should be up and running tonight." He dropped his burden untidily on the desk and turned to Rafe. "Ah, our pilot's here."" He offered his hand. "PO Thompson, MIT." He had a rich Californian accent and a friendly tanned face. He looked like he had barely started shaving. "O'Rourke," Rafe replied, pumping the man's hand.

"Thompson here will serve as navigator and operate the interception equipment. He's from the research labs in Massachusetts," said Beckett.

"Pleased to meet you, Mr. O'Rourke." Thompson grinned, revealing a mouth full of bright white teeth. Rafe found his hand was now smeared with oil and kerosene. "Right!" Beckett stalked out the door. "Let's get to the ops room for the briefing, then."

As the three men walked, Rafe lit himself a cigarette and found his hands were trembling with excitement. "How does this interception stuff work, Thompson?, I mean... is it tested?"

"Yessir, we've been chasing each other's tails up and down the country for a month now. The concept is proven, it just hasn't been used in combat yet. It works just like your Chain Home defence network, but miniaturised to fit an attack aircraft." Rafe understood the Chain Home equipment well enough; miraculously, the radio masts constructed along the coastline allowed fighter command to 'see' across the Channel, pinpointing the position and altitude of the attacking waves of bombers. When they were detected, the interceptors on standby were scrambled and directed to the targets by ground control. The techniques were still top secret and speculation was discouraged by command. "Radio waves?" Rafe asked.

"Yes, something like that," Thompson replied thoughtfully

"So we can see the blighters in the dark... like a cat..."

"Well, more like a bat, really." Thompson's blue eyes sparkled with enthusiasm. "You see, bats find their prey in darkness by sending out waves of sound that bounce back, like an echo." His slim hands gestured the action. "We do much the same thing, with pulses of energy."

Rafe began to warm to the idea. "If you can find them in the dark, I'll be happy to send them to hell for you."

The ops room was empty, save for the Met officer updating the weather board. The flight roster was empty and the switchboard was unattended. A large octagonal table dominated the centre of the room with a chart of the Channel and Western Europe. Rafe's first impressions were of a simple fighter sweep: cross the Channel, head southwards across coastal France, turn north towards Holland, then return to Rochford at 0800 for breakfast. Rafe had to swallow his disappointment: he was hoping for a specific target to attack.

Beckett began outlining the flight plan and charting the waypoints. Thompson seemed flustered and kept consulting a handbook while furiously scribbling notes.

"You are to fly low and level once you cross the Channel line at around eight hundred feet. Thompson will operate the AI set and call out height and bearing to close. If you make contact, establish a visual and then disengage." Beckett leaned forward and held Rafe in his witheringly icy glare. "Under no circumstances are you to engage with the enemy. This is a test flight; make visual confirmation and get out of it. Am I clear, Rourke?" Rafe was incensed. "What's the bloody point of this thing if we don't..." Beckett stopped him with a raised hand. "This is a classified piece of equipment. We can't run the risk of it falling into enemy hands. Furthermore, if you are shot down over occupied territory, you must destroy the AI unit and aircraft. There is a demolition kit in the inventory." Rafe bravely fought off a nasty attack of the vapours. Eight guns and no firing allowed. He was merely to fly this little egghead and his radio set around in the dark. "Any questions?" Beckett asked rhetorically. "Good, take-off at 1800, that's in two hours. Meet Chief Engineer Radcliffe outside Hangar Two in fifteen minutes. Good luck, gentlemen."

The massive hangar was unoccupied, except for a small circle of men in boiler suits smoking and arguing spiritedly. A very short man in the centre gesticulated as if acting out a bizarre pantomime. He spotted Rafe and pushed through the throng to meet him. "Flash suppression!" he shouted. "Ever fired a twenty-mm cannon at night, Rourke?" He didn't wait for an answer. "Blinding white fucking flash like the second coming of Christ!" This elicited a round of guffaws from his mechanics. He had a coarse Antipodean accent and the florid complexion of a dedicated whiskey drinker. They shook hands warmly. "So they finally let you back in the club, eh Paddy?" Radcliffe was the powerhouse behind 32 Squadron. The Kiwi was a God-gifted mechanical engineer and a master of improvisation, and he loved his aircraft like his very own infant children. You would be lambasted in the most colourful language if you landed hard or overheated an engine, and God help you if you received any battle damage. "I suppose they finally came to their senses. Where's this bird I'm taking out tonight, then?"

"Follow me, Paddy, she's out here getting her guns seen to."

Silhouetted against the russet afternoon sky like a great black crucifix, the aircraft was quite different to how he recalled her. Bereft of any identification markings, she was doped completely in funereal black, her wings spread wide like a great angel of death. A team of mechanics had just finished welding shrouds over the cannon muzzles. "Without those, you'll be blind up there. Those explosive rounds burn white like magnesium."

"We won't be needing them tonight. This is a field test of the AI set," Thompson observed.

"So I hear... just in case, then." Radcliffe winked wickedly at Rafe." Defensively, you know."

They clambered untidily up into the tiny cockpit through an aperture below the fuselage. Radcliffe stood on the wing root and gestured through the open canopy. "All the flight controls are how you will remember; the only difference is the landing lights and gunnery, and of course, the interception equipment." The cabin was filled with the pleasant scent of freshly sawn spruce and mineral oil. Every instrument was brand new, fresh, and crystal clear.

Rafe flushed with pleasure: this was his element. Thompson folded himself into the navigator's seat. He had two box-like imaging scopes in front of him, and they were peppered with switches and dials that he constantly adjusted. He pulled a pair of spectacles out of his shirt pocket and pulled them over his ears. They were almost an inch thick. Rafe and Radcliffe exchanged a quick glance of concern. "I say, Thompson..." Rafe began.

"Call me Billy," he replied absently, not looking up from his work.

"When did you rate for the D.H98?" Billy froze for a second. His cheeks bloomed a deep puce.

"Er... last week, in fact..."

"This will be your first nav ops, then?"

"Yes er... indeed, it will." Billy's blue eyes were magnified to the size of sovereigns behind the deep lenses. "Is there a problem?"

#

Rafe had caught Beckett at an early supper. He listened to Rafe's monologue silently as he tucked into a plate of steak and kidney pie. "... this is his first time in the bloody thing, and, what's more, the boy is blind as a bat, so what happens if he loses his spectacles, eh? Shall we drop a trail of breadcrumbs to follow home?"

Beckett leaned back from his meal and dabbed his moustache primly with a napkin. He finished chewing his mouthful leisurely. "Look here, Rourke, fighter command wants this interception business proven before committing resources to it." He struck a match with his thumb and puffed on his pipe thoughtfully.

"All our Nav boys are being re-trained in Suffolk and we have no one to spare for this operation." He produced an officious-looking document from his desk drawer and passed it over to Rafe. "Thompson has been given special dispensation by the doctor to serve as navigator for this flight." Rafe gave the sheet of typewritten paper a brief once-over. It mentioned something about completing a coastal navigation exercise with vision aids. "Fact is, Rourke... he is the only man in the country who can interpret those blasted instruments." Beckett was losing patience quickly. "Look, man, just take him up, and once he thinks he's seen something in his crystal ball, turn about and head straight back, and with any luck you'll be home in time for a pie and a pint down at the Lionshead."

The sun was setting fast as they completed the final pre-flight checklist. Rafe pulled his pistol out of his thigh holster again to check that the magazine was full—it was an American Remington .45 automatic; he had swapped it for his Webley revolver with a Canadian who wanted a souvenir. It was a fearsome weapon, firing a slow fat round that could stop a train. Radcliffe appeared by the hatch. "You'd best put your toys away now, Paddy." Radcliffe's breath had more than a hint of Chivas Regal on it. "Time to go lift some French skirts." He took Rafe's cigarette and popped it into his own mouth before he secured the canopy. Billy had the systems checklist on his lap and had already broken two pencils crossing off the stages. Rafe set the mixture and started the magnetos. There was a high-pitched hiss as the gyros spun up to speed behind the firewall. Rafe hit the starter switch for the port engine, the propeller spun lazily at first, and there was a reluctant mechanical whine until the engine caught spark and exploded into life. A great cloud of white smoke belched from the exhaust shroud and the whole plane shuddered like a giant bird shaking off sleep. Billy's face was set in a grey mask of fear. With both power plants lit, the noise was unholy, and Rafe gestured for Billy to plug in his headset as they taxied to the upwind run. "What crate did you train in, Billy?"

"Well-ing-tons, s-ir" Billy's voice was staccato as they bounced down the uneven field.

"Wimpys, eh?" Rafe smiled wolfishly. "I think you'll find this an animal of quite a different stripe."

Rafe eased the twin throttles forward and the mechanical cacophony rose to a skull-splitting crescendo as the machine surged across the field. Billy was thrown backwards and pinned against his seat as Rafe forced the stick into a thirty-degree climb. With the twin supercharged engines howling like dire wolves, the war plane pitched up and clawed for the heavens.

At one thousand feet, he levelled out of the climb and glanced across to Billy. The young man was flushed pink with adrenaline and his head swivelled about like a startled kitten, scanning the horizons for enemy fighters. He leapt almost out of his life jacket when Rafe called over the intercom.

"Vector to waypoint please, Nav."

Billy hurriedly consulted his compass and made a bearing on the chart in his lap. He mouthed something inaudible as Rafe gestured patiently to his mic in the mask. Billy's voice was very small as it crackled over the earphones. "Er... vector... one eight zero... height... one five zero"

"Roger that, Nav." Rafe dipped the port wing over and began a slow turn towards the coast.

Rafe revelled in the responsive feel of the controls. Airborne, he left his troubled mortal life on the earth. When he was in the sky he was deified, like a winged god, gazing down upon the trivial lives of lesser beings.

As they levelled out at five thousand feet, the patchwork quilt of rural England rushed beneath them, uneven squares of every shade of green and yellow. Farm workers rose from their labours to stare up at the strange plane, shielding their eyes from the sun with soil-caked hands. In the harsh red light of dusk, the cottages and villages looked like the toys of some giant child, peopled with diminutive animals and tiny men, vulnerable and helpless. The temperature dropped steadily. Rafe felt a frisson creep along his skin, an odd sense of foreboding descending upon him. The sky burned blood red, and across the sea, Europe churned in the storm of war.

A fat gibbous moon rose high in the spring sky, casting a cool icy light on the Channel waves. They kept well away from the coast, first heading south at one thousand feet, then turning north at barely tree-top height. The fortified coast of the continent squatted menacingly off their port wing. Rafe fancied that he could make out concrete bunkers and anti-aircraft batteries on the shore, waiting for them to stray within range. Göring had boasted about his Atlantic Wall. Rafe felt like winging over to have a poke at it, just to see its fearsome teeth.

After the sun had set to the west, Billy calmed somewhat and settled into his work. He was covered by a thick, black drape so as not to hamper Rafe's night vision, prompting Rafe to think of a Gypsy soothsayer in a traveller's caravan, looking for signs of portent in a glass ball. Billy muttered to himself and occasionally peeked out from under the curtain to take a compass bearing and call a heading. They flew on northwards at wave height, the turbulent air demanding Rafe's full attention so that his arms and legs ached as they approached the sandy dunes that marked the northern coast of Holland. "Vector, one eight zero... height one zero zero," Billy called the last waypoint. Rafe pushed the throttles up and began a climbing turn southwards on their final leg down the coast. "Not a sausage, then, Billy?" Rafe asked. "Not a what?" Billy answered distractedly from under his curtain.

"I said, no sport for us tonight, then?"

"Oh, yeah, well, I am getting a great deal of noise from the ground level. This higher azimuth could give us a clearer return signal."

Rafe levelled her out at one thousand feet and reached for the trim wheel. At this height, he could adjust the elevators so she would fly level and give his aching limbs some rest.

"Coffee?" he suggested.

"No, thanks."

Rafe shrugged and rummaged through his kit bag to find the thermos of strong sugared black coffee. Gingerly, he reached into his flight suit and produced a slim silver flask. He poured a generous slug of scotch into his cup and held up a toast. 'To the gods of war! " He knocked the sweet aromatic mixture down and immediately poured another; this time he savoured the mouthful and sighed as combined effects of caffeine, sugar, and alcohol made his blood sing. They were down to their last five hundred pounds of fuel and on the home stretch. Rafe was resigned to the night being just another test flight. Whatever potential that device promised, it had failed to produce any results. Rafe leaned back and poured another drink.

"Contact!" Billy shouted gleefully under his curtain. Rafe dropped his coffee cup and grabbed the control stick. "Heading?" he demanded.

"Standby... er... shit...hang on."

Rafe felt his pulse rise and thunder in his head.

"Four two four... height three zero zero." Rafe kicked the rudder and turned out to sea. He knew from the tactics brief to approach from beneath the target, using the brighter sky as a backdrop. "What's the range, Billy? What's their vector?"

"They're heading east... about eight zero miles south of us... strong profile... they must be... a formation," Billy's voice trembled. "I'll give you an intercept vector at interval."

The moon was setting behind them, casting a spectral blue light on the cloud front to the south, which would provide an excellent field on which to pick out enemy aircraft. Billy called a vector every forty-five seconds and Rafe formed a mental image of the formation's direction and speed. They must have been bombers returning from a night raid in England. He felt his blood flame, and a deep bitter anger gripped him, a wave of heat rushing up from his gut and flushing his face.

The range shrank steadily... five miles... then three... two. Rafe's eyes were the best in the Squadron and they served him well here: first, a tiny speck, small enough to be a fleck of grit on the glass. Then it gradually took form: the edges of a wing, the bulge of a wheel. "I see them." Rafe half-smiled, half-grimaced.

"What? Visual?" said Billy as he threw off the drape and peered myopically through his glasses. After staring at the glow of the monitor all night he saw nothing but green blobs pulsing in the darkness. "Where?"

"Eleven o'clock high." Rafe pointed with his chin. "Stukas, five of the bastards." The dark shapes grew and coalesced, silhouetting against the cloud bank. It was a flight of five Ju 87s. Stuka, the most feared and hated flying machine in all Europe, and Rafe knew the type well: inverted Gull wing frame, fixed streamlined undercarriage, Spandau machine gun jutting from the aft cabin. The lethal dive bombers mercilessly pounded the BEF to dust at Dunkirk. Rafe felt his hate squirm in his guts. "Visual confirmation, we've done it!" Billy gleefully began entering the contact in his log. "0235. Five enemy aircraft tracked and visual confirmed by FO Rourke!."

"Arm the weapons, please, Nav," Rafe said matter-of-factly over the com, and there was a long pause.

"Sorry say again, pilot."

"Repeat, arm all weapons, please." Rafe eased the throttles up and gently pushed the stick forward; the plane pitched down and accelerated.

"Er...that's a negative; we are instructed to make visual only... no engagements."

"I bloody know what we were instructed to do, now arm the weapons, please."

The two men locked eyes across the cabin.

"You've been drinking, sir," said Billy timidly.

"Look here, Pilot Officer Thompson, am I in charge of this flight?"

"... Well, yes... but Beckett was quite clear about that..."

"Sod Beckett! You wanted to find the enemy, now there he bloody is!" Rafe jabbed his thumb out across the closing gap. He had turned right angles to the target and was positioning the Mosquito for an attack run. "I'll be damned if I let these smug Nazi pricks sail off after hitting our boys at home." Rafe reached down between Billy's legs and flicked open the two circuit breakers that powered the guns. In the same movement, he leaned forward and wound up the projected gunsight. "Jesus, sir... Beckett will have your head on a stake... my head... I'll be sent home!"

Rafe craned his neck around and judged the timing carefully. When the enemy formation reached the last strut on the canopy, he stamped on the left rudder and pulled the stick hard to port. The Mosquito banked sharply until the port wing pointed directly at the sea. There was a loud clatter as the contents of the cabin (pencils, rulers, and callipers) scuttled across the steel floor. Billy clutched the scope monitor to prevent it from landing in Rafe's lap.

The Mosquito creaked and shuddered in protest at the violent manoeuvre. Rafe tipped her nose down and shoved the twin throttles fully open. She threw off the near stall and responded to the power surge, the controls becoming light and sharpening to a razor point. The crews in the formation obviously had no idea what was hunting them, since the raven black Mosquito would have been near invisible against the sea, and they showed no sign of evasive action as they cruised casually inland, side-by-side. Rafe chopped the throttles back and floated in, patiently waiting until he was close enough to read the squad markings aft of the wing root. At the last moment, the other pilot turned his head and a look of utter disbelief slowly began to form on his face. Rafe pulled back both triggers.

The effect was sudden and savage, and the cabin shook so violently that Rafe thought they themselves had been hit by flak. Rafe's vision blurred and his teeth rattled in his head. He released the triggers, and the world resolved itself into one image again with the immense power of four thirty-mm cannons firing simultaneously directly beneath the cockpit, which made long strafing fire inaccurate. The effect on the enemy machines was even more profound. Billy watched in grim fascination as the aircraft and crew of the first two Stukas shattered and crumbled away like coal dust, the bodies of men and machines shredded to bloody rags. Rafe lined up the now-panicking Stukas and unleashed another short burst, and the third in line detonated in a massive concussion.

The shock wave rocked the plane violently and fragments of steel and glass spattered against the cabin like hailstones on a tin roof. Rafe, momentarily blinded by the flash, instinctively jerked the Mosquito away. "Christ... Nav, can you see?"

"Hang on..." Billy stood shakily in his straps and pressed his head up against the glass. 'He's diving for the deck... Eleven o'clock low."

Rafe was forced to wait until his night vision returned, vital seconds in which the enemy put speed and distance on them. Now they were over land, heading eastwards through enemy territory. The landscape below was heavily forested and a dark mottled green like Irish moss; the camouflage-painted Stuka was almost invisible. "Let him go... you just killed six men for God's sake... Let's just call it quits, eh....!" Billy was badly shaken, and his voice broke like a schoolboy's.

"We can't let him escape... he could tell tales. Top secret, remember?" Rafe was in a battle frenzy: his blood fizzed like champagne and his heart pounded like a war drum; his vision grew so acute that every detail of the ground below stood out in razor-sharp relief. Something caught his attention on the horizon... what he had initially dismissed as fog seemed to be changing direction. With a savage grin, he realised he had hit the dive bomber in the last attack and it was trailing steam from a pierced radiator about two miles east of them. The pilot was a crafty one, zig-zagging at right angles from his original heading almost at grass height. If it wasn't for the steam, he would have gotten away clean. *Too bad for him*, Rafe thought. As he set the Mosquito into a shallow attack dive, he saw the Stuka react immediately. "This one's a clever bastard..."

"Look...sir, I've lost the last waypoint; we're off-course over enemy territory." Rafe barely heard him; he was contemplating the German pilot's tactics. It was ill-advised to close slowly upon a Stuka astern, since the MG 15 rear-facing gun added quite a sting to its tail. This was exactly what the enemy pilot was anticipating. He was staying as low as possible, trying to draw Rafe into a pursuit position. Rafe glanced at the fuel gauge: he had no time for a protracted engagement. "Sir, please." Billy was pleading now. Rafe felt his resolve weaken, but the fleeing Stuka was just too tempting a target.

Rafe made a snap decision to dive on him and count on the powerful cannons to kill the rear gunner before he could receive any real damage. "Sorry, Billy, can't let him go." Rafe put the Mosquito into a steep dive, and as they floated off their seats, Rafe felt the blood rush up and fill his head. The Stuka pilot immediately saw the manoeuvre and jinked left and right. Rafe had one chance once he was committed to the dive attack. He would have to pull out before five hundred feet to avoid tearing the wings off the Mosquito and ploughing into the earth like a spear. The Stuka grew alarmingly fast as Rafe pushed the rudder bars and tweaked the stick gingerly to keep the nose on target. In a surreal twist, time slowed to a dream-like slur, the sound of the screaming engines dropped down an octave, and he could just make out the man in the rear gunner turret squinting over his machine gun at him, a sheen of sweat glinting on his freshly-shaven upper lip. At the critical range, both men opened fire simultaneously.

The cockpit rattled as the two planes closed in a mortal embrace. The heavy shells thudded and bloomed into hot red florets of flame across the doomed Stuka, whose canopy was torn to shreds. The pilot and gunner rapidly cut into arcing ropes of gore. The last act of the crew was to empty the rear gun into the Mosquito's cabin. The seven-mm rounds pinged and popped around Rafe's head as he hauled back on the stick and squeezed his lower body with all the force he could muster. His field of vision began to recede, the dark grey edges of perception creeping inward as the blood was drained out of his brain by the enormous force of the dive. For a moment, he hung suspended on the edge of consciousness, then magically it seemed as though the whole universe recovered its reality, like a reel of film winding up to speed. The darkness fled, his vision was once more bright and clear, the sound of the Merlins raised up to its familiar note, and time returned to its frantic pace. Rafe shoved the throttles to the wall and the Mosquito surged skywards once more. Rafe banked over just in time to see the wildly-spinning wreckage of the Stuka crash into the earth in a wreath of bright orange flame and black smoke.

Rafe made a shameful gesture with his fingers out the canopy. "That's five in the bag, eh, what!" He turned with triumph to Billy. He was just coming to from the dive. "Wake up, son! 'Rafe reached over and gently smacked Billy's downy cheeks. His eyes slowly rolled down and blinked into focus, and he was clearly disorientated. "Sorry about that, old bean..should have warned you about the dive."

"Where the hell are we?" Billy slurred.

"Somewhere over Holland, I suspect." Rafe began a banking turn westwards and immediately felt that something was wrong with the ailerons. The stick felt spongy and stiff in his hands, and she was refusing to bank sharply. He gave her a stiff boot full of rudder to have her turn. He leaned across Billy and peered through the canopy. A pale slash of raw ply was exposed under the black paint, a ragged strip of fabric fluttered in the slipstream, and as he waggled the stick, he saw the damaged control surface twist awkwardly. What he saw next fell like a cold stone on his chest: a small plume of white mist jetted from the wing surface, trailing off into the night. Rafe sat heavily back in his seat and took off his mask. "Fucking bastard cunt!"

"What was that? Say again, pilot." Billy looked pained. Rafe replaced his mask before replying cooly, "It seems we have a fuel leak in the starboard tank." The gauges indicated less than two hundred fifty pounds. Rafe did some quick mental arithmetic; it would be a close-run race, but they could make it if they made a direct line for Rochford. He didn't fancy taking a dip in the Channel this time of year. "Vector to base, please, Nav."

Billy bent over to retrieve his glasses from the cabin floor and came up sharply with a loud hissing inhale. Instinctively, he clutched at his side, and they both looked with horror as his trembling hand came back thickly coated with blood, black as ink in the moonlight. "You're wounded, Billy. Is it bad?"

"Don't think so, sir," he replied bravely. "Just a little shrapnel."

"We need a straight line back home. Billy, or we'll be in the drink. Are you up to it?"

"Yes, sir, just give me a minute." Billy wiped the blood off his chart and tried to focus. His face set in a grey mask of pain as fat beads of sweat sprung out from his forehead and trickled down his nose. He began to shiver miserably.

Rafe had seen this before; the boy was going into shock. If they had any chance of navigating home, Billy would need to concentrate. "Look here, Billy, take a deep breath and try to calm down a bit." He proffered his flask. "Take a wee dram. It'll warm you up."

"No, thanks, I'll be fine." Billy wiped his spectacles on his shirt and brought them up to the moonlight to squint through the lens. They were smeared with blood. "Jesus, Billy...." Rafe pulled open Billy's jacket and was horrified to see that he glistened from chin to lap in dark arterial blood.

"Must have hit me while I was unconscious." Billy trembled, almost apologetically, and Rafe suddenly felt his body slump as if he were made of stone. The post-combat euphoria melted away, replaced by a gnawing panic, and now Rafe faced a half-killed navigator and a plane rapidly leaking fuel and damaged controls. The only way forward was to head west, and by the time they hit the coast, he would know if it was worth attempting to cross the Channel.

"My lungs," Billy coughed miserably. His laboured breathing had developed a nasty popping rattle. "I think my lung is punctured."

"Hold on, Billy, we're sailing home. Can you give me a heading for the last waypoint?"

Billy looked around the cabin blankly, his eyes refusing to focus as his brain struggled to make sense of his surroundings. "Try to stay with us, Billy, don't give up." Rafe checked over the instruments and stared in horrified disbelief at the fuel gauge. He tapped it with his finger to be sure it read true: less than eighty pounds of the four hundred capacity. Outside on the wing, the tiny white plume had grown to a great mare's tail. It was show over. They'd have to climb and find somewhere to ditch the Mosquito.

Rafe eased the throttles forward and climbed to fifteen hundred feet. He had only a scant few minutes of flight time in the tanks, and he had to find a flat, wide-open space and make a test pass, then turn for the landing. There was no room for error: he had one chance. The moon was setting fast to the north, casting a grim grey light on the rural landscape. Narrow dirt roads linked farm houses and windmills loomed over neatly-fenced fields. As they got further west, he saw more of what he was praying for: tulip fields. These were flat as billiard tables and some ran parallel to the levies for almost a quarter mile. Rafe's eyes flitted madly between the fuel gauge, Billy, and the earth below, his desperation now bordering on panic. Sweat trickled down his side under his flight suit, he was gripped by waves of nausea, and the cabin now reeked with a sweet sickly funk like a slaughterhouse. Billy sobbed softly and muttered to himself, as if praying for deliverance. Rafe could feel the black wings of doom slowly folding around them.

A glint of reflected moonlight caught his eye, and for a terrifying moment he thought they were being fired upon, as the yellow moon shimmered and flashed briefly on the surface of a long straight canal. There was a tulip field that was completely denuded of crop, and though from this height it was impossible to tell its length, it looked flat and even. Rafe struggled with the controls and the Mosquito pitched and rolled around its axis, clumsy as a drunkard. "I'm going to try for that field, Billy. Hold on, will you?"

From here, Rafe balanced the two opposing forces of gravity and velocity; if he was too slow and stalled, there was no fuel to power off for another pass; if he was too fast and failed to stop the plane in time, they would certainly die in a fiery collision with the woodland beyond the field. Right now, they were descending sharply and gaining too much speed, so Rafe chopped the power and cranked the flaps all the way down, and the air hissed around him. She dipped and pitched like porpoises, the landing gear lowered and locked into place with a thump, the plane shuddered, and her damaged wing dipped suddenly under the drag. The Mosquito tottered briefly on the edge of a wing stall, then recovered, banked over, stalled, and recovered again, the wings seesawing up and down as Rafe fought like a wrestler for control. The field surged up from below to meet them. At the last possible moment, Rafe pulled back on the stick and shut the engines off; the aircraft nosed up and flared like a kite, dropping the last few knots off her speed. For a graceful beat she hung suspended, then floated softly down to the earth; the gear tyres met the dry flat hard-packed soil, gentle as a lover's kiss, and they were down, bouncing along the field towards the woods.

Rafe kept her straight with the rudder while modulating the wheel brakes, pulling the cable 'till they locked and slid, then releasing and locking again. The wooded end of the field grew alarmingly fast in the wind shield, and Rafe saw with relief that it was new growth, the saplings barely taller than a man. They slapped the underside of the wing as they trundled to a stop just ten metres short of a copse of apple trees. Rafe locked the brakes and frantically shut down the aircraft while tearing off his mask and harness. "Billy, wake up, old boy, we're down!" Billy rolled his head from side to side, moaning softly, and Rafe's ears rang. It was deathly quiet after the thunder of Merlins died. He reached over Billy and opened the tiny hatch under his seat. "Can you get out, man? Can you manage it? Rafe's next fear was fire, as the gasoline fumes stung his nose and eyes. He grabbed hold of the extinguisher pin. "Get out, man. Fire! Fire!" Mention of the airman's worst nightmare seemed to rouse Billy; he tore off his harness and dove awkwardly head-first out of the hatch. Rafe yanked the pin and had just enough time to grab his knapsack and kitbag before there was a loud pop and hiss as the entire aircraft filled with a dense cloud of freezing carbon dioxide. Rafe tumbled out of the hatch and landed hard next to Billy. Rafe was dusted head to foot in the cold white powder, like he had been frozen in a snow storm.

"Billy, wake up!" Rafe sat him up in his lap and cradled his head in his arms. Billy gurgled and spat out a thick wad of blood, his young face crumpled in a rictus of agony. Rafe fished in the kitbag for morphine. "Don't leave me here...." Billy rattled and popped with each intake of breath. 'Don't talk rot, I'm going to get you to a doctor." Rafe couldn't bring himself to look at his face, so he busied himself with preparing the morphine. "Look at me!" Billy grabbed Rafe by the collar and pulled him down to face him with surprising force. His eyes were huge and swimming with tears in the weak dawn light. "Don't bury me here, get.. me... my body.. home. Promise me!" Rafe had looked into these eyes before, not so long ago, eyes he would never forget. 'I promise you, Billy." Rafe held his gaze as he stabbed the little syringe into his thigh. Billy squeezed his eyes shut and two oily tears oozed down his face. He stiffened, then relaxed, going as limp as a newborn in Rafe's lap. "Can't stay here," he croaked, his face grimacing with every rattling breath, a pink froth foaming out of his wound.

A frenzied yapping startled him. Rafe turned and was astonished to see two stout figures: a rotund man with a thick, grey beard held an ancient-looking double barrelled fowling piece pointed at Rafe's face. He was dressed in a white nightshirt and wooden shoes. The equally round woman was bundled up against the cold morning air and she stood half behind the man, holding a very sharp hayfork. "*Deutsch*! "the man barked, and motioned for Rafe to stand with a wave of the gun, while a little yellow stable dog yapped and snarled at his heel '*Deutsch*?" The man repeated. '*Nien....Engländer*." Rafe pointed to the plane. "RAF."

The woman stood on her toes and whispered something into the old man's ear, and after a moment he nodded and took a step back, still covering Rafe and Billy with the shotgun. The woman cleared her throat and paused to consider. Then, she began in halting English, 'You..are.. lost?" She had a tiny voice for such a large woman. "No, dear, no fuel...he is wounded." Rafe indicated Billy with a head jerk. "We need help.. he is very bad....*sehr krank*!" Rafe struggled to find the words in his schoolboy German. These people were surely Dutch farmers, but he knew that the two tongues were close enough to be understood. There was another hushed exchange—the man looked doubtful and he eyed Rafe and Billy warily. "He needs a doctor, or he will die.....*sterben*!"

Rafe ripped off his glove and felt Billy's pulse on his neck. It was very weak, and his breath smelled bitter, like rusting iron. His body was losing the fight, slowly shutting down, and with a gurgle he lost control of his bladder, sobbing softly in indignation.

The pair seemed to come to a decision, and the fat woman stepped forward and knelt beside Billy. From behind an apple tree, the man led a huge chestnut mare pulling a weathered oxcart. The woman lifted Billy's legs. "We need to get him inside, there are soldiers.."

"He needs a doctor; is there one in the village?"

"No doctor, no village, come.." As they lifted him, a fresh torrent of blood gushed onto the frosty grass, steaming in the frigid morning air. Together they man-handled him onto the back of the oxcart and set off across the field. Rafe looked back and saw that the Mosquito was well-screened from the road by the wood. He hoped it would be the same from the air.

The big woman cradled Billy's head to her ample bosom, making soft cooing sounds as the cart crunched along the frost out of a wooden gate. Rafe trotted alongside with the big man seated in the traces, the sky blushed pink, and the light grew steadily, illuminating an orchard and a large thatched farmhouse guarded by a flock of snow-white geese. Rafe lifted Billy off the cart and carried him like a child through the doorway. "Here, follow." The woman led him to an enormous ceramic-tiled hearth. Rafe gently lowered Billy to the rug before the fire, looking on in grim fascination as the big woman seemed to instinctively know what to do. She lay down beside Billy and gathered him up in a warm embrace, stroking his forehead and rocking him gently like an infant. Billy stared into the flames, his breath coming in broken, jerking spasms, each one weaker than the last, and his mouth working like a landed fish. The woman soothed and hushed, and finally he stopped shivering, relaxed, and the grimace of pain melted from his face. Rafe had witnessed this phenomenon once before, by his wife's deathbed, the flesh transformed before his eyes, becoming as frozen and inert as a marble statue. In a final macabre twist, Billy's eyes swivelled and locked onto Rafe's as the final moment came.

Rafe leapt to his feet and fled the room. He reeled and stumbled outside into the cold air. He drew his flask and emptied it down his throat. He gripped the door frame and waited for the whiskey to take effect, guilt and anger raging through his mind like a wildfire. The boy was dead, and he was to blame. The ground lurched beneath his feet like a ship in a swell. He stumbled forward, and, falling to his knees, vomited onto the grassy lawn. He knelt there panting while the pinwheeling world slowed and finally came to a stop. Rough hands dragged Rafe to his feet and frog-marched him indoors. He was led through a narrow doorway to a small windowless room with a rope bed. The door was shut and locked behind him.

The room was lit by a single old-fashioned gas lamp, and it smelled oddly familiar, a pleasant aroma like soap and rosewater mingled with freshly-sawn timbers. Rafe stripped off his parachute and collapsed on the soft bed. He was dimly aware of a heated exchange on the other side of the wall in coarse Dutch, but they were speaking so fast that he could not make sense of the conversation. Rafe closed his eyes and tried to think of what to do next. He had promised Billy not to leave him here, and he resolved to himself that, whatever happened, he would keep that promise. Fatigue descended on him like a leaden blanket, and he had a sensation like sinking backwards into the floor. A thick mental fog drifted in, and Rafe let it come.

34

#

The smell of baking bread roused Rafe from a deep death-like sleep. He sat up and found that someone had taken off his boots and put a thick woollen blanket over him. He shrugged it off and sat on the edge of the creaky bed. He felt stiff and sore, and his empty belly moaned and bubbled.

Rafe had an odd sensation that he was being watched. The door stood open a crack and a little face peered around it at him. The small eye suddenly grew wide and vanished, followed by a patter of running footsteps and the high piping voice of a child in the next room. Rafe pulled on his boots and followed his nose through the tiny, narrow passage to the kitchen. It was late afternoon on a sunny spring day and the kitchen was filled with a warm carmine glow, while the hot oven and streaming sunlight conspired to make the room sultry as a sauna. A young woman was busy with her back to him over a big iron stove, up to her elbows in flour. She was barefoot, stripped down to a lacy cream camisole in the heat, and her coal-black hair was piled on top of her head in a tousled bun. Her slim pale shoulders, wide for a woman, worked up and down as she kneaded a large clump of dough. A little girl, no older than about nine, clung to her skirts, tugging at her apron and gesticulating wildly in Rafe's direction. The woman turned, and seeing Rafe, dropped her lump of dough and reached for a pile of discarded clothes on the kitchen table. Rafe recognised the thick blue pea coat, heavy woollen scarves, and padded petticoats from the night before. His mind spun. "Oh! *Meneer.*" She hurriedly shrugged into a blouse and fussed with her hair. "You gave me a fright."

"Where is he?" Rafe croaked, his voice breaking.

"Who?" She dusted the flour from her hands distractedly.

"Billy! he snapped. 'What did you do with him?" She flushed and her expression turned grave. '*De Heer Groost*, is making a... *kist*..a..box for him."

"He can't be buried..not here."

"Not buried, he is in the cellar." Her face softened. "Sit down, you must be hungry."

Rafe sat wearily at the simple oak table. He didn't feel much like eating; the fact that he sat in the very room in which he had watched Billy die mere hours ago did little for his appetite.

"I need a drink."

"Food first."

He found he could not tear his eyes away from the young woman; she had been disguised last night, wrapping herself in padded clothing to hide her shapely young body, but from whom? He looked on as she prepared a simple meal of bread, cheese, and thick pea soup. Her hands were slim and delicate, with long tapered fingers and shaped nails—not the hands of a farm girl. Big brown eyes so dark as to appear black, her skin was milky white but glowed beneath with the translucent golden luminescence.

She set a porcelain plate of food before him, and the smell seemed to arouse his hunger. The aromatic crusty bread was fresh from the oven, and the cheese was rich and creamy. Rafe fell upon it with a will.

When he had finished, he was aware that the two girls were sitting and gazing at him from the end of the table. The little girl sat on the woman's lap; her eyes were huge, and she stared with rapt attention as Rafe mopped up the last of the soup with a piece of bread. Rafe realised he had not even properly introduced himself. "Good lord, I have been rude." He stood and smoothed back his hair. "My name is O'Rourke, Raphael O'Rourke. Everybody calls me Rafe." He broke out the old charming grin and extended his hand.

"I am Rachel." She ignored his hand, stood, and hoisted the child onto her hip. "This is my sister, Anne." Her accent was heavy

Dutch but her English was well-learned. He noticed she had a light sprinkle of acne on her chin; she wasn't any more than a schoolgirl herself. "Raff!" the child piped, and she squirmed out of Rachel's hold and skipped around the table singing, "Raff! Raff! Raff!"

"Anne!" Rachel scolded gently. An indulgent smile slowly broke over her face like a sunrise. Her teeth were slightly crooked but white as snow; she caught Rafe's eye and turned quickly away, busying herself with her dough. Rafe awkwardly began to gather his kit bag and webbing. "I ..er, must get out to my plane." He turned and made for the door to the courtyard. 'No! " Rachel crossed the room quickly, blocking the doorway." You must wait until dark; there are police, soldiers."

"Even out here?"

"Yes, many, please..." Rafe was shocked by the change in her demeanour; her face drained of colour and her hands shook. She was terrified. "Very well, I shall wait."

Rafe hadn't thought much about the occupation of this part of the Netherlands. He had read about the rumours circulating Poland about the way the Nazis had rounded up dissenters and local officials to be relocated and re-educated, and Hitler had made no secret of his contempt for Jews. But surely the mighty *Wehrmacht* had better things to do than hunt around the countryside for Jewish schoolgirls. "So you are in hiding?"

"Yes."

"From the Nazi party?"

"From the SS and the police."

"And they are hunting down all the Jews, in cooperation with the government?"

"Yes, we are all hiding. My parents are in Rotterdam, I am here."

"So what will happen if you are discovered?"

"We don't know; the trains leave, we never see them again. My Father says they are taken to a labour camp to be worked to death making shells—some say even worse, to be slaughtered like cattle."

Rafe stifled a derisive snort. *This must be fantasy, surely. How could the Dutch government be complicit in mass murder?*

Rachel held Anne close; the little girl spoke no English, but she sensed the mood and clung to her tenaciously. She must have been close to ten or eleven, but acted much more like a younger child, timid and watchful. Rafe lit a cigarette and took in the room around him. It was not as modest as he first thought. The furniture was of the highest quality. The dining suite was exquisitely worked and detailed. A walnut cabinet sat in the corner of the room, holding an impressive range of Delftware and other various decorative objects. Even the walls were panelled in dark teak, an extravagance for a humble farmer's cottage. Most impressive of all was the parlour grand in the next room. Rafe was no piano expert, but it must have been worth a king's ransom.

"So this is Erik's farm?" Rafe asked.

"He is retired here, and he only harvests tulips in the summer. He is, how do you say in English.. *houtbewerker...?*" She gestured about the room.

"A woodworker, yes, I can see. He has great skill." At that moment Erik appeared at the kitchen window, knocking on the thick old-fashioned glazing. Rachel opened the window and he passed through a freshly-plucked chicken. "*Laaste kip!*" he said, and peered past Rachel at Rafe. "Ah! *Hij is opgestaan!*" Erik walked around to the door, closely followed by the little yellow terrier, kicked off his dusty boots, and offered his hand. "Erik van Hoost, pleased—to—meet—you." He spoke in rehearsed English. His hand was rough as sandstone and held Rafe's in a grip of iron. His weathered face crinkled up in a warm jolly smile, the skin folded up as if it were used to assuming this expression on a daily basis for many years.

"I am Pilot Officer O'Rourke, RAF." Rafe's smile barely disguised a wince as he felt the bones in his hand grind together. "Please call me Rafe."

"*Ja!*, Raafe! Erik slapped him so hard on his shoulder his teeth rattled. "Tonight, we drink to your friend. *Komm*"!

Erik led him through the house to a workshop built off the eastern side. The walls were lined with hanging tools of every shape and form: planes, saws, hammers, clamps, files, and chisels. Neatly-stacked towers of freshly-sawn oak, teak, and fine walnut veneers shared space with jigs and partially-completed cabinets, glued and dowelled, awaiting assembly. The room had a pleasant natural aroma of sawdust and wood glue. On the main workbench, a long pine box held a neatly-wrapped bundle of white linen. Rafe's heart twisted as he lay a hand on the cold shroud.

"What vas his name?" Erik had removed his cap and stood, head bowed beside the coffin.

"William...I think. We called him Billy."

"Dat is *Herr* William's." Erik pointed at a respectfully folded and assembled collection of clothes and effects across the room. "We can bury him at sunset."

"No...we can't," Rafe sighed. "I made a promise, I will bring him home to his mother. Is there somewhere we can leave him, cool and dry?"

"*Ja,* I have just the place...*Komm mit mier*!.

Together they laid the lid on the box, and amid much difficulty and swearing of oaths in Dutch and English, manoeuvred it down a series of stone steps deep in the earth to a cellar beneath the workshop. As they descended, the air became so frigid that they blew clouds of steam from their mouths as they laboured under the heavy burden. At last they set down the box and covered it with hefty stone blocks that were cold as ice to the touch.

"Dis is my *lager*," said Erik proudly. The room's rough walls were hewn from solid rock, and from a timber-framed ceiling hung various sausages, hams, and bacon hocks. A shelf on the back wall groaned under the weight of dozens of big, green bottles with wire-lightning stoppers. Erik handed two to Rafe and took two himself.

When they climbed back up into the warmth of the house, the sun had set.

"Look, old boy, I would really like to get out to my plane. There are important matters I must attend to right away." Erik cocked his big shaggy head quizzically until Rachel translated.

"*Ja*! Soon! First, we drink." He carefully poured the bright amber beer into tall glasses that glistened with dew and held up a toast 'William, *rust in vrede.*"

"Rest in peace."

Rafe took a deep draught and licked the foam off his lips; it was delicious, cold, and crisp. Rafe then raised his glass in another toast. "Death to the Nazi bastards!" Erik vigorously nodded in agreement and they both drained their glasses. He refilled them and offered another "*De Koning van Engeland!*" Rafe felt he was obliged to drink deeply to that.

"Long live Queen Wilhelmina! God bless her!" Rafe returned the favour. Erik puffed up his chest, set his jaw, and bravely downed a whole glass in one swallow.

Many similar toasts followed: to the RAF, to the Dutch Army, to Rafe's father, to Erik's, and to Cork United FC. Erik poured the last from the fourth bottle. "Now we go to plane, but first, more beer for walk." He made his way unsteadily back down to the *lager* singing *Het Wilhelmus* in a booming stentorian baritone.

Erik lit two bullseye lanterns and led Rafe to the stable where he bridled the big bay mare. "Dis is Frieda, she is a good horse. *Ja*, strong horse." She pricked her ears up at the sound of her name and whickered softly, stamping her great hoof on the earth. Erik led them through the orchard and into the field. It was a crisp, cool spring evening, the apple trees were in bloom, the white flowers almost iridescent in the dusk. They passed through the ancient stone wall and into the tulip field. Rafe cringed and caught his breath when he saw the Mosquito's naked tail sticking rudely out of the little copse of elm trees.

"Frieda will pull her, you will see." As they walked up to the plane, Rafe saw that Erik had cleared a path through the wooded area. Tree limbs and sawdust littered the ground where he had cut an artificial glade wide enough to accommodate the thirty-foot wingspan of the aircraft. The canopy was intact, providing thick cover from the air.

Together they lashed the thick hemp cable to the tow points on the nose gear. Erik wound the cable about the horse's massive shoulders. "I've got to get up and release the wheel brakes. Erik, give me a hand." Erik bowed his powerful back and laced his fingers under Rafe's boot, lifting him easily up to the hatch. Rafe scrambled inside and was immediately hit in the face by a thick swarm of blow flies. The bloody floor of the cabin was seething with a carpet of fat, grey maggots. The cockpit buzzed loudly as the hoard of insects sought escape, seeking out his nose and mouth. Covering his face with the sleeve of the smock, he reached under the firewall and released the wheel brake lever, snatching up his flight bag before making a rapid and graceless exit through the hatchway.

With the aid of a carrot, Frieda overcame her initial reluctance and walked slowly forward. The cable creaked as the great bands of muscle in her hindquarters swelled and bunched under her glossy coat. She nodded her head, and in a series of powerful surges, the great black plane was swallowed up by the wood.

They walked back in a companionable silence. Rafe was racked with uncertainty as to what to do next. He had been ordered to destroy the aircraft, along with the interception equipment, if forced down, but the plane was clearly salvageable. Rafe inspected the damage by lantern light and was satisfied that the critical structures were intact. An evening's work at Rochford and the wing could be repaired, the fuel tank patched. Rafe was reluctant to demolish a perfectly serviceable aircraft, but he resolved to do his duty and follow the order. First thing the next day, he would set up the demo kit and destroy the Mosquito.

When they returned, they were greeted with the savoury smell of roasting meat. "Our last hen, in your honour, Mr. O'Rourke." After a lengthy and heartfelt saying of grace from Erik, they dined on a simple but hearty meal of roasted chicken, potatoes, and sauerkraut. Despite his predicament and many thoughts troubling him, Rafe found he could barely take his eyes off Rachel. She had set her hair up, and he marvelled at the soft white perfection of the skin on her neck and the way her full mouth formed a bow shape as she chewed. She must have felt his gaze as she struggled to keep a half smile from her lips as she fussed about Anne, who wriggled and fidgeted on her chair.

After clearing the dishes, Rafe retrieved his navigation charts from the flight bag and laid them out on the table. Erik soon located the farm on the map; they were about twenty kilometers northeast of Haarlem, just below the horsehead-shaped peninsula of Holland. Erik spoke rapidly in Dutch, while Rachel translated. "Tomorrow Erik will go to Amsterdam; we have friends there who helped us and they will surely put us in contact with the *Engelandvaarders.*" Rafe had heard of them, an underground railway of sorts. They arranged the smuggling of adventurous young Dutchmen to England, usually via convoluted routes through Belgium, France, and Spain. Once there, they would sign up with the armed forces. The process could take months.

"We are so near the coast, I could make my way there, either find a boat or steal one?" Rafe knew that was hopeless as soon as the words left his mouth. Ever since the commando raids in Norway, the SS had sworn to shoot any Englishman out of uniform as a spy. "Don't be too hasty, we can hide you while we decide what is best here..." Erik pulled back the walnut Delftware cabinet covering the entrance to a large bedroom that had been partitioned. Rafe recognised the pattern of wall covering. The double bed was neatly made and the walls were covered with glossy magazine clippings, mostly portraits of Matinée Idols and popular singers, like Clark Gable, Frank Sinatra, and Carole Lombard, who shared space with a pantheon of black-suited concert pianists, composers, and virtuosos. A little writing desk against the wall was piled with well-thumbed books of sheet music and gramophone discs, and next to it stood a beautifully-crafted dresser crowded with all the personal accoutrements of a sophisticated young woman: fine bottled perfumes, face powder, hair brushes, and hand creams, the scent of which aroused conflicting instincts deep within him.

"This is my room. Last night you slept in Anne's room, but she can sleep with me for now."

The partition was carefully made to appear like part of the original construction. A hinged section allowed access to the smaller room that Rafe had occupied the night before. Another narrow doorway opened out onto the kitchen, which was also cleverly concealed as panelling between two cupboards, and, when closed, the entrances were all but invisible to a casual observer.

That night Rafe's body rejected sleep. He tossed and turned on the little bed, his mind visualising over and over the attack on the Stukas and Billy's last moments before the fire. His own voice in his head badgered prodded and nagged him mercilessly, *"Why dive on the Stuka?, Stupid! So reckless! Beckett was right about you, foolish! A better pilot would have pulled out sooner! Everybody who trusts you ends up dead!* Like snapshots, the faces of his wife, their stillborn infant, and Billy's empty death stare floated behind his eyes. He sat up and lit his last cigarette. He felt sure that he would drive himself mad stranded here for weeks, or months, on end with nothing to do but think about his sins and be haunted by nightmares. And tomorrow he would have to destroy the Mosquito, his only means of escape. The thought made his bowels churn.

At dawn, Rafe woke slowly from a half-remembered dream: angels were playing their harps and each note seemed to be a solid object in his head, gold and shining like flaming copper. As he woke, he realised the music was real; someone was playing the piano in the next room. He rose stiffly and stepped out of his windowless room into the morning sunlight. Rachel sat at the parlour piano, her slim fingers dancing lightly over the keys, sure and firm. Each note was clear and perfect, the player and the instrument in sublime harmony. Erik, dressed in a dark woollen suit, stooped under the soundboard, making adjustments. "*Beter?*" his voice was muffled under the board. Rachel played the last few bars again. "*Ja*, much better, thank you." She played the full passage, something wonderfully chromatic and ornate. Erik listened intently, casting a critical eye over the exposed hammers and chords as they shimmered and rippled. When she finished, Rafe felt suspended in the air for a moment, like he had been levitated by an unseen force.

"You play beautifully, Rachel," he said, his voice breaking like a schoolboy's.

She shot him a coy smile over her shoulder. "Thank you, *meinheer.*" She ran her hands over the polished maple wood lovingly. "It's a beautiful piece. *Heer* Hoost has done a work of wonder to repair it. It's a miracle, really." Erik beamed with pleasure, "*Ja*, how could we let this old girl die, eh."

"It belonged to my school, in Rotterdam," Rachel sighed wistfully. "The conservatory took a bomb and burned, and this was the only piano to survive."

"You studied at Pijepr's?" Rafe was amazed; it was the most highly-esteemed school in western Europe. "Ha! Studied!" Erik scoffed. "Rachel teaches there! She is a virtuoso!"

"All that is over now." Rachel closed the lid with a grave finality. "Jews are forbidden."

After a breakfast eaten in uncomfortable silence, Erik summoned Rafe outside. "I am driving to Amsterdam to contact our friends. Stay indoors and near the annex, keep an eye on the approach road. It is long and dusty at this time of year so you should have plenty of warning of a vehicle. If anybody comes up the drive, you and Anna lock yourselves in the annex. Do not come out no matter what happens."

"What of Rachel?"

"She is posing as my sister-in-law, so she will see off any visitors." Rafe raised a sceptical eyebrow. "There will be none, don't worry yourself about this. We are quite isolated here." They walked around the back of the house to a gloomy stonewalled shed. Inside, under a dust-laden canvas cover, was an elderly Peugeot coup.

They pushed her out into the morning sunshine and Erik directed the starting procedure, which involved many complicated and esoteric steps—some involving prayer and the invocation of saints.

Finally, Rafe was allowed to crank the starter handle. After a few skinned knuckles and choice words of encouragement, the little motor burst into life with a huge cloud of blue smoke. Erik leapt in and shouted above the clattering noise." I will be back tomorrow morning, stay out of sight..... and don't drink all my beer." He winked wickedly at Rafe and bounced off down the rocky road, veiled in a cloud of yellow dust.

Rafe moped about the house all that morning. He checked and rechecked the action and load of his .45 automatic. He pulled back the slide and ejected the magazine, blowing on the breech and snapping it home compulsively over and over like a metronome. After lunch, Rachel appeared with a white towel and a bar of soap. "You need a bath, you stink to high heaven."

Despite courageously debating the merits or otherwise of bathing during the day, Rafe found himself folded up in a small tin bathtub next to the stove. He sat in barely six inches of soapy water, with his knees about his ears. A strategically-placed wash cloth preserved his honour while Rachel helped him shave.

"Are you related to Erik?"

"No, he worked at the school, a craftsman. He was a member of the Communist Party with my father. After the capitulation, we went into hiding." Rachel shaved his cheek with a straight razor, scraping the creamy whiskers off, then rinsing the blade in the bathwater, uncomfortably close to Rafe's business end.

"Why not just leave?" Rachel paused and gave Rafe a scornful glare. "This is our country. We want to defy the enemy. We are not just going to roll over and surrender." Her pretty young face took on a fearsome mien, cheeks colouring and dark eyes flashing with anger. She reached down and whisked the blade between Rafe's legs; he felt himself wither and flinched away slightly. An impulsive thought occurred to him. "What if you could leave now, you could come with me.... back to England." He saw he had caught her off-guard. Her face softened and a sad wistful shadow passed over her eyes. "What about Anne?" she asked, her voice small and doubtful.

"She could come with us."

"The way is hard, dangerous, and she is but a delicate child."

"We won't go with the *Engelandvaarders*. I will fly the plane, we could be in London within two hours." The idea that had been half-formed in the back of his mind for the last two days resolved itself as he uttered the words. With Erik's workshop they could repair the damage to the aileron, then they could shut off the aft wing tank and fill the port tank. It held about two thousand pounds of fuel, and if they were careful they could easily make it home. "Is the plane not damaged?"

"Only a little. The wings are made entirely of wood. A master craftsman like Erik could fashion the replacement parts we need." Fuel was the problem. Where could they get three hundred gallons of aircraft-grade petrol? It didn't matter, he would find a way.

He could see he had planted a seed of hope in her mind; it had taken root and was now blooming behind her eyes, though she tried to hide it. Her face suddenly seemed very close; he could smell the scent of her. Her breath, her hair, clean and unsullied. Her face was maturing; she had the poise and aspect of a woman, but she was still to shake off the last vestiges of girlhood: the little freckles on her nose, and the subtle mischievous glint in her eyes. He saw she was studying his face, her eyes darting left and right, searching his eyes for any sign of deceit or false hope.  Rafe felt the devil take him and he leaned forward to kiss her full on the lips. She pulled back, wide-eyed with shock, and fell with a bump onto her backside, a blob of shaving soap forming a little peak on her nose. As they sat and looked at each other in stunned silence, a tiny sound hummed in the distance.

Rachel scrambled to her feet and dashed to the tiny window overlooking the approach road. *"Oh mien Got!"* The thin, distant buzz grew into a steady thump, the unmistakable sound of a German Zundapp motorcycle. Dripping wet with a towel about his waist, Rafe joined her at the window. Far down the drive, a German motorcycle sidecar weaved and jostled as it negotiated the rough-cut roadway. The driver was a scrawny little fellow wearing goggles and a leather helmet. The big man in the sidecar bounced and wobbled along as he held his cap on his head with one hand and shielded his eyes from the bright afternoon sun with the other. "It's Jaap and his lap dog."

"You know these two?" said Rafe, hopping into his breeches. "The big one, Jaap, he's the local bully, and his family are influential in town; they own this farm and most of the land from here to the coast, and he visits occasionally to throw his weight around. The little one is Max, his poisonous little sidekick. Shit! Why now! " As the bike got closer, Rafe could make out the black and silver uniform of the SS ."Looks like he has joined the Nazi Party; that's perfect. They love petty thugs like him; he's come to show off."

"Will he cause trouble?" Rafe cleared and holstered his .45

"Maybe. I'll tell him Erik is in town, so hopefully he will come back tomorrow. " She grabbed Rafe by the shoulders, looking straight into his eyes; her face was pale and her voice stern. "Stay in the annex, no matter what happens. If you try to intervene we will be uncovered and Anne will be deported. Do you understand what that could mean?"

"Yes, but I'm not about—"

"The worst he will do is arrest me, and he won't even do that. Stay hidden and quiet, yes?"

"Yes."

Rachel got into her padded coats, while Rafe hurriedly gathered his things and bolted for the annex, slipping and sliding on his soapy feet. Rachel knelt at Anne's eye level. "Now, you remember how we play dead?." Anne nodded gravely. "We play now, go under the bed and don't come out until I say. Me and no one else, okay?"

"Okay!"

Rachel pushed the tall cabinet shut with a thump; the windowless room was suddenly gloomy and suffocating. Rafe heard the machine's engine come to a stop outside the front door. As his eyes adjusted to the darkness, he noticed motes of dust dancing in a bright shard of light. At its source was a two-inch crack where the ceiling beam joined the wall timbers. He found that if he stood on his toes he could observe most of the kitchen area through this gap in the panelling.

Jaap strode in without invitation, pounding the dust from his trousers with his cap. He was a big man, tall and corpulent; his high and wide Sam Browne belt struggled to hold back the great mass of his gut. He lowered himself onto one of the kitchen chairs, mopping his sweaty face with the silken monogrammed kerchief about his massive neck. His companion ominously stood guard by the doorway. Rachel came up from the *lager* carrying a pewter jug of beer. "*Mevrouw* Hoost! So good to see you again." For a big man, his voice was high and shrill.

"Erik is gone for the day, he will be back tomorrow. Come back then." Rachel poured the beer, not making eye contact. Jaap's greasy lips receded, revealing a mouthful of orange tobacco-stained teeth held together by bright gold bridgework.

"I know this; I saw him leave this morning in his motorcar, and there is a checkpoint now, on the Landsmeer Road." He leaned forward, trying to catch her eye. "You see, I am an officer now, my girl. Of the SS *Nederlandsche.*" He stood and preened, hooking his thumbs into his belt and jutting his chin out aggressively. He exchanged a lewd grin at his little friend standing guard by the door. Rafe didn't like where this was heading. Jaap strolled lazily about the kitchen, casually inspecting each item he encountered. "Things are going to change around here, *Mevrouw.* There will be obedience and honesty!" He came closer to the stove where the bath stood, and Rafe stiffened when he saw his soapy razor next to the gently steaming tub. "There is talk, my dear...about certain people, shall we say...wanted people, being sheltered out here in the countryside." He took another step closer to the tub. This time his boot came to rest in one of Rafe's shiny wet footprints on the polished pine boards. Craning his neck, Rafe could see the smudges and smears of glistening water that led to the Delftware cabinet, and he felt his guts bubble like a witch's cauldron. "Yes, of course, *Herr* Hartman..." Rachel saw the danger so she proffered a cold glass of beer at his back; he turned on his boot heel, his face splitting into a reptilian grin as he took the glass. He advanced on Rachel, invading her personal space, and drained the glass in a few giant gulps, never taking his eyes off her. She retreated before him, walking backwards towards the kitchen table, and when she could go no further he pinned her there with his hips. "You wouldn't know anything about this sort of thing, would you, my dear?" He reached behind her and set the glass on the table. Rachel had to bend backwards, almost in half, to avoid his face.

Rafe's heart thundered against his ribs while he reached down and drew his weapon. Jaap started unbuttoning Rachel's coat. "Why so wrapped up, my dear? It's so warm in here.." He fumbled with the big horn buttons, pulling back and releasing her from the pressure of his body. Rachel took her chance and slapped him hard across the face, swinging her shoulders into the blow with all her strength; the smack was extremely loud and echoed through the house. Jaap staggered back, stunned. For a second, he seemed to be confused as to what had just happened. He blinked and gaped at Rachel like a half-wit; a great crimson hand-shaped weal bloomed on his chubby face and a thin trickle of blood meandered over his lip and down his chin.

Rachel took a deep shuddering breath and tilted her head up. "Erik is not here today..." She calmly turned and walked around to put the heavy table between them. "Please come back tomorrow."

Jaap trembled, shaking his head in disbelief. Tears sprang up in his eyes, and to Rafe's utter amazement, he sobbed, just once. His face screwed up like an infant and he choked tears back. He caught himself, and with visible effort, returned from the brink of total humiliation. His henchman stared, mouth agape, from the window. Rafe had witnessed men like this before, and from here they either walked away like nothing had happened or  flew into a murderous frenzy of violence.

Jaap dabbed at his eyes with his neckerchief, sniffed back the snot in his nose, and smeared the blood from his chin with his knuckles, then cleared his throat and walked out the door without a word.

Rafe's pulse throbbed so hard in his skull that he saw black dots blink at the edge of his vision. He realised he had been holding his breath, and exhaled gratefully through puffed cheeks. The Zundapp crunched away down the drive in a cloud of dust. For a full minute they both stock still, half-expecting the bike to return down the road, perhaps leading a full Panzer division. Rachel appeared to gather her courage and stepped outside.When she returned, she stripped off her coats and knocked on the wall panel. "It"s okay, they"re gone....heading to the Coast Road." Rafe slowly pushed back the cabinet and stepped into the kitchen. "Rachel...."

"I am fine, really." She looked at the ground and hugged herself while her whole body quaked; he could hear her teeth rattling. He took her in his arms. She didn't return the embrace but Rafe held her all the same. Anne emerged from the room and joined them, and slowly Rachel's trembling subsided and she was still.

Jaap was in a sour mood, not at all in the mood for a party. He was so looking forward to this evening; it was to be the first time he presented himself to the *Waffen* SS Area Commander, Gustav von Leeb, whose birthday party they were attending.

It was to be quite an occasion. Gustav von Leeb was a popular figure, one of the original members of the *Totenkopf Waffen* SS division that fought like demons during the conquest of the Low Countries. He led a *Panzergrenadier* mechanised infantry assault that had stormed over the French and British defensive lines within thirty-six hours, playing a key role in driving the English into the sea and mauling the French into submission. After being wounded in Spain, he was rewarded for his aggressive vigour by being promoted and installed in a lucrative administration role as SS Area Commander Nord Holland.

Jaap had gone to great lengths to impress. He spent a great deal of his allowance buying the cursed machine he bounced along in, a small fortune tailoring the uniform, and an advance on next month's allowance to procure the Spanish leather saddle and harness as a birthday gift—not to mention the basket of sweet meats, cheeses, and liquors in his lap—and that morning he had set off with a spring in his step and a song on his lips.

Then he had ruined it all by visiting that bitch. He touched the side of his face; it still stung, and was hot and red as a beet. He had boasted to Max that she would bend over and lift her skirts for him when she saw him in his uniform. Now his fevered mind replayed the encounter over and over in his head like a scene from an American film, fantasizing about what he should have done, what he ought to have done, what was his right to do.

He should have caught her hand before the blow and kissed her, just like Rudolph Valentino. She would have struggled at first, but then she would succumb to her passion, pulling him down to her on the table, where he would take her deftly, drawing cries of pleasure from her while Max watched, struck dumb with admiration. In another scenario, he imagined he would take her by force, smashing her face with his fists until she was senseless, then tearing the clothes from her body. Then he would mount her from behind like a stallion, his powerful phallus driving her into throes of ecstasy despite her pain. Then, his favourite one, he would draw his knife and cut the clothes from her; then he would force her to her knees and he and Max would share her, like a pig on a spit. Afterwards, he would cut her and bleed her slowly; she would beg for her life, he would laugh languidly, savouring the sensation. So engaged was he in his lurid fantasy that he barely noticed they had come to a stop outside the Klaas Hotel.

Klaas had the finest dining and ballroom north of Amsterdam, and it was a masterpiece of Baroque excess: triple Gable roofs and tall ornate window frames in a formal setting of Romanesque gardens populated by fountains and nymphs. The entire building had been taken over for Gustav's birthday, and the ground floor was thronged with guests from all levels of the Party. Max brushed Jaap's uniform down with a horsetail brush as he gathered up the saddle and gift basket.

"Park over by the other cars and wash this mess," snapped Jaap as he kicked the tyre of the dusty sidecar. "I want it gleaming and polished when I call you back to pick me up." Jaap puffed out his chest and crunched off across the pea gravel drive to the entranceway.

A brawny *Heer Sergeant* acting as doorman smiled and held the door for him. As he entered the lobby, Jaap was overwhelmed by a solid wall of sound and smell. The cavernous room was packed with guests; every type of officer's uniform and ladies' eveningwear was on display. *Heer, Kriegsmarine, Luftwaffe,* SS. All resplendent in glittering buttons, medals, polished leather, boiled and starched cotton, brass gold and felt, feathers, and sequins. The air was pungent with a heady mix of tobacco smoke, pomade, perfumes and colognes, spicy sausage, beers, and liquors. Huge intimidating red Nazi banners hung from the high ceiling, some thirty feet across. They loomed over the foyer like immense Zeppelins, while beneath them, the air hummed with a myriad of conversations, punctuated by the occasional burst of laughter or hearty greeting. As accompaniment, a four-piece played the Führer's favourite, the "Merry Widow Waltz", as a handful of couples swayed and twirled under a massive crystal chandelier.

Jaap stood awkwardly on the fringe of the crowd, searching desperately for a familiar face.

"May I help you with that, sir?" A short fellow in immaculate black coat and tails gestured to the saddle. "No," Jaap snapped, craning his neck around to catch a glimpse of the birthday boy. "It is a gift for *Herr* Leeb. I wish to present it to him myself. Where can I find him?"

"I am afraid all gifts must be taken through to the security room." He smiled humourlessly and bowed with a flourishing gesture to follow. "If you please...Mr....?"

"Hartman, Jaap Hartman, SS *Nederlandsche.*"

"This way, please, *Herr* Hartman.." They threaded through the crowd to a side door that led to a huge cathedral-like dining room. The concierge shut the door on the noisy gathering and waited patiently for Jaap to add his offering.

Jaap stared in disbelief at the Aladdin's cave of treasures it contained. An enormous banquet table, almost seventy feet long, bowed under the weight of gifts. Jaap saw Delftware, silverware, and fine bone china, hunting harnesses, duelling pistols, oil paintings, statuary, and glassware. Numerous bottles of fine wines, magnums of champagne, and a great many gift baskets filled with fruit, flowers, and chocolates of every shape and form. Jaap bristled; he had imagined presenting the saddle to Gustav personally, astonishing the other guests with his generosity and taste. Now he saw that his grand gesture was just one among many. It seemed that many wealthy and influential people wanted to curry favour with the new commander and were willing to go to great expense to do so.

A strange voice boomed from behind him. "Impressive, is it not..?" Startled, Jaap spun around, searching the room for the speaker. He was standing in shadow, his face wreathed in cigarette smoke. "Most of it stolen, of course..." He stepped out of the darkness. The mysterious man was impeccably dressed, wearing a well-tailored double-breasted suit with a crimson vest and white gloves, but there was something odd about his face that Jaap couldn't quite put his finger on. "Well, confiscated, we should say." The man smiled cruelly, like a wolf. Most of his teeth were silver and gold; they twinkled in his mouth like jewels.

"Confiscated from whom?" Jaap was intrigued; this was clearly a man of great wealth and import. During his lifetime of privilege, Jaap had learned to stick close to gentlemen of this type, since they often proved useful. "The Jews, of course...." He took a dainty puff of his cigarette from the end of a long ivory holder. "A man in the right position can acquire a great deal in the current, shall we say, climate." He nodded almost imperceptibly at the insignia on Jaap's lapel.

Smiling sweetly, Jaap stepped forward and offered his hand. "I am Hartman, SS Standard 8 *Nederlandsche*." The gentleman squeezed Jaap's hand in a palm-down, feminine grip, his fingers cold as ice and iron-hard under the soft silken glove. "Kurt Schroeder." Now that he was closer, Jaap realised what was strange about this man: he had no eyebrows. They were painted on like a doll's; underneath, his skin was powdered white while there was a distinct line on his jaw where the skin colours clashed. Jaap shivered a little involuntarily as if he had touched something loathsome. "So, *Heer* Schroeder, which gift is yours? "

"Oh, mine," he chuckled gently to himself. "Mine is out by the lake."

The Klaas Hotel backed onto Meer Zandput, a still-blue lake surrounded by elm trees and privet hedgerows. The celebrations spilled out onto the manicured lawns, and groups of guests milled around in the warm afternoon sunshine, black-tied waiters weaving among them and balancing wide silver trays crowded with champagne glasses. Jaap took a flute in each hand every time one passed by. He was determined to soak his bruised ego in booze, and he was playing catch-up with the other guests. "So where is this magnificent gift of yours?" Jaap asked dubiously. He expected to see a sailboat in the lake or a shiny new sedan. "Ah, here he comes now...." said Kurt, gazing off into the distant lakeshore. There was a faint thudding deep in the earth and a murmur of excitement ran through the crowded guests like a wave. The rhythmic pounding grew stronger and Jaap strained on his toes to see over the heads of the throng.

A uniformed officer came thundering down the shoreline at a full gallop. He half-stood in the classic hunter position, his head pushed forward over the animal's neck. He was clearly an expert horseman, his body in tune to the muscular rhythm of the animal's motion, flowing together in perfect synergy like lovers. "She is an Arabian charger, the finest Polish stock." Schroeder's mask-like face broke into a gruesome smirk. "Courtesy of our vanquished foes at Antoniny." Jaap was impressed. Such creatures were the playthings of princes, but he was more taken with the man astride it.

Gustav von Leeb was a paragon of Aryan masculinity. Backlit by the last rays of the sun, his crown of curly blond hair burned with a fiery glow. The shirt he wore had been blown open by the wind and revealed a wide, muscled chest and flat belly. He stood in his stirrups and saluted the crowd with his crop, a beatific grin spread across his face. "The best Arabians are bred in Poland, you know..." Schroeder went on smoothly. "When we took over the military, we found their royal cavalry very well-appointed. All one had to do was bribe the right person."

Jaap looked on with enchantment as horse and rider rapidly approached a five-foot hedgerow that marked the lawn's boundary.

Rather than slow down, Leeb gave the mare a sharp spur and she bounded forward, kicking up a shower of grass and dust in her wake. There was a collective gasp as the rapt guests realised he was going to take the hedge at full tack. The lithe animal smoothly took to the air like a bird, sailing gracefully over the earth a full foot clear of the hedge, landing neatly as an Olympic gymnast. The crowd burst into a spontaneous round of applause, cheering as Leeb paced her up the lawn. She danced around in a neat circle and he dismounted with a high leap, landing with uncanny cat-like balance and precision.

Leeb pushed through his adoring crowd straight towards Jaap. His heart jumped, and for an exquisite moment, Jaap thought he had caught Leeb's eye. Up close, Jaap could see why this man was chosen as a true son of the Reich. His icy cerulean eyes twinkled like jewels in his smooth, lightly-tanned face. The features were precise and had the mathematical proportions of a Grecian Adonis—only his mouth seemed out of place, too full and soft, like a cherub's. It stirred erotic sensations in Jaap that confused and confounded him. He was in such a trance-like state that he barely noticed being gently nudged aside and passed over. Leeb gathered Schroeder in a bear hug, nearly lifting the little man off the ground.

"She is perfect, my old friend; you know my tastes so well. It's supernatural!" Schroeder was only lightly ruffled as he smiled effusively and smoothed down his crumpled jacket. "Of course, you deserve the best this world has to offer; nothing less will do." The two men were quickly swept along by a tide of well-wishers. Jaap stood rooted to the spot for a moment while he pondered his next move. Somehow, he must ingratiate himself with these people. If he was to keep his privileged lifestyle and wealth through this war, he had to do better than just cooperate; he needed to be an active participant in the occupation.

As the evening wore on, he circulated the room, moving from one group to the next. Quietly hanging about the fringes of the clusters of conversations, picking up salient points of topics he knew little about, after steeling himself with more drink, he'd move in and add his own voice to the discourse. There was much talk about the fortification of the coast and where they were to find the workers needed to build them. The aborted invasion of England, the Jewish problem, the properties they had acquired in Holland and Belgium. Some of the officers discussed military matters, tactics, personnel, boring details that Jaap could not quite grasp. But without fail, the conversation would turn to money matters, a subject Jaap well understood.

At first, he found he could imitate the German accents quite well. His attitude, mode of speech, and opinions were accepted with grave nodding and murmurs of agreement. But as he took in more and more wine, his brain became fuddled. He struggled to get his tongue around German without his Dutch accent creeping in. He was beginning to forget his manners, interrupting senior officers mid-sentence and bursting into irritatingly loud cackling laughter at even the subtlest humours.

Jaap was becoming aware that his presence was unwanted among certain circles, as he approached the conversation would die off. They would stand there awkwardly, sipping from their glasses, or suddenly change to trivial topics until he took his leave. At one stage, he sat down with a group of young *Heer* officers as they passed around a bottle of apricot schnapps. In a fit of bravado, he upended and drained it, the potent liquor burning his throat like liquid fire. The men clapped and cheered, slapping him on the back and chorusing, "Dutchie! Dutchie!" When he stood to bow, he toppled over backwards and went sprawling on the floor. They cheered louder still and dragged him to his feet. He swayed, and his head swam while the grinning faces blurred and danced about like reflections on a pond. Jaap pushed them aside and stumbled out into the night, seeking fresh air to clear his buzzing brains. The world spun like a pinwheel, the lawn chairs and close-cut grass whirling about the axis of his vision. Finding an elm tree to cling to, he finally relented to his boiling guts and gushed out onto the grass.

After a few minutes voiding his belly, the spinning sensation abated, and he mopped up his face and looked about to get his bearings in the darkness. He had wandered some way into the grounds and his sodden brain struggled to make out any familiar pathways. He sensed some light and laughter to his right and set off in that general direction.

As he approached, he realised he had come across an outbuilding to the main hotel. It seemed to be a lakeside cottage built in Bavarian style, half timber with plaster walls. There was definitely a party in full swing. Bright light, music, and revelry spilled out into the night. Jaap blundered around, looking for the front door; he came across a ground floor window, glazed with thick glass tiles.The interior drapes were open a crack, and squinting drunkenly through one eye, Jaap peered through the gap.

At first, he could barely comprehend what he was seeing; he blinked and pawed at his eye with his knuckles. The thick glass distorted the light. He tried his other eye and the twin images wavered and resolved into one.

The scene was reminiscent of a Hieronymus Bosch painting he had once seen in Amsterdam. Nude bodies grappled in lamplight, their anatomies blending and blurring together. He saw patches of hair and pink flesh, glistening with sweat and other juices, rhythmically pulsing and gyrating, caressing and plucking at each other. It took him a moment to realise he was witnessing some sort of orgy. The wavy glass bent the light and made a mockery of the forms engaged. He moved his eye to a flatter piece of glass and the scene took on a more familiar shape. What he first took for a scene from hell now aroused a new sensation. His eyes greedily took in the heaving breasts, red nipples, and dark crevasses of the men and women. He felt his own flesh swell and thicken in response. He giggled to himself, "Well, then..looks like I have found the real party, eh, Schroeder?" His hot breath misted up the glass, making it hard to see any familiar faces in the scrum of bodies. He staggered around the building until he came to the front entranceway. The huge oaken door was locked and there was no welcoming staff to greet him.

Jaap licked his palm and greased his thinning hair across his forehead, knelt and spat on his shoes, polishing off the specks of vomit with his trouser legs, rose up to his full height, and knocked firmly on the door.

There was a long pause and a muffled moan. Jaap waited a full minute and knocked again. This time there was an annoyed curse followed by heavy footsteps, and the door was opened a crack. A half-naked man scowled at him from the inside as a gust of hot, sweet-smelling air washed past him. "Who the fuck are you?" The young man looked Jaap up and down contemptuously. He wore the riding breeches and knee-high boots of a cavalry officer. "Hartman, *Herr* Hartman. I am a guest at the Leeb party." Jaap tried on his best Berlin accent. There was a long, awkward pause as the young officer looked unmoved. Jaap looked to his left and right, then leaned in close. "I'm with *Herr* Schroeder." The man winced at the stench of Jaap's breath, then he sighed, half-turned into the cloak room, and called down the hallway, "Hey, Kurt, you know a Dutch SS stooge called Hartman?

Jaap took a chance to peek around the door. The hall was gloomy, candlelit with pools of orange light. Jaap could just make out Schroeder seated in a plush leather chair at the entrance to the living room. His face was flushed with drink, and a sheen of greasy sweat glistened on his face. A naked young boy squatted between his knees, his head bobbing up and down in Schroeder's lap. At the sound of the man's voice, the child's small head rose and swivelled towards the door, his eyes dead, blank like a doll's. Schroeder idly stroked the boy's sandy blond hair, as one would a pet cat. He glanced momentarily at Jaap and shook his head.

"Schro—" Jaap was cut off as the door was slammed in his face.

For a moment, he stood trembling with rage and indignation on the doorstep; he knocked again. Surely this was a mistake? After a minute standing stupidly on the step like a spurned cur, he turned and stalked off back towards the hotel in a blind fury. This latest humiliation was too much for Jaap's already fragile ego to bear, and his mind now seethed in a tempest of violence. He paced backwards and forwards across the lawn, grinding his teeth and wringing his hands, cursing and spitting. His outraged psyche writhed like a pinned serpent, frantically snapping at its tormentor. Jaap was a man who was used to getting what he wanted: he was the son of a wealthy family, an heir to a legacy of privilege and prestige, and he could have any woman he desired—or boy. "No, no, no. This will not do..." he slurred to himself, squeezing his fat fists until the blood oozed from his palms; he felt the sting of tears in his eyes. First, his amour was rudely rejected by a Jew bitch, an illegal Jew bitch, who must know he could have her deported with a single word. Then, he was refused admission into the exclusive circle, a world of which he was once the centre. Jaap pouted like a great petulant child, took a deep jagged breath, and wiped the bitter tears from his face. Glancing at his fob watch, he saw it was still early. There was still time to salvage something from the evening.

He stumbled to the scene at the main party, where many of the guests had left or were leaving. Some mingled about the driveway as they waited for their cars, singing and swaying about in a drunken riot. Jaap stormed through the throng, shouldering his way through the mass of uniforms, dinner suits, and fur shawls, and as he passed the banquet table, he gathered up two bottles of gin and stuffed them under his jacket.

"Max!" he bellowed over the heads of the mob. The frontage was a bustling traffic jam of armoured staff cars and gleaming black Mercedes coachwork. Jaap found Max on the edge of the scrum, furiously polishing the fenders with his sleeves.

"Don't bother with that now!" Jaap squeezed his bulk into the little sidecar and slammed the door angrily. "Just get us the fuck out of here."

"Heading home, sir?"

"No." Jaap took a swig of gin and handed the other bottle to Max. "Let's go and visit that sweet little Jew cunt again, see if we can't coax her skirt up this time."

They huddled around the old radio set in Erik's workshop, surrounded by the pleasant aromas of pine sawdust, oils, and glue. A single candle struggled to illuminate their faces in the warm flickering apricot light. Rachel slowly turned the tuning rotor, her eyes closed as she carefully felt for the frequency amongst the hisses, pops, and squeals. Anne sat on Rafe's lap and sucked her thumb like an infant. She had barely left his side since the incident, and was quiet and watchful as an owl. Rachel seemed to brush it off and carry on as usual. Rafe admired her pluck, but he felt he could also sense a change in her. There was an underlying sense of urgency in her now.

The radio burst out into a series of familiar tones: the BBC broadcast from London.

"This is it! Radio Oranje!" Rachel beamed in triumph. She hopped over to the bench and sat next to him and Anne. Rafe revelled in the exquisite warmth of her thigh against his leg. He leaned further over, the bare skin of his arm next to hers. She didn't move away.

"*V is for victory!*" The announcer's thin electronic voice spoke Dutch against a backdrop of crackles and snaps.

Rachel had explained how all domestic stations had been taken over by the NSB, and broadcast nothing but propaganda. This service from London was the exiled government's only voice, and sole reliable source of news. It was naturally forbidden, but everyone with access to a radio set listened religiously every Sunday.

The show began with a news bulletin: "*A great battle has been won by the Royal Navy in the Atlantic! The battleship Bismarck has been sunk!*" "Jolly good show!" Rafe shouted suddenly, pumping his fist in the air and startling both girls. Tomas, Erik's stable dog, yapped excitedly and danced in a circle. Rafe jumped up and paced the room, as if he were listening to a football match, pausing now and then to clarify a point of Dutch with Rachel as the story of the battle unfolded. Rafe's enthusiasm began to infect Anne and she followed him back and forth, giggling and mimicking his actions. *"...and we are pleased to announce that the Bismarck sank by the stern at ten-forty!"* Rafe spun around and lifted Anne high into the air, making her squeal with delight. "Rule Britannia! Britannia rules the waves!" Rafe chanted and swayed her to the rhythm in his arms, like a sailor hoisting a yard. Rachel went down to the *lager* and came up with two bottles of cool beer and a box of Belgian chocolates.

The broadcast ended with a singalong of an old Dutch favourite with a twist; the lyrics had been changed to a patriotic anthem, extolling the virtues of staying true to the nation and using passive resistance to foil the invader, finally urging the people to hold on and persevere until the day when liberation would come. They all swayed in time while Rachel and Anne sang along joyfully.

Afterwards, they indulged Anne and let her stay up late. She dozed in Rachel's lap by the fire with chocolate smeared on her face and hands. Rafe lit his last American cigarette and watched them caper around the room; they looked so harmless and vulnerable. He inwardly cursed the conflict that could turn such innocents into fugitives in their own country. What callous, cruel men plotted to do such things? Rafe never was one for believing in evil, true biblical evil, but now he wondered... Just what kind of enemy were they up against?

Far out on the road, a weak light flashed. The trees lining the track were briefly lit with a cold white light, and a dreadful sound followed: the steady, rasping beat of a motorcycle engine. Rafe's blood froze to ice in his veins. Rachel's small face appeared in the window, a mask of fear. She stood and carried Anne's sleeping form into the annex. When she emerged, they watched the light approach. There was no doubt now: a single headlight bounced down the drive towards them like a winking Cyclopean eye. "That swine has come back for more, " Rafe hissed. "No doubt with a belly full of drink to pluck his blood up."

Rachel threw on her coats and they raced to extinguish the oil lamps. Little Tomas began barking furiously, snapping and snarling at the door. Rafe grabbed Rachel by the elbow and spun her around to face him. "I won't let those pigs touch you, not again." Rachel put both hands on his chest and pushed him backwards through the narrow aperture in the panel. "Stay silent! Whatever they do to me can't be as bad as all of us being arrested." She slammed the panel closed just as the bike came to a long sliding halt on the gravel outside; the bright headlamp shed a cold, white light into the house, casting long, twisted shadows on the walls and floor as the men approached. Tomas redoubled his fury, rasping and yapping, the spittle flying off his jaws like a rabid fox.

Silhouetted against the kitchen window, Jaap tapped on the glass with a half-empty gin bottle. "Hello, hello, my dear..... time for a little drinkie!" His high voice was slurred and thick with lust; the other man hooted with laughter and stumbled about in the background. From his peephole in the wall, Rafe watched Rachel huddled in the shadows; he guessed she would wait and feign sleep first, hoping they would give up. But Rafe knew what these men were here for, and they would not leave without it. He thumbed back the hammer on his .45 and flicked off the safety; there was no way in hell he was going to hide behind this wall while these swine raped Rachel.

This time Jaap hammered his meaty fist on the doorframe, making the windows rattle. "Wakey wakey, sleepy head....time to get up!" he sang sweetly. Anne tugged at his trouser leg; he stepped down and pulled her close to him. "Be silent now," he whispered in her ear. "Please don't fight the men..." She trembled in the darkness, pulling him away from the wall. "Play dead with me."

There was a sudden thunderous crash as Jaap kicked at the door. Rafe felt a shot of adrenaline go through his guts like a hot lance.

"OPEN ZEE FUCKING DOOR IT'S ZEE FUCKING ES ES! he screamed, and both men burst into fits of giggles. The darkness in the annex was lifted by a weak yellow glow as Rachel lit a kerosene lamp.

"Come back tomorrow, Erik is in Amsterdam...." she croaked, trying to sound roused from sleep. "He will be back in the morning..."

"We don't want to see Erik, you stupid bitch." Jaap panted against the glass, fogging it with his hot breath. "Now open this fucking door or I will smash it the fuck in.."

"Come back tomorrow—"

She was cut off by a house-shaking thump as Jaap slammed his full weight against the door; the latch buckled and twisted, but held firm. He cursed and stepped back; this time he took a run up and threw his shoulder into it. With an ear-splitting crack, the old frame timber split and the door flew open wildly, shattering the window's glass and sending plates, crockery, and ornaments crashing onto the floor. Jaap's massive body careened through the room, and unable to check his momentum, slammed into the opposite wall of the annex. The thin panelling bowed and plaster dust sprinkled down on Rafe's head like snowflakes.

Jaap regained his footing and swayed in the centre of the room, too drunk to notice the buckled wall.

"Ah *mien Leif.*" He leered at Rachel with one boozy eye. "Come and see what *Herr* Hartman has brought for you!"

He tossed the empty bottle aside and lumbered at her. She was quick and ducked around the heavy oak table. Tomas snapped and snarled at his heels, his barking becoming high-pitched and desperate in his outrage. With her back to him, she clutched a small paring knife; she circled the wide table slowly, keeping it between them.

"Come on, pussycat....." Jaap grinned. "Just a little fun, eh?"

Tomas got a hold of Jaap's trouser leg and fiercely worried at it like a terrier on a rat. Jaap brought his leg up, and with a great kick, flung the little dog across the room. He cartwheeled through the air and landed with a painful squeak on the stone floor.

Suddenly Anne grabbed at Rafe's pistol; she put herself between him and the wall.  He had to take his eyes off Jaap and fight her off. Her eyes were wild with panic in the half-light, tears streaming down her face. She fought with surprising strength as she struggled to wrestle the weapon from his hand.

"No fight!" she hissed. Rafe gathered her up and lifted her in a bear hug. He stumbled to the bed and fell upon her, smothering her cries with his chest.

"What the hell's got into you girl?" he breathed.

"No fighting!" she sobbed, squirming and bucking wildly under him.

Out in the kitchen there was a yelp, followed by a clattering of pots and pans. Rafe tried to stand, but she clung to his clothes with the grip of a maniac.

"For Christ's sake, girl, let me go!" He shrugged out of his flying jacket and she collapsed on the bed, hysterical.

As Jaap advanced on Rachel, she inched her way backwards to the door. She brandished the knife, stabbing at the air. "Erik is back tomorrow, he will..."

"What will he do, eh, pussycat?" Jaap grinned at Max. "We know your little secret, *mein Leif* .. "

Rachel backed straight into Max. He pinned her arms around her waist and hoisted her high in the air. She shrieked and kicked at Jaap's face with her bare feet, the crushing force of the man's grip pushing the air from her lungs. She gasped and choked, unable to draw breath, and finally he threw her to the ground, slamming her on the hard stone floor. With her arms pinned, she had no way of breaking her fall. There was a hollow crack as her skull impacted the ground.

Jaap stomped one huge booted foot on Rachel's thigh and dropped his pants; his erect penis sprang free and nodded menacingly side to side above her unconscious form like the head of some ribald purple serpent. Jaap hacked up a mouthful of yellow phlegm and lathered up his member.

"This is what you want, eh, pussycat? He knelt before Rachel and pushed up her skirts, panting and wheezing as he forced his face between her thighs, huffing and snorting like a boar at the slop.

Tomas hit a new crescendo of rage; he began to howl and bay. His eyes bulged out of his head and he swung from side to side in frustration. Jaap's saturnine face appeared over Rachel's skirts. "Shoot that fucking dog!" he screamed, his greasy head red as a beet. Obediently, Max drew his Luger and aimed drunkenly at the little red dog. He closed one eye and swayed as he tried to draw a bead on the dog's head.

Rafe turned to the smaller panel next to the pantry, and with a mighty kick, sent it spinning clear off its hinges. In the same movement, he stepped into the kitchen and went smoothly into the classic stance of a pistol marksman, right arm straight out and shoulder pointing at the target. He had Max dead to rights. '*Overgeven!*" Rafe shouted in Dutch. Max reacted instinctively; he pivoted about and aimed at the new threat. Rafe's .45 crashed out, the gunshot obscenely loud in the small room.

A dark red spot appeared magically in the middle of Max's brow; at the same time a cloud of pink vapour bloomed behind his head and the top of his skull leapt up like the shell of an egg. In a great spasm, he pitched forward and crashed face-first onto the floor with a loud slap. For what seemed like a full minute, the kitchen was silent as a tomb. Gun smoke drifted in the beams of the lamplight while Max twitched rhythmically and Rachel wheezed, half-conscious on the floor.

A sudden blood-curdling scream shattered the silence as Jaap leapt to his feet and charged at Rafe. The big man threw himself forward with arms outstretched; he was naked from the waist down, and the sign of his arousal swung wildly beneath his bulging belly. He barely took two steps before his pants caught around his ankles and he flew like a diver across the gap. The momentum of his massive body crashed into Rafe, driving the air from his lungs. The two men smashed through the flimsy annex wall in an explosion of splintered timber and plaster, landing with a nauseating crunch on the solid stone floor.

Rafe was stunned. A bright white light flared in his head like a star shell as his skull bounced on the ground with the full weight of Jaap's bulk on his lower body. Blazing hot pain shot across his palm. As his starred vision resolved, he saw with horror that Jaap was gnawing on his gun hand like a savage cur. Warm blood welled from the ragged wounds across his knuckles as the .45 escaped his grip and went spinning across the polished floorboards, vanishing into the shadows.

Squealing like a sow, Jaap clawed his way up Rafe's body into a full mount and went for his eyes with jagged, yellow nails. Rafe's vision cleared just in time to catch Jaap's fingers inches from his face. Though he was a big man, Jaap had the soft hands of a glutton too long given to rich food and idle play, while Rafe had spent much of his youth boxing and wrestling with the local lads on his father's estate, and he had certainly learned quickly how to deal with a larger opponent.

Rafe twisted his thumbs under Jaap's palms and forced his arms apart. He bucked his hips up and slid under, looping his leg around Jaap's thigh and levering himself across until he was seated on the fat man's belly with his forearm across Jaap's flabby neck.

Rafe drew himself up and came down with a vicious headbutt. Jaap's nose burst apart like an overripe fruit in a spray of blood and mucus. Rafe then changed his grip, forcing one forearm under Jaap's chin, with his other across the back of his neck in a vice-like choke. Howling in outrage, Jaap forced himself up into a seated position, lifting Rafe clean off the ground. In a desperate bid to free himself from the death grip, he reached behind and grabbed a handful of Rafe's testicles. Shouting in indignation, Rafe was forced to relinquish his advantage. He seized the offending hand and prised it open, kicking himself away and rolling out back to the kitchen, bent double in agony. Rafe's whole body was paralysed as he fought back waves of nausea and tunnel vision.

The brief respite gave Jaap a chance to struggle to his feet, blood dribbling out of his ruined nose like a tap. He whimpered and moaned like an old maid. Rafe watched as he fumbled drunkenly in his boot and brought out a *Waffen* SS dagger. It was brightly polished and nearly as long as a bayonet. Rafe rolled neatly to his feet and swung his leg around in an arc, catching Jaap full on the jaw with his boot. Jaap's head snapped back and he rolled forward, making a hollow sound like a coconut as it thumped off the stone floor. His eyes rolled back he began snorting softly through his shattered face.

Rafe found that Rachel had come to. Her lips were rouged with blood, and her face was white as a sheet.

"Are they dead?" she croaked. Rafe snatched up the dagger and slid it under his belt loop.

"This one's dead, I'm afraid," he panted, nudging Max with his boot. "This one's out, but he won't be for long, so you'll need to help me tie him up."

They found Anne and Tomas huddled under the bed with Rafe's .45. He secured the weapon and they left them there to calm down while they dealt with Jaap.

Together, they dragged Jaap's dead weight down the steps to the lager. They hoisted him onto a dining chair and Rafe strapped him tightly to the frame using his belt. They left his pants round his ankles and stuffed a sock in his mouth to stifle his moans. When Rafe reached the top of the stairs, he felt his vision narrow and his head float off his neck. His hands were slick with sweat. Adrenaline raced through his blood like venom, making him tremble and twitch like a puppet. He threw the table cloth over Max's ravaged head to save himself from the sight as much as Rachel.

Rafe had killed men before, but always in the sky. Behind the instruments of an aircraft, thousands of feet in the air, the joining of battle is a sterile, impersonal engagement. The reality of the act at close quarters appalled him. The kitchen stank of cordite and blood, and the floor was riven with the fluids and waste of the man's body, which also lent their familiar stench to the miasma. Rafe gripped Max by his still-warm heels and dragged him out into the cold air, leaving a trail of brain and gore in his wake.

Gathering his wits, Rafe pushed the sidecar behind the house and covered it with straw from the stable. When he returned, Rachel was talking in hushed tones on the telephone.

Her colour had returned and her voice was steady. ".....yes...okay, one hour." She hung up and scowled at Rafe. "Now we are in a real mess.."

"You called the police?"

"Don't be stupid, the police are full of N.S.P. That was a friend of my father's, a member of the resistance group. They are sending some people to help us. We are in great danger now, and we have put them in great danger also."

She snatched up a broom and began sweeping the broken glass, refusing to make eye contact.

"Rachel, I had no choice. Those rotten bastards would have had their way with you, and Lord knows what after..."

"Well.... now one man is dead, and we have an officer of the SS tied up in our cellar. Where do we go from here?"

Rafe's head spun thinking about it. They could dispose of the dead man, however unpleasant it might be, but the prisoner was a different matter altogether. "Your friends...they can help us, yes...surely they have ways to make people...disappear?"

"But what happens after that, when people come looking? There will be an investigation, questions will be asked. You didn't think of that before your heroic act, did you?"

Rafe was dumbfounded "Would you rather I let them violate you? Then kill you, most likely—"

"Of course not!" She rounded on him, her eyes overfilling with agony and fear in the weak yellow lamplight. "But now that we are finished, we can't stay here—look at this place!"

She threw the broom aside in a fit of frustration." You men are all the same. You blunder in, all guns blazing, never thinking of the consequences, the bigger picture. People like you are the reason why we are in this ridiculous situation." With that, she turned and stormed off down the hallway in a fury.

"Like....like me?" Rafe stammered. It was all he could muster; he was not accustomed to being spoken to in such a manner, especially not by a girl barely out of school. Her words sorely wounded him, and he struggled to understand what she meant. He felt wretched. What he needed was a stiff drink to knock the edge off him.

He took the half-empty bottle of Jenever left on the table, and after wiping the neck on his shirt, took a solid pull. The strong juniper flavour was sharper than British gins, but the powerful liquor had the desired effect. Gradually, his muscles ceased quivering and snatching; he felt like a tightly-wound steel spring in his core beginning to release its tension. Outside in the cool, sweet air, he felt his shock and confusion slowly turn to anger. How could she berate him for doing his duty as a gentleman? Had he not just saved her from the worst of all violations? What the devil did she mean? As his body relaxed he felt the pain of his wounds increase. He poured a liberal dash of gin on his mauled hand and miserably massaged his aching manhood.

Crunching gravel roused him from his reverie. A car with its headlights off was slowly creeping up the drive. Rafe ducked into the moonlit shadow of the orchard wall and watched it approach. The little Peugeot struggled up the stony trail with its engine churning asthmatically. It seemed to be listing to one side, and the driver was forced to correct its steering every now and then as it crabbed along. When it emerged from the line of elm trees into the moonlight, Rafe could make out Erik's bearded face in the driver's seat. The car drew to a halt behind the stable and the occupants got out: first Erik, with his familiar gait, followed by what looked like a young woman, and finally a massive giant. The man unfolded himself from the front passenger seat as the coupe's springs creaked and the car righted itself. He moved with the smooth economical power of an athlete as he jogged around the farm house, obviously securing the scene. Rafe saw he was armed with a British Sten gun, and he carried it with purpose. Rafe thought he had better go in and introduce himself before he got shot.

They all stood around the kitchen as Erik poured them neat gin in tin mugs. No names were offered and none asked. Erik clicked his tongue and shook his big, shaggy head as he surveyed the damage.

"Yes, I am dreadfully sorry, old boy.... the rotten bugger came at me like a bloody train."

Rafe eyed the strange couple suspiciously over his mug. The woman was short and lightly built. She wore an expensive wool overcoat and shiny patent leather shoes. Long copper red hair sprung out from under her head scarf. She stood directly in front of the giant with her arms crossed and her finger on her chin. A small frown of concentration wrinkled her brow as Rachel quietly explained the situation in a mixture of Dutch and Yiddish. Rachel talked quickly and forcefully, elaborating with frenetic hand gestures and dramatic facial expressions. Rafe sensed that it was the young woman who would decide the next move.

The colossus towered over them all, his bald head stooping under the huge oak beams of the ceiling. He was an odd-looking creature: his dark brown eyes appeared too small for his face, peeping out above his long equine nose, and he had a cavernous mouth lined with tiny milk teeth. He stood silently, smoking a pungent cigarillo and regarding Rafe with a curious half-smile.

"So, where is Mr. Hartman?" the woman demanded. Her voice, though feminine, had the stony edge of authority.

Rachel shot Rafe an awkward glance. "Bound ...down in the *lager.*"

Rafe led them down the steep, cold steps, his gun drawn and cocked in his hand. The room stank with a sharp mix of body odour and the rusty tang of blood.

Jaap was still seated on the chair, shivering half-naked in the cold. His nose resembled a giant misshapen plum, and dark crimson dried blood caked his lips and chin, while both eyes were swollen almost shut. As they crowded into the tiny room he began growling and wheezing against his gag, bucking and squirming on the chair.

"Please remove that gag, Mr. Rourke," the woman asked calmly.

Rafe obliged by drawing the SS dagger and cutting the blood-stiff sock off Jaap's head.

Jaap coughed and hacked up a thick wad of clotted blood. He burped and retched through a tirade of curses and expletives.

"You'll all hang for this.. " he raged behind a cloud of flying spittle. "Every last one of you...my father..---"

"Your father is a traitor to his nation. You are a family of traitors" the woman said slowly and deliberately.

"Who the fuck are you?" Jaap squealed. His flabby face was slick with sweat, despite the cold. "This man attacked me, he.. he fucking shot my driver dead!" He went a deep crimson colour and the veins in his neck sprung up, thick as hemp ropes under his skin.

"You are a traitor and a defiler of women." The girl spoke softly, thoughtfully, and she gazed up at the single naked bulb that swung from the ceiling as if talking to herself. "You have shamed us all with your cowardice and greed."

Jaap's head swivelled about as he searched desperately for a way out. "You are all fucking crazy!" he shrieked. "Untie me, for Christ's sake'.

The woman turned to Rafe. She spoke in heavily-accented English as Jaap raved on in the background.

"Please give us some time alone." She gave the giant's broad buttocks an affectionate pat. "Henk and I wish to have a private word with our countryman here."

Her breath smelt faintly of cinnamon and tobacco. She held a small, delicate hand out and nodded at the dagger.

"Of course." Rafe shrugged, handing over the blade and starting up the steps.

Henk stopped him with a massive, warm hand on his shoulder. "Don't worry, mister." His rich voice was deeper than the thunder of God. He handed Rafe a cigarillo and broke into a wide, friendly smile. "We'll take care of things."

At the top of the stairs he found Rachel, Erik, and Anne huddled around the door like a family of castaways. Anne clung to Rachel's skirts with her thumb in her mouth. She was drawn and sallow. Rachel gave him a questioning look.

"They want some time alone. I left them to it." Erik lit Rafe's cigarillo with a trembling match. They were all wound up tight like coil springs in a clock.

Rafe spoke to Rachel in English. "What's wrong with that child? She pounced on me like a tiger when I went for you."

Rachel instinctively pulled Anne closer in a protective embrace. "She saw her...our... father leave us one night with a pistol in his hand to..." A shadow of regret passed over her face." We never saw him again."

She looked across to Erik; he avoided her gaze and tugged on his ear nervously. He inhaled as if to say something but seemed to stop himself with great effort. There was an uncomfortable silence as they stood awkwardly in the hallway. Rafe was surprised when Rachel snatched his cigarillo from his fingers and took a dainty puff. As she blew the fragrant blue smoke through her bow lips, Rafe thought she looked like a Hollywood starlet, dramatic and beautiful. A pang of desire plucked at his heart, and he felt a powerful urge to kiss her again.

A heavy crash from below broke the spell, followed by a series of terrible choking and wet slapping noises. Rafe charged through the door, gun drawn, and ran straight into Henk halfway down the steep stairway. "Sweet Christ, man, what's happened?" The big man shook his head and pushed his way past. He was pale and looked rather in a hurry for some fresh air.

At the bottom, Rafe was met with a horrific scene. Jaap had been pitched over onto his back, still strapped to the wooden chair, and his huge, white, blubbery body shuddered and wobbled obscenely in the weak light. The SS dagger stuck hilt-deep into his chest; it twitched in a weak rhythm with the final beats of his heart.

The woman picked a bottle off the shelf, pulled the cork stopper, and raised it in a toast to Rafe. "Such is the fate of traitors." She took a long, deep drink. "This one has gone to join Judas in the ninth circle." Jaap's body sputtered and blubbered as it voided itself across the dusty floor. The room was immediately filled with the sour reek of death.

"My name is Hannie." She smiled sweetly and offered the bottle to him. Rafe stared mutely at the now-steaming corpse. He felt an unclean oath rise into his throat, so he grabbed the bottle and drowned it.

Upstairs, the smell of brewing coffee welcomed them into the kitchen. The first blush of dawn was visible on the horizon. Rafe sat down heavily in a chair by the hearth and stared at the glowing embers. His head throbbed in time with his rapidly-swelling hand. He heard Rachel arguing with Hannie somewhere in the background, but his mind failed to decipher the rapid exchange. He only looked up when Henk appeared in the doorway, holding Jaap's body. The corpse was shrouded in a thick canvas sheet and the giant held him easily in his arms like a child. "We need to bury them before the sunrise," he rumbled.

"I'll help you." Rafe stood and reeled on his feet. "No, you rest, Raf.." Henk called him R-A-F like the acronym. "No, I must insist; it's my mess, I shall clean it up."

In a secluded corner of the orchard, they dug a single grave in silence. After a few shovelfuls of the heavy, dark earth, Rafe gave up and watched Henk work. The man was gifted, and within ten minutes an eight-foot-deep chasm yawned beneath them. Henk gently lowered the two bodies in and said a short prayer in beautifully-enunciated Latin before backfilling the void expertly to level, replacing the cut turf carefully. When he had finished, the ground looked pristine and undisturbed in the pale dawn light.

Sunrise brought with it a freezing squall off the North Sea. It howled hauntingly through the cracks in the walls and shook the window frames. Rachel was packing a sea trunk with her clothes and books while Anne sobbed gently on the bed.

"You're leaving.." Rafe croaked. "It's too dangerous here now," she shot back. "They will come looking for Jaap. His family has influence here." Her tone was accusatory.

Hannie tugged on his sleeve and led him into the hallway, where she sat him on the piano stool. "We will take Rachel and Anne with us today in the car. You will stay here with Erik and Henk. Tonight, we return with the *lijkwagen*."

"A hearse? Good lord, who is that for?"

"For you; you have no paper, you have no Dutch, you ride in a casket." She saw the look on Rafe's face and stifled a chuckle. "Don't worry, *Herr* Rafe, we do it many times. The German won't look into a sealed casket, but you will breathe, I promise."

"Where are you taking us? I have a plane here..."

"I know all this," she cut him off. "There is a safe house in Rotterdam, you go there—

"—I will stay with Rachel." Rafe stood and folded his arms. "She's coming with me, back to England." Hannie smiled up at him, "Shh, *minnaar.*" With a gentle hand on his shoulder, she sat him down again. "Rachel tells me this. When we are in Rotterdam, we will find your gasoline."

"Rachel told you?" His heart leapt. She still had hope.

"*Ja,* she tells me." Hannie smiled indulgently. "But first we get to Rotterdam."

There was little time for a fond farewell. Rachel embraced Erik and all but ignored Rafe. "Your hand is festering; clean the wound," was all she said to him. In the driving rain, they bundled into the little coupe. Rafe watched as they bounced down the muddy track into the haze of the storm. At the last turn before the road, Rachel finally turned around to the back window. Through the rain and distance, he could just make out her pale little face bobbing in the back seat. He felt his heart might break.

Rafe pulled hard on the oars of the little skiff. Every time he pulled, the distance was decreased, only to fall off again as he went forward for another stroke. The scene was a familiar one. They charged down the Cam together; he in his father's skiff, wearing his Cambridge blazer and boater hat, her in a wide punt, holding the infant to her breast. This dream was so frequent, it was like an old friend. A lovely sunny summer's afternoon, groups of students picnicking on the riverbanks, dandelions and laughter drifting through the air. It was a scenario from his carefree youth. Halcyon school days spent drinking and dallying the long summer evenings away. The school, the river, seemed to be real places in the landscape of his psyche, peopled with figures from the past. Places he visited often in his dreams, usually soft pleasant memories. Only this time, he was being left behind; this was the version of the dream with his dead wife and child, the one he dreaded. She sat facing away from him, her broad sun hat obscuring her face, the nursing infant suckled on her breast.

Rafe pulled on the oars with new desperation; it seemed absurd, the sleek skiff would do four or five knots on the punt, he should overhaul her easily, but his arms felt weak, the blades of the oar skipping over the surface of the water, twisting out of his grip. The man in the punt was unnaturally tall and dark; the pole in his hands was similarly outsized, and it seemed to reach way up into the sky, pushing the punt a full furlong with each mighty plunge. "Slow down, please! I'm falling behind!" Rafe's voice was that of a child, high and piping. His wife and the dark man ignored his plea. They pulled away smoothly, rapidly disappearing into the distance. Up river, Rafe saw the scene was changing, a thick fog enveloping the banks, the neatly-shorn grass giving way to a gloomy verdant jungle.

Towering trees bent over the water, twisted with vines and heavy with fat hissing insects.

The current was strong now; like a tidal surge, it creamed up over the bow of the skiff, pushing him further back. He screamed now, "Mary!" Her name came out a ragged roar; his arms were wasted, thin sticks of bone under his blazer, they bowed and cracked under the pressure of the waves. "Mary!, I'm sorry, I can't follow you!" She seemed to hear him, her head jerked up, and she shuffled around slowly on the seat. Only it wasn't her. The hat blew off her head, and her dark hair cascaded out in the breeze; the dead infant ceased its suckling and glared at him, pointing a bony, accusatory finger. Its shrunken mouth was full of blood. It grinned savagely. "No! Not her!" Rachel smiled lovingly and drew the monster to her bleeding bosom. The river became a torrent of worms. Rafe felt a burning pain in his hand and realised with horror that a giant maggot was chewing on his fist. The fat white worm had a human face. Pale blue eyes peeked out from the folds of pale flesh. Overcome with revulsion, Rafe released the oar and shook his hand in a spasm of panic. A scream tore at his throat.

When he awoke, his scream still rang in his ears. Erik suddenly loomed in the doorway of the little room, short of breath. "Jesus Christ, man!" he panted. "You were screaming bloody murder."

"It's nothing," Rafe sighed. "Just a bad dream."

"Best get ready, the wagon will come soon after sunset." Erik was backlit by a halo of deep golden sunlight. Rafe must have slept for most of the day. The knuckles on his left hand had swollen to twice their size; the bite wound was a hot crimson crescent, crusted with dried yellow pus. It pulsed in time with his throbbing head.

Erik drank black coffee from a pewter mug and puffed on his pipe. The kitchen was blue with rank tobacco smoke and hot as an oven. Rafe pounded down a whole pitcher of water and belched painfully. "I could bloody murder a cup of tea." Erik didn't seem to hear him; he sat staring out the window across the field where Henk stood watch, his face gaunt. He seemed to have aged ten years since he arrived back from Amsterdam; the humour had left his eyes, and deep wrinkles furrowed his forehead and bracketed his mouth.

Rafe cleared his throat and broke the grim silence. "Have you a pencil? I need to draw you a picture."

Erik watched as Rafe drew on the plywood with the square grease pencil in quick slashing strokes. When he finished, he stood back and tapped his lips with the pencil.

"Can you guess what that is?" Erik stooped over the drawing and tugged at his beard.

"It looks like the hull of a yacht, the ribs and a central spar, but it's too flat." Rafe nodded with approval. " This is a plan view of the port wing of an aircraft; namely, the plane hidden under an elm tree in your back paddock. We call it the Mosquito."

Erik raised a sceptical eyebrow. "Why do you show me this...I am no engineer, I make clavier, piano, furniture."

"Oh.... but you can, Erik. You see, this wing is not metal, or steel; it is entirely wood. Spruce to be exact." Rafe saw a spark of the old twinkle return to Erik's eye. "You see, we needed a fast bomber, one that could outrun Göring's fighters, and for that we needed a lightweight material, but with the strength of modern aluminium alloys. Spruce was the answer, old boy...wood! " Erik squinted quizzically at Rafe through dusty spectacles.

"Plywood, layered like a strudel." Rafe stacked his hands together. "The grain crossed like thatch, and glued with resin—strong, very strong, and lightweight." Rafe took a broad sheet of brown paper and outlined the wing cross-sections in more detail. He had watched the prototypes being assembled at the De Havilland plant in Salisbury two years ago and knew the patterns well. Erik began to nod his head in recognition of the familiar forms.

For the rest of the afternoon, they paced about the aircraft, assessing the damage in detail; the Stuka's gun had racked across her port side, peppering the leading edge of the wing and cabin with widely-spaced shots. The first thirty-mm round had tumbled through the wing and torn off an interior section upright that attached to the aileron, while the crucial control surface hung limply off its pivots. They found the steel control arm inside the wing undamaged. If Erik could copy the shape of the damaged section it would be a simple matter to repair.

The main problem was the rounds that brought her down, one puncturing the aluminium fuel tank and another piercing through the radiator body. Erik would have to strip off the plywood panels and patch the holes with pitch and canvas, with none of the specialised tools available. It would be a tough job. Rafe made some quick calculations in his head and surmised that they could fly to Dartmoor using only the central and starboard wing tanks, leaving the port wing empty.

"Can you manage it, old boy?" Rafe asked as he dusted his hands on his trousers. Erik took a finger-sized splinter out of the wing and sniffed it thoughtfully. "Spruce?" he questioned

"I believe so, yes, from Canada.."

"Hmm," Erik clicked his tongue and shook his head doubtfully, He paced around the wing, bending and peering into the bullet holes, running his rough hands over the canvas surface. Finally he crumbled the splinter in his calloused hand and sighed, "I can try to do it....for Rachel."

As they walked slowly back through the orchard in the half light, Rafe heard a low distant rumble. He felt the familiar vibration in the soles of his feet, then in the depths of his breast. He grabbed Erik by the back of his coat and dragged him quickly under the cover of a nearby apple tree. The tremor grew rapidly into a mechanical cacophony; the air around them beat and throbbed that their teeth rattled in their jaws. A fight of low-flying Heinkels thundered overhead, brushing the treetops, in the familiar arrow formation. One was running rich, and it trailed a stream of oily black smoke as they passed barely sixty feet above them. Rafe savoured the carbon smell as the cloud descended about them. It was the scent of blood to the hunting hound. He felt the hackles rise on his back. "Looks they're changing tactics," he mused. "Low-level, high-speed attacks." Erik did not hear him; he was bent double under the apple tree with his fingers jammed in his ears, his face screwed up in outrage at the deafening racket. After a minute or so, the thunder receded into the east, leaving clouds of disturbed seabirds and geese cawing and flapping in their wake. A seed of an idea began to form in Rafe's mind. He quickly abandoned his train of thought when he saw the tiny twinkle of light flash between the trees: there was a vehicle approaching.

The gigantic Buick hearse crawled up the drive. It was an American beast, almost twenty feet long, shiny obsidian in the twilight. Henk sat hunched over the wheel in the old-fashioned open drivers cab covered in dust. He grinned and waved as the monstrous car lurched and creaked its way forwards. The expansive rear coach was hidden behind drawn black curtains that swayed morbidly with the rolling motion of the rear axle. Henk swung the hulk around and backed it right up to the front door of the house, coming to a juddering halt in a cloud of dust.

Henk threw open the double rear doors and wheeled out the casket on a large wooden frame with castors. Rafe was immediately hit with a powerful gust of malodorous air. The stale chemical reek of formaldehyde, and beneath that, a sweet, sickly pang of decaying flesh. Rafe felt his gorge rise and pinpricks of sweat spring out on his brow.

On a count of three, Erik and Henk lifted the heavy lid. Rafe winced when he saw the oily stain on the satin lining. "Sorry, Raf, we can't afford new ones." Henk put a huge hand on Rafe's shoulder and handed him a neatly-folded black mourning suit. "Put it on. It's not new, either, I am afraid, but I am sure the previous owner won't mind." The ripe funk stung Rafe's nostrils and made his eyes water; he shrank away in disgust. "Sweet Christ, man, is this really necessary? I mean, they won't be looking into a sealed bloody casket, will they?"

"They have before..." Henk nodded sympathetically. "Sorry, Raf, it's the only way to be safe; they are getting harder to fool around Rotterdam, but this little trick hasn't been uncovered....yet."

"We need to get moving if we want to beat the curfew," Erik interrupted. "Go empty your bowels and get changed. It will be a long drive."

As he undressed in the chilly air, he became aware of just how swollen his left hand had become. He had to unbutton his shirt cuff to pull it out of the sleeve; a sudden flare of pain shot up his wrist as he did so. The skin on his knuckles was bright purple and stretched tight as a pig's bladder over the bulging wound. Vivid scarlet streaks weaved outward, tracing spidery threads across his skin; his whole hand felt heavy and foreign on the end of his wrist.

Rafe pulled on the stiff white cotton shirt. The fabric was soaked with beeswax and stained a pale yellow; the jacket and trousers were two sizes too small, the hems hovering over his ankles and wrists. He shuffled stiffly over to the casket, gathering his resolve. "Here." Henk handed him a small, slender glass vial with a cork stopper. "This is laudanum; if you feel yourself panic you can take two drops, and it will calm you down. If we are stopped and searched you must take it all; it will put you to sleep, a deep sleep."

"Will I wake up?" Rafe held the vial up to the light; the contents glowed a thick venom-like red. "You will!" Henk boomed with laughter. "Whether you will see my face, or God's, who knows!"

Rafe clutched the glass vial in his sweat-slick fist and lowered himself into the narrow space. His knees trembled a little as he sat down. "Steady on, old boy," he said to himself. "Just a little prank we'll play on the bosch, eh?" As he lay back, he found his broad shoulders barely made it between the sideboards. He was forced to assume the pose of the dead, arms crossed on his chest. "There are spacers, here in the top." Erik pointed them out as he lowered the heavy oaken lid. "You will have some light, and plenty of air, so don't think we are trying to kill you."

"The thought never crossed my mind," Rafe quipped weakly as the casket was closed and the lid screwed down into place. Thin slivers of weak lamplight leaked through the gaps in the timber. If he concentrated hard, Rafe could just make out his hand in front of his face.

Rafe was jostled and bumped around inside the cramped space. He found he had to brace his forehead and knees against the lid of the coffin to keep his nose from grievous injury as the giant hearse lumbered down the rough side road. They soon reached the main graded highway and things settled down enough for him to relax slightly. Now there was nothing to distract him, only the first pangs of panic setting in.

Rafe was not a man easily given to phobias or hysteria; he had spent many an hour inside the tiny, cramped cockpit of a single-engined fighter plane; under the duress of combat; facing enemy bullets, flames, low visibility, and all the stresses of war, undaunted. But now, locked in this sarcophagus, he faced his most hated enemy, an adversary whom he feared more than any man, bullet, or bomb: his own idle mind.

It began as a tingling on his lips, which spread to his face. His heart thundered in his breast, and his bowels boiled. Rafe wrung his hands and tried to hum a cheerful tune, but his voice came out ragged and broken, the words dying on his lips as he struggled to recall them. In the total darkness, tiny white spots bloomed in the corner of his eyes with every heartbeat. His thoughts raced, careening out of control, images flashing before him— Billy's anguished face, contorted in the agony of death, the fat Dutchman's bloody grin—and leered at him from the utter darkness. It seemed his mind was intent on tearing itself apart. Rafe bit down on his lower lip, hoping the pain would distract him, but the riot continued.

Blood welled up in his mouth and trickled back into his throat. A sudden urge to scream out for help gripped him, but would they even hear? In desperation, he fumbled for the vial, and Erik's words came back to him, *"Don't think we are trying to kill you."* Rafe's fevered mind probed the possibilities: was this the plan? Would they bury him alive? Rafe tried to dismiss the notions as soon as they occurred, but the doubt lingered.

He drew the vial to his lips; the powerful drug had a harsh sour smell, and whatever it was, it was potent. Rafe hesitated; was this the end for him? Drinking poison, locked in a coffin on the way to Rotterdam?

The utter absurdity of the situation made him chuckle bitterly as he upended the vial and sucked down the fluid: it was acrid. He fought to keep it down; he coughed and retched until he gasped for air, but the drug took hold quickly, smoothly. His body relaxed, time seemed to slow, he felt the sweat cool on his face. He had a soft, sweet feeling like he was dipped in honey. A big, soft, dark blanket was drawn over him, and finally, Rafe slept.

Kurt Schroeder stepped carefully out of the giant porcelain bathtub and stood steaming in front of the floor-to-ceiling window. His buttocks glowed bright pink in the dull morning light as he padded across the marble tiles and seated himself neatly on the stool before the dressing suite. The three mirrors reflected three different angles of his face like a triptych portrait. He studied the images carefully, turning his head in the light, examining the tortured surfaces of his skin. The terrible affliction that plagued him in his adolescence had long since cleared, but it had left its mark.

Schroeder's face was riven with deep scars: his cheeks and chin, forehead and neck, churned about like the landscape of some volcanic moon. The heat of the bath water had turned the craters and valleys an angry crimson, multitudes of broken blood vessels and capillaries weaving outward like lava flows, forming a web-like mask that radiated down his throat to his chest. Schroeder knew every hill, valley, and lake intimately, like the map of a familiar country, a nation of one that he could never escape no matter how far he had come.

And how far he had come, he thought as he patted his skin dry with the soft Egyptian cotton towel. He was not yet forty and he had more than tripled the family fortune. When the war was won—if it was won, he really did not care either way—he would be there to profit from it. It was his way, his *modus operandi*. Other men waged war, started war, ended war. Kurt Schroeder merely made it his business to profit from it, and war was the most profitable business of all. His father had taught him that, before he lost himself to the drink, cards, and dice. When he finally succumbed to his vices, the greater part of the Schroeder empire had been squandered away. Mortgaged, gambled, fucked, and pissed up against the wall.

His father was a weak man; he was haunted by the ghosts of Somme, Passchendaele, and Ypres. They drove him to despair by way of guilt. Fortunately, Kurt had not inherited his father's self-indulgent compassion. "My only vice is my vanity," he sighed to himself as he unpacked his make-up kit.

The pearl- and ivory-inlaid box contained tools of the art: brushes, sponges, pencils, grease paint, powder, colour sticks, oils, creams, and palates. First, a base coat of pale tone applied with a sponge; he worked quickly and efficiently, expertly blending the colour down his throat and across his neck. Next, a layer of powder, followed by a subtle rouge under his cheekbones and filling in his eyebrows with pencil. When he was finished, he sat before the mirror for a full minute, turning his head in every conceivable angle, grinning then scowling, puffing his cheeks and working his jaw like an actor preparing for the stage.

Next. he prepared his hairpiece, carefully oiling and combing it on its spherical stand before placing it on his balding pate and brushing it into his own remaining natural hair.

Then, from a marble pill box, he took his partial denture and polished the solid gold teeth to a high gleam with a leather burnishing cloth. The delicate piece was skilfully sculpted by his personal dentist to fit perfectly against the roof of his mouth.

Finally, when he was satisfied with the transformation, he regarded himself in the polished glass. The thick layer of greasepaint completely obscured the lurid colour of the scars. His skin glowed with a lustrous pale sheen. The veneer could not completely mask the deep wounds on his cheekbones and forehead. Though dulled, the texture remained. In the right light, Schroeder looked unmarked, like a fresh-faced young man of means.

Donning a silk bath gown and slippers, he strode across the marble tiles to the gas fire and rang the service bell. Almost instantaneously, the double doors to the dining room opened and a five-foot-long brass clothes hanger sailed smoothly in on well-oiled castors, and a small, neat man emerged behind it. Gunther, Schroeder's personal aide, was a man of many useful talents. With a minimum of fuss and great economy of movement, he set out an arrangement of freshly-pressed and -laundered shirts, gloves, and monogrammed handkerchiefs on the dressing table.

Schroeder had a busy day ahead: tonight he was hosting a dinner party for the great and good of Amsterdam's business community, and he was personally seeing to the details of every aspect of the evening. One guest in particular was the target of his attention, a banker of great esteem and discretion. A discerning gentleman like himself who, it was rumoured, held exotic tastes in after-dinner entertainment.

"Will you be taking the Bugatti this morning, sir?" Gunther asked, his Bavarian-accented German was clipped and very formal.

"Not today. You will drive me in the Grosser; the Bugatti is running like shit again." Schroeder selected a royal blue Hugo Boss jacket from the rack and a creamy silk brocade shirt. "Just the thing for a casual luncheon, sir." Gunther complimented his choice as he adjusted the jacket lapels and dusted the shoulders with a felt block.

"We shall be visiting the Zwart house at ten, then we meet Colonel Detzner for lunch at one-thirty."

"Very good. Sir, shall I collect some notes from the safe?"

"Yes indeed. Five thousand guilders should do." Schroeder crinkled his face up in disgust. He rather disliked dealing with cash, it was the currency of the under classes, but that NSB sow at the Zwart House only accepted guilders. The thought of spending the best part of a morning with her made Schroeder feel slightly queasy. It was a necessity, of course; he must be the one to judge the produce. It was a delicate matter that he could not leave to Gunther, a question of good taste more than anything. Schroeder considered himself a man of fine judgement when it came to the visceral joys in life: wine, food, fine art, horseflesh, human flesh. He had an especially good eye for flesh, he was commended on that score many an occasion. It was at times such as this that he must step down amongst the muck to pluck out a tasty mushroom.

"Get the Grosser warmed up and bring it around the front, will you? It's bitter out."

The pale ghost of winter still haunted Amsterdam. Although it was mid-morning, an icy mist clung tenaciously around the wide tree-lined boulevards of the wealthy *Oud Zuid* quarter. They shared the neatly-cobbled streets with handsome electric tram cars. Row upon row of monotonous and very tidy brownstone buildings marched shoulder-to-shoulder, block after block, seemingly forever. Tall plane trees stood like sentries along the edge of the roadway, their naked branches just now reluctantly beginning to sprout tiny green buds.

As they headed north through the *Centrum*, passing over a series of canals, the wide streets gave way to a warren of narrow one-way lanes. Gunther skillfully guided the big Benz around the unsighted corners, occasionally stepping on the brakes or leaning on the horn as one of the multitude of cyclists that swarmed the city got in the way. It was a particular plague of this city, Schroeder thought. He had never seen a people so taken with this crude mode of transport, the bicycle. In this cold spring morning, the streets were crammed with bicycles of every shape and size, since the Dutch used them for everything: delivering bread and coal, and using wide three-wheelers with huge boxes filled with milk, flowers, and even paying passengers.

It had been a bleak winter in a dull city. The Queen, Wilhelmina, had long fled to England, and the army had capitulated after a brief but violent struggle when the *Luftwaffe* destroyed most of Rotterdam in a single afternoon. The populace seemed content to struggle on through the occupation stoically. They went through the winter with a kind of dead-eyed, bovine resignation. But with the change of season came a renewed sense that things were moving forward again. Kurt Schroeder had plans for this city. He knew there was real wealth here, a fatted calf fed by centuries of colonial trade and commerce, ripe for the slaughter. And Schroeder would be first to the feast.

The malodorous funk of the fish markets and the clatter of the railyard marked their arrival at their destination. This part of the city was seldom visited by motorcars of this size and style. Everyone stopped what they were doing and stared as the sedan wafted along gracefully. Kurt stared back through the inch-thick window of toughened glass, his scented kerchief held to his nose to filter the rank of the working class: sweat, diesel, and cod fish. This was the district on the edge of the river that was the workhouse of the great city, and here the many trade barges from the continental interior stopped to offload their goods, along with coastal fishing boats and seagoing trade ships from the harbour.

The narrow medieval lanes were crowded with sailors, merchants, bankers, rail workers, and of course now, soldiers of the Reich. A throng of *Kriegsmarine* seamen politely parted as they swung into the arched entrance to the Zwart house.

This grand sixteenth- century mansion had once been the residence of a great family of traders, members of the mighty Dutch East India Company. The weathered stonework above the archway still bore the coat of arms in crusted green copper. Beneath the ancient stone arch hung a more recent wooden sign, "*WEESHIUS*", carved in elaborate gothic script. Whatever its illustrious past, the grand old Zwart house was now an orphanage, a last refuge for unwanted children run by the Dutch government. Since the invasion it had become a ward of the NSB. The National Socialist Party of the Netherlands was very busy of late, and it seemed to have little time for the administration of institutions such as this. So the task was set to the lower orders of the party, small-minded, self-important bureaucrats like the one marching triumphantly up to Schroeder's window now.

Margaret Witlam was a short, rotund woman of about forty; she had thick black hair drawn back in a severe bun. Her NSB uniform was cut very tight and struggled to contain her fleshy bulk, her ample bosom jutting out in front of her like the prow of a tall ship; her stern was equally proportioned. Schroeder had the impression it was more muscle than fat as it jostled around under her skirt. She beamed enthusiastically while he emerged from the back seat of the Benz. "*Godemorgen, Herr* Schroeder!." Her round, moon-like face flushed pink with ardour as she flung a pudgy arm out in a convulsive fascist salute.

"*Hiel* Hitler!" she barked.

Schroeder raised a half-hearted hand in return and started off in the direction of the cook-house. "Let's get this over with, please. I have a lunch appointment."

"*Ja Herr* Schroeder!."

She scrambled on her stubby little legs to overtake him and unlock the thick, iron-banded door at the rear of the building. The dingy ground floor room was part of the old kitchens; it seemed to be three degrees colder than outside and stunk of boiled cabbage and greasy mutton fat. A withered old crone sat hunched next to a smoky pot-belly stove drinking gin from a bottle. The thin white house coat she wore was discoloured with age and an old patched woollen shawl hung about her shoulders like a dead animal. Witlam shouted out orders in low Dutch that Schroeder could not understand, and she sprang to her feet and dashed out of the room and up the staircase with surprising speed.

There was a long awkward silence as they waited. She seemed to sense Schroeder was reluctant to make small talk and held her usually-flapping jaw closed with visible effort. Schroeder drew a thin, silver cigarette case from his jacket pocket and lit a Dunhill without offering her one, then glanced pointedly at a wooden bench across from the stove and coughed gently.

"Oh, of course. *Bitte,* forgive me, take a seat, please. 'She shrugged off her own coat and tossed it across the bench with a flourish. Schroeder sat down and crossed his legs elegantly, instantly assuming a languid, almost feminine posture. "*Danke,*" he whispered under his breath. Margaret took this gesture as an opportunity to start a casual conversation. " This spring we will be putting the men to work, *Herr* Schroeder, yes indeed." She nodded her round head gravely. "Every male of age will be issued with a work order. We will send them to the coast to build the Atlantic Wall; there will be no more sitting around idly getting silly ideas...they will either join the *Wehrmacht* or serve the party....."

As she went on, Schroeder scrunched his eyes shut and pinched his nose between his eyebrows with his thumb and forefinger. The woman was giving him a headache.

There was a shriek from upstairs, followed by clambering footsteps on the wooden stairs. The old crone appeared, dragging two scrawny, bedraggled children by the elbows. She pulled them protesting across the dusty floor and fussed about their clothes and hair, pulling up their socks and tucking in their shirts. "Never mind that, woman...bring them closer into the light so I can see." The old woman prodded them forward with a bony finger to the ribs. "Stand up straight!" Margaret growled.

Both boy and girl were about ten, though without the hastily-tied ribbon in her greasy hair, there wasn't much telling between them. They wore the same rough-cut grey woollen uniform and Roman-style sandals. The boy had a crop of unruly copper hair and huge pale, watery blue eyes set rather too close together. The girl was rail-thin with mousy-brown hair cut short to her ears. "Come closer, boy...take your shirt off." The little urchin stared ahead blankly, not comprehending the command in German. Margaret lunged forward and wrenched the boy almost off his feet; with her powerful ham-like fists she tore the shirt off his back and yanked his shorts down to his ankles. He stood terrified, shivering in the cold. His elbows and knees were scraped and scabbed. Schroeder grabbed him by the shoulders and turned him around gently; his back was criss-crossed with raised purple scars, and they continued down his buttocks and across the back of his legs. Most were healed but there were a few fresh ones across his thighs; this was the sign of a wilful child, one who would not, or could not, be beaten into submission. Schroeder clicked his tongue and shook his head. "No, this will not do." This one was a scrapper; some liked them to put up a fight, but Schroeder and his guest preferred submissive playmates.

"The girl, now, come forward," he ordered. As the child stepped into the weak light of the only window, Schroeder could see she had dried mucus crusted around her nose and her hair was plastered to her forehead with sweat, and a manifest odour of sickness rose off her tiny body. Schroeder recoiled in disgust, clamping his handkerchief over his mouth. "This one has the *grippe*! Get her out of here before she gives it to all of us!"

The old witch quickly herded the little pariahs back up the staircase and promptly returned with two more equally wretched creatures. The boy sobbed pitifully as he undressed, exposing a shrunken left arm and skin pockmarked with ringworm. The girl was even less desirable than the first, gypsy-dark and covered in flea bites. "Christ, woman, is this all you can bring me? The crippled and the sick? "

"My apologies, *Herr* Schroeder." She wrung her hands and exchanged a subtle glance with the old crone. "It has been a hard winter here."

Schroeder smelled a rat. This woman was baiting the trap, perhaps angling him for a sudden rise in tariff. It was a hoary old horse traders' ruse: wheel out the nags and plead poverty of stock, then lead out a shiny thoroughbred for a special price. Beneath his ire, Schroeder found it amusing that she would think him so naïve as to fall for such a clumsy maneuver. He decided to play along, for now. "Okay, *Frau* Witlam, let's not waste any more of this fine morning." He ground his cigarette out theatrically with the heel of his boot.

Margaret nodded and the old woman scurried up the staircase once more. While they waited, she avoided eye contact and her lips twisted as she held back a triumphant smirk. Schroeder contemplated what he would do to her for this little game. She obviously had no idea whom she was dealing with. He had crossed blades with some of the most devious, powerful men in Europe; he had negotiated settlements that had taken decades and involved sums of money that this woman could scarcely imagine.

A young Jewish merchant banker from Geneva had tried to play the ringer with him once, he recalled fondly. Schroeder had him drowned in his bath. He also saw to it that the corpse wasn't discovered until the following autumn, even penning telegrams to his family to assure them all was well while he putrefied. When his corpse was finally discovered, he was more of a melange than a man. He smiled warmly at the memory. *I wonder how long your fat carcass would take to liquefy?*

There was a polite knock on the side door before the old woman entered. This time she led two enchanting creatures by the hand. All thoughts of revenge were temporarily put out of Schroeder's mind and replaced with a sudden and overwhelming warm flush of arousal. "We have just received them this very morning," Margaret enthused. She leaned in and whispered behind her hand, " Their parents were arrested for espionage against the Reich; you know what that means.." She made a small slicing gesture with her thumb across her throat. The boy and girl held hands and looked about the room with innocent, trusting eyes. Both mirrored each other beautifully, like matching dolls. They were plump and clean, their flawless skin glowing pink with health; the girl's long, thick flaxen hair was artfully knitted into twin braids that hung all the way down to her waist, ending in a powder-blue silk bow. She wore a heavy, fur-lined tweed coat against the cold and on her feet she had little polished leather boots and lace-trimmed knee-high stockings. Someone obviously had loved her dearly and spared no expense to dress her in the latest fashions.

The boy was slightly older. Schroeder estimated his age as about twelve, and just the type of boy he wanted. Like his sister, he was well-nourished, apple-cheeked, and chaste as a spring lamb. His head was crowned with thick, curly golden-blond hair like a cherub, and his huge, clear blue eyes glittered like sapphires.

Schroeder produced a bag of boiled sweets from his coat pocket and the children  immediately skipped over to him and held out their hands expectantly. "My name is *Herr* Schroeder, " he sang merrily, his face splitting into a crocodilian grin. "You two will be coming to my house for a party tonight." The girl looked slightly pensive; she popped a sweet into her mouth and sucked thoughtfully for a moment. "Is it a birthday party?" the boy asked in high, piping Dutch. "Yes it is, my darling boy, and it will be ever so much fun." Schroeder ruffled the boy's hair playfully, savouring its silky softness.

"Will *Moeder* and *Popa* come too?" the girl asked hopefully.

Schroeder lied around his grin. "Maybe, we will see."

Margaret shook her head regretfully. "Of course, we will have to bribe the officials if they come back to question them tonight; their family may come here looking for them also."

Schroeder knew where this was going, but he was so mesmerised by the boy that he could barely take his eyes off him. "Very well, how much?" Schroeder pulled the thick wad of guilder notes out of his coat pocket and began counting them out on the bench beside him. He watched Margaret's little porcine eyes sparkle with greed.

"Oh, f-four, 'she stuttered as Schroeder continued peeling notes from the bundle; this trifling amount of money meant absolutely nothing to him, he would throw away one-hundred times this in a card game and barely notice it. "F..five thousand will do fine.." She took the cash in her fist and it vanished into her pocket like a conjurer's trick. Schroeder quickly took the children by the hands and led them out to the waiting Mercedes. Margaret hurried after him, closely followed by the old woman, who began muttering something about her share when Margaret silenced her with a vicious glance. Schroeder settled the two children in the backseat and shut the door gently; he then turned to face Margaret, who was peering past him into the passenger window. "You will, ah, return them..safely...tomorrow?" Schroeder set his face into an unreadable mask, and he stood staring down his nose at the shorter women. He let a moment pass and then responded coolly, "As usual, I can't promise anything, but you will receive the agreed-on compensation if something unfortunate should happen." A shadow of concern briefly flitted over her eyes like a bat in flight. "I see.." She let the matter drop and smiled sweetly up at him. "Well, have a pleasant evening, *Herr* Schroeder...*Heil* Hitler!" The business concluded, Margaret dashed off to her car at a rapid waddle. The old woman hitched up her filthy skirts and curtseyed awkwardly before joining in the escape.

Schroeder left Gunther strict instructions to return directly to the house without stopping and bring the children through the servants' entrance in the rear of the building. He then had Gunther drop himself off at the *Witte Tuinen* restaurant in the centre of Dam Square. The restaurant was an impulse purchase for him, but it had turned out to be a worthy investment. He himself had chosen the staff and had them sent over from Munich. They served a selection of Bavarian dishes and Franconian wines, presented on the finest hand-painted china and solid silver cutlery. The style of the food and décor pandered to the tastes and exuberance of the new officer class in the Reich, a tidal wave of urbane young men, graduates of the military academies in Berlin and Nuremberg who wanted a taste of the fatherland in Amsterdam. They were well-trained, well-paid, and completely convinced of the superiority of all aspects of Teutonic culture. In fact, Schroeder was sure he could count the number of locals dining here on one hand; the rest were all uniformed or off duty officers of the Reich.

The *maître d'hôtel* and head chef were at the front entrance to greet him; they stood stiffly to attention as he breezed past them into the dining hall. It was already almost full to capacity with Saturday lunch patrons. The place was humming with polite conversation and the tinkle of tableware and utensils, the steamy aromas of meat, fish, and pickles mingled with tobacco and sweet fruity wines.

"We will take my usual table by the window."

Schroeder had a carefully-chosen spot next to the picture window. He sat with his back to the view so that he was silhouetted against the light; this allowed him to scrutinise the faces opposite him in better detail, while partially obscuring his own. It was also set slightly apart from the other diners, an insurance against curious listeners.

When seated, the *maître d'* lit Schroeder's cigarette and began a carefully-contrived monologue describing the available wines, beers, and liquors. Schroeder silenced him with a casual wave of his cigarette. "Did you procure the Dutch sausage for tonight? What's its name..?...*Ossen* something.." The head chef stepped forward, beaming with pride. "Yes indeed, sir, we have turned the district upside down to find a freshly-slaughtered oxen; the  sausage is slowly smoking as we speak, although if you don't mind me saying so, sir, it is clearly inferior to our own provincial varieties." Schroeder bristled slightly at the query, but let it pass.

"Indeed, you are correct, my friend, but tonight I host a native of this city and I wish to make him feel comfortable."

The *maître d'* made a timely interruption. "Of course, sir, your judgement is impeccable, as always."

"Bring me a bottle of Brut, ice cold, then a pretzel and mustard. Area Commander von Leeb will be joining me at one-thirty. He will almost certainly order the *steckerlfisch* with potato salad, so have it ready to serve at two." Schroeder went on to detail the whole luncheon dish by dish, the *maître d'* making notes in a tiny order book, every now and then pausing to compliment Schroeder on his exquisite taste and discretion. Once he had sent them off to the kitchen, he sat back and contemplated the hours ahead. He had much to think about.

The events of this evening could set in motion the wheels of the great wealth-harvesting machine he had spent the winter planning, a juggernaut that could make him one of the richest single men on the continent within a matter of months. Once the terrible device was set in motion, Schroeder could sit back and simply watch the crop pile up. It was elegantly simple, audacious, and undeniably diabolical.It was a work of true genius.

The familiar rattle of a *Kübelwagen* heralded the arrival of the first part of the machine, the scythe that would reap Lieutenant Colonel Leo Detzner.

Detzner was second-in-command of the seventh SS *Panzergrenadiers*, the unit assigned governorship of Nord Holland and led by Schroeder's personal friend and hero of the Reich, Commander Gustav von Leeb. Schroeder had first considered von Leeb as his prospect, and indeed he had gone quite a way to groom him for the role. But over the months, he realised that Leeb, although a fearsome warrior, was too much the military man. Born of ancient Prussian nobility, Leeb considered himself an honourable Germanic knight of old, bound by foolish notions of chivalry and nobility. The lives he took in battle were sacrificed in the name of the Reich; he had no stomach for the wholesale extermination Schroeder had in mind.

Detzner, however, was a natural predator. He was born and bred in the German East African Colonies. The only son of the infamous Governor Detzner, the Butcher of Buleago, at the tender age of twelve, Detzner had taken part in putting down the uprising of the native Maji Maji people. It was a brutal campaign lasting months. In the end, the small German government militia and a dozen score loyal Afrikan troops armed with Maxim machine guns had massacred tens of thousands of insurgents. Detzner himself once boasted that he had killed at least one hundred Maji Maji before his twenty-first birthday. It was an auspicious beginning to his career as a soldier.

Through the picture window, Schroeder watched him park the *Kübelwagen* on the pavement right outside the entrance, scattering cyclists and pedestrians as he skidded to a halt. He leapt out and strode purposefully through the entranceway. Ignoring the fawning *maître d',* he burst into the dining hall and picked out Schroeder immediately. He cut a powerful figure. He was at least a head taller than anyone else in the room, dressed in the full field uniform of the SS *Obersturmfuhrer*: black cavalry breeches and knee-high riding boots, starched black tunic, and ankle-length black-leather trench coat; the uniform was cut tight around his massive shoulders and thick neck. His huge bald head was permanently stained a deep mahogany by the harsh African sun, lending his face the colour and texture of untanned rawhide. His features were broad and simple: small muddy green eyes, a bulbous nose, twisted and misshapen from being broken in innumerable brawls. The other diners and staff gave him plenty of space as he crossed the floor to Schroeder's table.

"Good afternoon, Leo. You look well today." Schroeder stood and gestured to the chair opposite. Detzner eyed the single table set for two suspiciously as he shrugged off his great coat and handed it to the waiting concierge. He seemed guarded, tense. The basis of their relationship thus far had been frivolity, carousing. Indeed, this was the first time he had seen Detzner stone-cold sober. "It's a bit early for one of your sex parties. Schroeder, what are you up to?" Schroeder chuckled behind his cigarette.

"All in good time, my friend. Let's take some lunch before we talk business, eh? My treat."

"Fine with me, I'm fucking starving."

"Good, good. Let's have a drink." A waiter appeared carrying two tall pewter steins overflowing with foaming suds. Detzner sucked down almost half the stein in a series of gulps and let out a thunderous belch. "*Ja!* This is the stuff!None of this Dutch donkey piss here, eh?"

"God forbid!" Schroeder agreed. He took a dainty sip and dabbed at his lips with a napkin. "You must try the fish today, Leo. It really is rather good." Detzner's leathery forehead crinkled up as he pondered the menu card. "I will take the *leberkase* first, then the fish." Detzner was a man of great appetites.

"Of course." Schroeder dismissed the waiter with a click of his fingers and lounged back on his chair, an open, easy smile spread on his face. "How is Gustav up there in Holland?"

Detzner snorted derisively. "Ha, we are all bored out of our fuckin' minds! The whole squad is getting the twitch."

As was the custom, they discussed the war at length, first nibbling on pretzels and mustard, then eating salty liver *knödel* soup with silver spoons; by the time the main course arrived, Detzner was on his third stein of strong pilsner. He had developed a distinct flush of rosy colour on his cheeks and seemed to let his guard down a little. He set to the steaming loaf of *leberkase* on his plate with gusto, smacking his lips and licking his knife with relish.

"I must say, I was surprised by your message, *Herr* Schroeder." Detzner spoke around a mouthful of potato salad. "What would a man like you want from a lowly-enlisted man like me?"

"*Bitte*, call me Kurt. I always have need for men like you, men with your, shall I say, Talents...., gifts." Detzner's muddy green eyes flashed. Though he was not an intellectual like himself, Schroeder saw he possessed a certain animal cunning, a nose for trouble, and an instinct for self preservation that had afforded him his rank and reputation as a dangerous man. "Gifts, you say?" Detzner replied.

"Of course..... unique skills, if you like, skills that maybe our good friend Captain von Leeb lacks." Schroeder paused and let that statement hang in the air as the second fish course was served.

"And, pray tell, what would these skills be exactly?"

"Leo...my friend, I think we need not go into details here and now. Let's just say that you and your brothers in assault group seven are...thorough. You like to do a thorough job. Like last year, in Wormhoudt, you know?" Schroeder let it slip so casually it took a moment for Detzner to realise the gravity of what he had just heard. To Schroeder's amusement, he controlled himself admirably, but for a moment his jaw stopped working and hung slack. His already-flushed face took on an even more purple hue while his eyes darted across the table to where his holstered Mauser pistol hung over the empty chair back.

Schroeder had extracted the gruesome tale from a moribund and very drunk petty officer from von Leeb's seventh assault group . The troubled young man had been given leave to attend his father's funeral and felt the need to unburden himself of the truth before he left the next day to face his family.

In the spring of 1940, the young officer was part of the armoured spearhead of the westward advancing forces, a fast-moving mechanised fist designed to punch a hole in the defensive formations of the retreating BEF and French, creating a gaping wound in the line for the masses of mobile infantry to pour in and roll up the front south towards Paris. The unit had been operating at full speed for almost a week, driven by the ruthless ambitions of Leeb to push further and further into the enemy's bleeding flanks and crush pockets of stiff opposition dug in around the north of the city. The men were nearing the point of exhaustion, fighting hard from dawn 'till dusk for days with little sleep. It seemed as though the more success Leeb had, the more it fuelled his desire for destruction.

Leeb's battle fever was infectious, and the men in his small unit matched his frantic, headlong rush stride for stride. The pace was taking its toll, though, and fatigue was starting to show. Among them, Detzner, who led the *5 Kompanie*—was on triple his daily ration of Pervitin tablets. The potent methamphetamine kept them all awake and alert, but it also made Detzner jumpy and even more aggressive than usual. Just outside of the *hinterland* of Paris, the column came up against a small group of British and French riflemen dug in around a farmhouse. They seemed stubbornly determined to fight to the last bullet, and only surrendered after a long morning exchanging fire with heavy machine guns and mortars. By the time the last men finally staggered out of the burning house, covered in soot and waving a pair of white bloomers tied to a broomstick, Detzner was already incandescent with rage.

Leeb sidled up and took in the situation quickly: a total of twenty-eight men streamed out of the ruins of the farm, and he would have to leave a detachment here to take them prisoner while he went on to Paris himself with the Panzer brigade. Detzner's 5 *Kompanie* got the job.

Schroeder recalled how the young officer looked when he described what happened next. His tunic was soaked with sweat, he shivered as if gripped with a fever, and he rocked backwards and forwards on his chair like a confused child. Detzner had waited until the column moved out of sight beyond the tree line and then had the prisoners rounded up and marched into a tumbledown hayloft away from the road. It occurred to the young man that Detzner had absolutely no intention of waiting here on guard duty while the rest of the unit rode triumphantly into Paris. It could take days for the regular infantry to catch up and relieve them, and by that time the party would be over.

The now-protesting prisoners were shut up in the hayloft and the door barricaded with a heavy wagon wheel. Detzner calmly ordered two *Maschinengewehr* crews to set up a crossing field of fire outside, then had the walls doused with petrol from the jerry cans.

Schroeder knew that he had his man cornered. Schroeder was a collector of men, and knew his subjects well. All one needed to do was to gather the right information and one could own men like cattle. Schroeder had become so familiar with the process that he could pinpoint the exact moment when the realisation dawned on the other man's face; he had seen it many times: across crowded boardrooms, card tables, parlours, and countless dining rooms. The look was always the same: heat and sweat, eyes darting left to right as if they were two rats searching frantically for a way out of the man's skull.

Although the *Wehrmacht* valued its experienced officers, it had strict rules regarding the treatment of prisoners. The massacre of twenty-eight unarmed men would be investigated. Detzner could be imprisoned, or at the very least he would surely lose his commission, be stripped of his rank, and sent to the *Ostfront.* A word from Schroeder in the ear of any of the many officials he courted could easily send the man down for good.

Detzner's slack jaw resumed its rhythmic stroke. He snorted and sat back in his chair, small muddy eyes set in a dead unreadable gaze over Schroeder's shoulder through the picture window outside, the shadows of pedestrians flickering over his face like the frames of a film as he quickly weighed his options. It didn't take long; undoubtedly, Detzner understood simple extortion when he saw it. Finally, he took in a deep breath and sighed effusively in a theatrical show of feigned defeat. Across the table, Schroeder was hit by a warm hoppy gust of beer and onions.

At this point, Schroeder decided to sweeten the pot a little; there was little to be gained by having a man over a barrel just to watch him squirm.

"Leo, *bitte,* I understand what happened down in Wormhoudt wasn't exactly standard playing. . .but neither is what I am proposing. That's why I want a man like you, a man who knows that to prosper in this..." Schroeder gestured around him with his cigarette holder. "....situation, one must now dance to his own tunes, take control, lead the polka." Schroeder smiled sweetly and began his pitch.

He considered himself a master of the classic switch game. It was a lure as effective as it was simple: lead your opponent to the edge of the desert and offer him a drink. He spoke around and around in circles, orbiting the obvious point of fact that Detzner's fate rested in his hands, all the while alluding to a way out, an escape clause. Detzner stared somewhere off into the distance, no doubt plotting his own options and weighing them up against the coming proposal. Finally, after the dishes had been cleared and the brandy poured, Schroeder made his point.

"Look around you, the great Jews of this city are cashing out. They are gathering up centuries of hoard and leaving in droves." Schroeder leaned across the table slowly and whispered, "Now is the time to act, my friend. Amsterdam is a fatted calf waiting to be slaughtered; it only needs a butcher to put blade to throat. If we don't do it, someone else will!" Schroeder thumped his small pale fist on the table lightly.

The action awakened Detzner from a trance. He blinked in wonder at the glass of brandy in his hand and the cigar in his lips that someone had put there.

"Money, Leo, millions of marks in gold, gems, cash, and bonds are being smuggled out of this city every day by a torrent of illegal, untraceable, vulnerable enemies of the Reich."

Detzner sipped his cognac and puffed on his cigar. "So what would you have me do about it? "

"Collect it, of course," Schroeder replied abruptly. "You and a handful of your most loyal men can deal with a few unarmed Dutch burghers and merchantmen."

"What if they refuse to hand it over?"

"Convince them, Leo. I think you can be a very convincing man when you want to be."

Detzner's lips twitched around the cigar in some semblance of amusement.  "How would I know where they are? It's a big city."

"I will give you addresses and dates."

"If word gets out that *Wehrmacht* units are robbing refugees..."

Schroeder's face darkened, giving up all pretence of joviality, his pale eyes flashing.

"That will not be a problem, my friend. We will conduct our business at a carefully-chosen time and place. There will be no witnesses, no evidence, and you will see to that."

Detzner's round face slowly spread open in a wolfish grin, only now he realised what Schroeder was alluding to: wholesale murder of unarmed, unsuspecting civilians.

This was a critical point in the tacit negotiation. Schroeder could not be one hundred percent sure the other man had the stomach for slaughter until he showed his hand clearly and gauged the reaction. From behind a shroud of cigarette smoke, he studied Detzner's face in the bright midday glare. The big man sucked his teeth and licked his lips, the greasy film of sweat on his forehead breaking free and trickling down his face to his collar.He dabbed at it with his napkin and chuckled heartedly, shaking his head in amazement.

"Kurt.... you surprise me with your generosity. You offer me not only fortune, but sport as well." He paused, clamping the cigar between his teeth and raising his glass in a salute.

"How the fuck could I refuse?"

On the drive back to the house, Schroeder was filled with a sense of awe at his own prowess. He cradled the warm *ossen* sausage in his lap and savoured its heat and aroma. Tonight he would feed it to his other collaborator, the esteemed *Herr* Wilhelm de Jong, attorney and chief officer of the newly-formed Schroeder de Jong Holdings Limited.

The company was formed as a legal apparatus through which Schroeder could acquire title deeds to properties that had been claimed by the banks in the event of a mortgage default. Herr de Jong managed the insurance underwriters to the bank and in that capacity knew which borrowers were vulnerable. He also managed the finances of many well-heeled Dutch-Jewish families, who were, owing to present circumstances, hastily pulling out of the real estate game in Amsterdam.

When Schroeder first put forward the plan last winter, Wilhelm was, of course, appalled by the idea of taking advantage of his clientele, many of whom he had known for generations and who trusted him comprehensively. Indeed, de Jong was a prominent member of the community in central Amsterdam, by all appearances a hard-working, stoic, God-fearing Protestant family man above reproach. But Schroeder knew different.Almost all men had a fulcrum from which they could be levered. For Detzner, it was cold hard cash, easily brought on the side. De Jong was already a very wealthy man, and thus a somewhat more complicated game. In the end, it was a chance encounter that put Wilhelm within his grasp.

One cold July evening, after an exceptionally dull National Socialist dinner party, Schroeder had accompanied some of the more adventurous guests to an after function in one of the district's colourful gentlemen's clubs. Late in the evening, Schroeder was on his way out to meet Gunther with the car when he heard something oddly out of place that caught his attention: the soft sobbing of a child. Intrigued, he followed the sound through a discrete panel door to a dimly-lit hallway, at the end of which a door stood slightly agar. A thin crack of bright yellow light reached across the carpet towards him. The pitiful sobbing grew louder, now accompanied by the ragged gasping and grunting of a man. Aroused now, Schroeder crept forward and peeked through the gap.

To his astonishment and delight, he beheld there, clear as day in the bright electric lamp light, none other than *Herr* Wilhelm de Jong, on his hands and knees performing a messy act of fellatio on the flaccid penis of a very young-looking rent boy.

Afterwards, Schroeder had Gunther accost de Jong while he tried to make a discreet exit and hustled him into the waiting Mercedes. By the time they arrived at de Jong's hotel in the pale dawn light, Schroeder had arranged the first meeting of the Zaterdag Club.

The first Saturday of every month hence, de Jong's wife took the train down to Antwerp to visit her mother, while Jong would spend the evening at Schroeder's villa.

Schroeder would provide the food and entertainment, while Jong agreed to listen to business proposals. At first it was a gentlemen's agreement that no word of Jong's 'hobbies' would reach the wrong ears, as long as he cooperated, and indeed the first meeting of the Zaterdag Club proceeded more like a wake than a dinner party. That was until the after dinner parlour playmates were introduced.

It only took a few discreet inquiries amongst Schroeder's friends in the National Socialist Party to secure a source for Jong's playmates; After all, the party now controlled most of the civil services. And in the current climate, there was no shortage of orphaned or abandoned children in state care.

That first night in February, Jong put up a front and feigned his disgust. He snatched up his coat and hat and stormed out into the night, only to return twenty minutes later, gushing tears and apologies. Since then, Schroeder had learned to cater to Jong's unique tastes and his ever-evolving level of perversion and depravity.

Schroeder was a man of the world, and had over the years attended his fair share of clandestine parties around Berlin and Munich that catered to exotic sexual tastes. When money was no object, and one had influence in certain circles, many of Europe's elite could indulge in all manner of extreme excess, sexual or otherwise. As such, he was well acquainted with acts of sadistic paedophilia, and although it was not really his cup of tea, he would occasionally take a very young boy, if offered one.

De Jong on the other hand was a ravenous beast for *die kinder.* His twisted lust was like a raging torrent, and once Schroeder had breached the fragile dam holding it back, it had exploded forth in all its grim savagery.

That night Jong looked agitated. He barely touched his meal. He stared down at the plate, pushing a pea around with his fork. De Jong had the aspect of a man who spent his whole life seated at a bureau counting money, hunched over the table with his huge belly overspilling his lap almost to his knees; his waxen skin had the pallor of boiled tripe, dotted with bright orange freckles. Periodically, he glanced over at the double doors that opened out onto the hallway of the east wing, where, after some brandy and coffee, the evening's entertainment would begin.

They sat opposite each other on a long mahogany dining table. Between them lay an impressive array of silver serving platters, each steaming gently over kerosene burners. The cavernous dining hall of the villa was too large for just the two of them, so de Jong preferred to eat in the interior parlour. It was deep in the structure, and no exterior windows looked out onto the world. They had both fallen silent while they ate; the only sound was a ticking, brass sea clock on the wall.


"Is the *ossenworst* any good?" Schroeder asked. "I had an ox sent up from Belgium for it."

"Hmm, what's that? Oh yes, very nice, thank you," de Jong replied absently, his eyes still fixated on the hall doors. Schroeder amused himself with the thought that he could have served him a fat greasy turd and he would have barely noticed. While he ate, Schroeder read through the documents Jong had brought with him: leger balances for various bank accounts, copies of title deeds, and lease holds on properties throughout the city.Occasionally he would turn to a small yellowed notebook and scratch down names and addresses in a neat Gothic script. De Jong watched him nervously over his gold-rimmed spectacles, a patch of oily sweat sprouting on his upper lip.

"They trust you, these...." He leafed through a log book "...Baums?"

"Of course," de Jong replied, filling his pipe. "They want to leave for Canada as soon as possible. As you can see, they have a large chunk of real estate to deal with."

"Indeed.... and they will sign over to my holding office, the first of next month, in exchange for our service."

"That is the understanding, with the option to buy back if the weather changes here for people like the Baums."

"That won't happen. People like the Baums are finished on the continent. All that was once theirs is forfeit." Schroeder rose slowly and strode over to an ornate mantle on the other side of the room.He clasped with gloved hands behind his back. "The only question is what becomes of the financial assets they leave behind them... Wilhelm." De Jong twitched like a cat's tail as Schroeder used his given name.

"You are a practical man; surely you can see the providence in taking prudent measures here. Trust me, I was there in Munich, and Berlin in thirty-sic, when the Nuremberg *Gesetze* really started to bite." Schroeder turned, his eyes sparkling greedily. "It was a blood feast—the wolves gorged, my friend. Millions of marks, trillions, drifted away like embers on the wind."

De Jong's head shook, his jowls wobbling. "That kind of thing can't happen here. There were promises made when we capitulated. We keep our national identity, our civil law..."

"Don't be naïve, Wilhelm," Schroeder scoffed. " It's simply a matter of time now; I know it, you know it, the Baums and every crummy Jew from Danzig to Damascus knows it."

De Jong gulped down his response.He fumbled his match and it fell to the floor, extinguished.

Schroeder's face softened.He sauntered over and proffered his own silver Dunhill lighter. De Jong's eyes once again found the hallway doors.

"That's enough business for tonight.You will be staying for a tipple, *ja*? I have something very special for you this evening," Schroeder purred. "I really should be heading home," de Jong replied weakly, his voice thick with lust.

"Nonsense, the night has only just begun," said Schroeder, pushing a crystal balloon of cognac into his hand.

Schroeder crossed the thick woollen carpet silently to the parlour doors, de Jong following meekly behind, swaying a little on rubbery legs.

Somewhere out across the stormy sea, Rafe heard the faint woman's voice speaking in French like his mother used to. The howling winds carried her words up and down the beach, so he could only pick up snatches of the dialogue, strange passages out of context, isolated, meaningless. He walked towards the voice. It was soothing, beckoning, and it grew stronger as he stumbled on through the night.

Dimly, he became aware he was dreaming. If he focused really hard, he could make the beach disappear; then he would be lying in a strange bed. Faces hovered above him, they seemed to be debating something. The woman's face was familiar. It was the source of the voice, he decided, and slipped back to the beach.

One evening, the woman's voice stopped and was replaced by a rhythmic rasping noise. Rafe found himself sitting up in the strange bed, looking across the room at the woman asleep in a chair. A book lay in her lap, her head resting on her fist, snoring softly. It was Rachel.

Slowly, the events of the last few days came back to him: the flight, the landing, the fight with the big Dutchman. Stiffly, he lay back down and let out a long, low groan. He seemed to be in a tiny attic room, where the thick timber beams of the roof met in an enormous V-shape about three feet above his head. At the foot of his brass bed, a single rosette window with blackout curtains looked out onto a wharf or harbourfront. In the fading twilight he could just make out the masts and rigging of clippers swaying gently on the horizon. Snowy white-breasted gulls called out and circled lazily in the distance. Rafe's left hand hung in a sling over his chest, a shapeless club of grey bandages and pins. He tried moving his fingers but felt them immobilized in the dressing somehow.

As his senses returned, Rafe felt the onset of a violent craving like he had never experienced before. His tongue felt swollen, like choking on a lump of chalk in his mouth. His whole being suddenly screamed out in a frenzied crisis of thirst.

He called out to Rachel, the first attempt coming out as a pathetic hiss of air. He was so weak that dark spots bloomed before his eyes as he struggled to sit up on one elbow. Fast asleep, Rachel had slid down in the chair, hitching her skirt above her knee. Rafe reached out with his good hand and touched her bare leg. She awoke with a snort and then almost leapt out of the chair.

"Water..... please," Rafe croaked. He began to roll off the bed onto the floor. Rachel caught his head in both hands and looked into his eyes. "Rafe, are you there? What's my name?" Rafe looked up into her face and saw her searching his eyes frantically for a sign of recognition.

"Yes, of course, silly. Your name is Rachel, and I'm in dire need of a bloody drink."

"Oh, thank God!" She wrapped her slim arms around his neck and squeezed him tight; the embrace had a positive effect on his ebbing strength. "I thought you would never come back to us."

Rafe had to drain two whole jugs of cold water before he could speak again. "What the hell's been going on?" he panted.

"Two weeks, Rafe; you had a fever. When we opened the casket you were delirious, raving like a lunatic. Father said it's an infection of the blood, from the bite on your hand, plus whatever it was that oaf Henk gave you to drink; it almost took you."

Rafe's head spun. "Where are we?"

"Rotterdam, one of the few blocks left standing after the attack; we are quite safe here, as most of the city centre is deserted." She shivered and hugged herself tightly, despite the warmth in the room. "I will fetch my father; he will want to examine you." With that, she turned and hurried down the narrow wooden staircase. There was some commotion below, followed by many heavy footfalls and what sounded like a small army pounding up the stairs.

Anne, closely followed by Tomas, the little dog who immediately jumped onto the bed and stuck a wet tongue in Rafe's face, then Henk, Hannie, and Rachel crowded into the tiny room, beaming awkwardly. Lastly, a tall, elderly man appeared and dispatched them all back downstairs.

He was almost as tall as Henk, with a rail-thin frame and unruly mop of snow-white hair. He peered at Rafe suspiciously over tiny pince-nez spectacles that balanced on his ample nose.

"So, our lordship has finally joined us!" His clear, sonorous voice spoke perfect English with a Dutch lilt.

"This is my father, Doctor Weiss," Rachel said, almost apologetically.

"Well, you might as well call me Jacob." His long arm reached across the small room and gripped Rafe's good hand firmly. "Let's have a look at that paw of yours."

Jacob unwrapped Rafe's wounded hand and carefully soaked the gauze dressing in warm, salty water. Rafe winced and blanched white when he saw a neat row of black stitches where a large chunk of his hand used to be. "I'm sorry, Rafe." Rachel touched his face gently. " The infection would have killed you."

"I wanted to take off the whole hand!" Jacob snorted. "She wouldn't have any of it!"

"Rafe is a pilot; he needs his hands." Rachel protested. She moved closer to him protectively, then checked herself and drew back. "Anyway, it was unnecessary; this isn't the eighteenth century anymore, Father."

"Hm, well it looks like we got away with it this time." Jacob bent over and took a long, deep sniff, savouring the fragrance like a connoisseur of cheese or wine. "Beautiful! It should heal up nicely from here, so it looks like you can keep both your paws after all."

Rafe felt close to passing out again. Darkness crept into the edges of his vision as his fevered brain struggled to understand the clamour of Dutch voices around him; there seemed to be some discussion about what to do now that he had survived. Rachel took charge and ushered them all out, finally shoving a reluctant Jacob through the doorway and down the stairs with a curse.

In the silence, Rafe slowly recovered his wits. With concerted effort, he stiffly rose from the bed and limped over to a tin washbasin with a small crackled mirror propped against it. A stranger stared back at him: deep crimson smudges under two sunken eyes, his cheekbones jutted out against dry, paper-thin skin. Someone had shaved him, at least, and they had also taken his carefully-cultivated moustache.

Trembling with weakness, he washed in the cold water, a wave of despair welling up suddenly; hot tears burned his eyes, threatening to un-man him. He fought them down, choking them back. "Shambles!" he croaked to himself. "Damn fool business, this!" Bitterly, he followed with some of his more creative oaths and obscenities, spitting the blasphemy and graphic smut into the basin.

When he had finished, he dried his face with the rough rag and returned to the bed, the sense of helplessness and shame abating, replaced by a numbing fatigue.

The next morning, Rachel returned with a steaming bowl of beef and onion stew, the meaty aroma filling the tiny room. Rafe was suddenly ravenous. Rachel watched him eat in silence for a time with a strange maternal expression Rafe had not seen before. When he finished and had licked the spoon clean, she produced some old clothes from a steam trunk and helped him dress. The rough cotton shirt hung off his bony shoulders and the woollen trousers almost wrapped twice around his waist. "Where's my shirt and battle dress?" Rafe protested.

"We can't have you wandering about in a British uniform. This is father's old college stuff. It will have to do for now. I'll have to go out shopping for you later."

Over the following languid days, Rafe fell into a routine of eating and dozing while Rachel read aloud to him. They finished the French translation of *A Tale of Two Cities, Twenty Thousand Leagues Under The Sea,* and then, at Rafe's insistence, the entire

*Selected Works of Jules Verne.* Steadily, the colour returned to his cheeks and his vision sharpened. Jacob removed the catgut stitches and gave him an old tennis ball to squeeze in his hand to recover some of its lost strength and dexterity. Nourished by copious amounts of potatoes, liverwurst, and meatballs, Rafe's natural vigour returned with force. He began performing push-ups while Rachel read. He then began to read to *her* in English from some old copies of *Life* magazine.

From the tiny attic window, they would sit and watch the sunset behind the ruins of the city. The hollowed-out shells of blackened stone buildings were silhouetted against the pale silver and gold of the clouds. Rachel explained how the whole of Rotterdam burned to the ground after the *Luftwaffe* bombardment. Wave after wave of low-flying bombers droned overhead like a great swarm of monstrous insects. The earth shuddered like a living thing, and the thick toxic smoke hung in the air for weeks afterwards. She pointed out where the landmarks of the city once stood: a cathedral, a post office, a hotel, a schoolyard. Rafe described his experiences in London the year past, how they almost pumped the Thames dry trying to extinguish the firestorms, how the flame-driven gales howled through the narrow city lanes, like the mournful wails of a banshee.

"I stayed in London as much as I could; all my friends thought I was mad as a meat axe, but I had the club, my father's club, and his father's club. I'll be damned if I'm going to let those bastards send me running off with my tail between my legs to the country." Rafe had to then explain the tradition of the English Gentlemen's Club, how membership was passed down from father to son and was considered a great honour and privilege, and how it was a "poor show' to stay anywhere else if one was "in town".

"My father is an Army man, you see, a career officer. He was horrified when I chose to sign up with the RAF. I think he would rather I was locked up as a conchie." Rafe went on to tell her about his childhood in Ireland, how his father was promoted to the

Foreign Office and moved to India where he attended school, and later returned to England and started reading law at King's College. In the middle of his second term, the Third Reich rolled into Czechoslovakia, and Rafe signed up the next day. "Was for the best, I suppose. I was failing anyway."

"In your fever dreams, you were crying out a name, a woman's name." Rachel looked sheepish. "Caroline. You were sobbing her name." Rafe felt his face redden, but somehow he kept talking anyway. In this little room with this girl, with all that was happening around them, the ghosts of his own past seemed remote, faded.

"Caroline was my wife; we were children, really, too young. I was a foolish boy, she was the daughter of a Major teaching at Dehradun. In India, the rules were different; we got carried away and suddenly she was with child. It was all a whirlwind." Rafe had never told anyone about it, not really everything. "Father flipped his lid, he chased me down the boys' hall and thrashed me black and blue with his riding crop in front of the whole form. Nevertheless, arrangements were made and we were hastily married just before Christmas in thirty-seven. Mr. and Mrs. O'Rourke, a family man at seventeen.

"She seemed pleased as punch at first, silly little thing, we had no idea what married life meant. We moved into a little officer's cottage by the river while I tried to finish school. After a week, I was going out of my mind; all I wanted to do was play cricket and drink cider at the club.

"That summer was hot, even more than usual. The heat didn't agree with her; she went quiet, withdrawn, something wasn't right. The army doctors we had weren't much chop with that sort of thing, you know. Women's problems." Rafe stared sightless at the floor; it was all playing back in his head now, like some twisted newsreel.

"I was out shooting with my father, stalking tigers in the bush. They told me the baby was coming. I was genuinely pleased. We drove the motorcar all night to get back in time, cigars at the ready."

Rachel had quietly moved over to where he sat on the foot of the bed. She put her warm hand over his. Rafe didn't seem to notice, and he went on.

"The midwife was an old crone, black as your hat she was. Wouldn't let me in at first. Caroline was already gone,; something had torn in her, you see, and the blood wouldn't stop. The boy was stillborn. Our son. She named him before she died. David." Shuddering, the tears came upon him suddenly, his breath coming in ragged convulsions. Rachel said nothing, but she drew him to her; he buried his head in her lap and surrendered.

After a time, he rose and washed his face in the cold soapy water of the basin. When he spoke again, his voice had renewed certainty. "They blamed me, all of them. Her mother never spoke another word to me. Father told me as much, through a fog of whiskey after the funeral. 'You are a curse," he said. 'Since the day you were born you have been a curse on me.'"

Rafe went on to explain how he was sent back home in quiet disgrace. On the long sea voyage, he crawled into a bottle of gin and stayed there. Somewhere off the skeleton coast he tossed a biscuit tin overboard; it contained the last remaining artefacts he had of Caroline: wedding photographs and love notes. Forlorn, it bobbed about in the wake of the ship, refusing to sink.

"Nobody ever asked me about it. It was like it never happened. I thought I could just forget about the whole thing." Rafe shook his head. "Maybe Father is right. You've seen what happens to people around me; they tend to end up in the ground before too long."

Rachel drew him closer; he nestled his head on her warm bosom and listened to her soothing voice as she began recounting her own past.

Her father, Jacob, was born into a family of bourgeois merchantmen in Amsterdam. Soon after graduating from medical school, he rejected his background and became active in the political scene, where he met her mother Sophia, a liberal woman of an entirely new era. Rachel kept a cameo portrait of her mother in a locket. Rafe could immediately see a very strong resemblance to Rachel, the stunning woman in the photograph with thick dark hair cut into a short bob and dark fierce eyes staring hungrily into some distant horizon. Much in contrast to the old stuffy Victorian style of his own mother, this woman was a child of a new century.

After they married, Jacob set up a practice in Paris, where Rachel was born. Rachel remembered growing up surrounded by bohemian artists and intellectuals, parties with jazz music, and flapper dancing. Jacob soon grew tired of the self-indulgent lifestyle and yearned to make a real difference in the world. When the Spanish Civil War broke out, Jacob found his cause and moved the family to Madrid for a year while he treated Republican casualties fighting the fascist Franco government.

Rachel was torn away from her friends and school, and plunged into a desperate fight for survival in an alien city. Despite the danger and poor living conditions, she found solace in music and was admitted into the Royal Academy, where she studied organ and piano under the great Jesus Guridi.

Rafe found himself engrossed in her story; he listened intently, stopping her now and then to ask for more detail here or explain something there. He was surprised to discover she was no silly schoolgirl after all, but a worldly young woman, travelled and experienced, educated and tested by life, and it only made him admire and love her more.

The tide of the war changed that winter in 1936 when, with the help of the *Luftwaffe's* Condor Legion, fascist forces besieged Madrid, threatening to cut the city off from Barcelona and the French border. After many days and nights of pleading, Jacob finally packed up his clinic and they made a desperate bid for the border. On the road to Valencia, Sophia contracted cholera. Rachel's voice thickened as she recalled the rapid course of the illness that took her beloved mother. With all his training and experience, there was nothing Jacob could do to halt the volcanic purge of fluid from her body. In forty-eight hours, Sophia had gone from a beautiful, healthy young woman to a withered bony husk, delirious with fever. At the end, she didn't even recognise her own daughters.

Jacob returned with Anna and Rachel to Amsterdam, where he began a professorship at the August Illustre Athenaeum University. He threw himself into his work. Driven by guilt and tortured with grief, he became isolated and unreachable. Despite her tender years and own grief, Rachel took on the role of mother, caring for Anna and Jacob as Sophia had done.

Rafe was astonished to see the first pale of dawn sneak into the room; they had been talking almost the whole night. Exhausted, they drifted off to sleep fully dressed on the covers. When he woke in the late morning, Rachel was gone, and she had left a note on the bed next to him.

*You are not a curse, Rafe. You are a blessing.*
*X Rachel*

#

Schroeder could just make out the sign through the drifting sheets of drizzle.

Fliegerhorst Deeleen—Restricted Area

The Mercedes bumped along the rough-hewn drive to the gatehouse. It was empty, the fence around the perimeter unfinished. Gunther drove on through the darkness towards the flashing lights of a *Kübelwagen* parked beside a huge pile of lumber. Detzner emerged and signalled for them to kill the headlights. He got in and sat opposite Schroeder in the limousine, his oilskin dripping wet on the leather upholstery.

"Good morning, Kurt, glad you could join us!" Detzner boomed. Schroeder bristled at the familiar address. "You have made the arrangements for our guests?"

"All is in order. It's three tonight, *ja?* An old couple and a lad?" Detzner slurred a little, a whiff of brandy hung in the air. "That's right, the boy shouldn't give you any trouble, he's a simpleton."

Detzner chuckled. "Ha! Jew blood, hey? Probably born to a witch." He pulled out a Walther pistol and snapped back the action. He then peered one-eyed over the sight. "You know I can take care of this myself; there's no reason for you to drive all the way out here every time."

Schroeder ignored him and stared out the window at the rainswept landscape.

They were right on the coast. An icy wind blew off the North Sea, spotting the window glass with drizzle and gently rocking the car on its springs. The airbase was part of the *Arbeitseinsatz* work programme, contract work for the *Luftwaffe* carried out by forced labour gangs. It was to be operational by the summer, at which point they would have to find another location for the disposal of guests.

"How about a drink while we wait, hey?" Without invitation, Detzner opened the little liquor cabinet and poured himself two fingers of Scotch whiskey; he downed it in one and poured another.

They waited in silence as the quarter moon rose to its zenith and the clouds thinned out, revealing a bleak and barren tableau of sand dunes and tundra grasses. Detzner had drained almost half the bottle of Johnnie Walker Red Label when they saw the lights of the van sweep across the field.

Gunther walked out to the gatehouse and paid the driver. He returned with the Baum family, burdened with several large pieces of luggage. Otto Baum, property trader, looked like he was attending a cocktail party; he wore a three-piece suit and white silk kremer. His rotund wife was similarly adorned, draped with furs and a floral cloche hat. The younger Baum followed, clutching his mother's skirts; he beamed and laughed merrily as he swatted at the leaves blown by the wind. They seemed most relieved when they saw Schroeder and his limousine.

"Welcome, *Herr* Baum, and you, *Mevrouw.*" Schroeder had to raise his voice against the rising wind.

"This is my assistant, Mr. Weiss." He gestured to Detzner, who bowed unsteadily. "If you would come this way immediately, please, we are quite late."

Schroeder led the way across the muddy field at a brisk walk; they headed for a copse of pine trees that lined the beach. "I must apologise, sir. My wife, you see, she couldn't decide what to take with us, and our son.. "

"No matter, come along now, not much further."

"We really do appreciate you making your personal plane available to us," Otto Baum panted as he struggled to keep up. He was a big man, and not used to physical exertion. "We should have gotten out last year, but my wife is so stubborn, she hates travelling, it makes her ill."

"I see." Schroeder glanced over his shoulder at Detzner, who was weaving slightly, coming up the rear. Casually, Schroeder interjected, "My good man, I trust you told no one about our arrangements here. Our continued operation relies on the utmost secrecy."

"Of course.. not a word, I didn't even tell the wife until... this evening," Otto wheezed.

"Excellent, this location must remain a secret. I'm taking a great deal of personal risk with this venture."

"You are a truly righteous man, a saint." Otto put his hand on Schroeder's shoulder; his round face was taut with genuine emotion.

They came to a small clearing facing the beach. On the shore side loomed an earthworks sea wall, and the view of the unfinished runway was obscured by a windbreak row of pines. A shallow trench about twelve-feet-long had been excavated hastily in the sandy soil.

Otto looked back through the trees nervously. "Your man, with the luggage, will he be joining us?"

"Later; he is setting the flares for the plane to land," Schroeder replied calmly.

The others emerged through the trees. Otto's wife looked terrified; she stumbled and fell over in the deep sand. Detzner helped her up, and they both swayed drunkenly for a moment. The boy chortled. "Come, Oskar!" Otto chided.

They waited as the tension built. Inwardly, Schroeder was savouring the moment, the calm before the tempest. He let the minutes roll by, it seemed to Schroeder that his senses were enhanced: crickets rasped in the grass, the air hissed through the pines, faintly in the distance waves foamed across the sands. He knew Otto was listening intently for the sound of an aircraft engine, and there was something delicious about his anticipation. He embraced his wife and son; he kissed the top of her head and gently soothed her. His son Oskar grinned up at him credulously.

The feeling of control was exquisite, but like all pleasures, fleeting. Schroeder made a show of consulting his pocket watch. It was almost two a.m. *If we finish this up promptly, I could make it back in time to have a reasonable night's rest.*

"Right, please line up here and face this way. Ladies first, we need to be ready to embark as soon as the plane touches down." Obediently, they shuffled about. "Mr. Weiss, if you please."

Detzner sauntered behind Otto and aimed the Walther at the base of his skull. He held there for a moment, squinting drunkenly; he closed one eye, then the other, and fired.

There was a sharp pop and Otto's hat jumped off his head. A mighty paroxysm gripped his body and he dived headlong into the ditch. Without taking a step, Detzner swiftly turned and shot Mrs. Baum through the ear. She pitched over backwards and sat down heavily on her backside. Her head nodded slowly onto her chest, and a thick torrent of blood spewed forth from her nose.

Still clutching a handful of her skirt, Oskar carefully sat down next to her. "Bang!" he said, and clapped his hands. He put his arms around her neck and they both fell over sideways.

Detzner snorted and shook his head. "Fucking Mongols." From where he stood, he pointed the pistol and fired two shots in quick succession, but both missed and kicked up clouds of sand in the ground behind Oskar. Detzner changed his stance, aimed carefully with a two-handed grip, and fired two more rounds. Both thumped into his head; he sighed and lay still.

Detzner flicked the safety and holstered the weapon. He drew a knife and began stripping the bodies. Schroeder watched his quick, efficient movements with mild amusement. He seemed well practised, like a professional butcher dressing a deer carcass. He ripped the jewels from Mrs. Baum's ears, then carefully unclasped and pocketed the string of pearls around her throat. Detzner then split the blouse and brassiere with the knife and found a wax paper package containing a wad of English pound notes. He quickly pocketed these and rolled her into the ditch.

A few deft strokes of the knife revealed a thin vest hidden under Otto's shirt, and carefully sewn inside was more currency: guilders, francs, and sterling notes. He also uncovered a collection of documents, birth certificates, and sentimental photographs. These he handed to Schroeder. Into Detzner's pockets went Otto's watch and wedding ring. When he was satisfied everything of value had been harvested from the Baums, Detzner laid them end-to-end in the trench face-up, arranging their limbs neatly to the sides. The identification documents were heaped on top with two tins of Shell kerosene.

They both stood for a time and watched the flames take hold. Detzner smoked a cigar and counted the bank notes by the firelight. To a man like him it must have seemed a small fortune. To Schroeder it was next to nothing.

"Sure, I'll be ready." Detzner didn't look up. Gunther appeared through a curtain of smoke. "All the luggage has been taken care of, sir," he said. "I found nothing of interest, except this." He handed Schroeder a heavy leather-bound ledger book gilded with gold filigree. Inside, barely decipherable by the wavering red firelight, all entered in the same neat cursive script, was the long list of waterfront properties and their tenants. Therein laid the real wealth.

The smoke was oily thick now; the fire had consumed the clothing and now fed on the skin and fat. Schroeder spoke through a handkerchief held to his mouth. "Don't try to contact me, I will get in touch with you for the next time." Detzner shrugged off his oilskin and hefted a shovel. As Schroeder strode away, Detzner called after him. "How many more, Kurt, how many more of these poor bastards are there?"

Schroeder stopped; he carefully folded his handkerchief and arranged it in his top pocket. When he turned, his face was impassive. With grim sincerity, he replied, "My dear friend, we have only just begun."

Rafe awoke to a deep thump; the light fittings rocked and the window glass rattled. For a brief moment, he lay frozen with fear. There was a muffled curse in Dutch, followed by a collective hushing sound. Momentarily, he heard Rachel's familiar light steps ascending the staircase. Rafe reached under the bed and found his webbing belt and pistol. She popped her head around the door. "Sorry about that; everything is fine, go back to sleep." Rafe checked his watch; it was half-past three in the morning.

This was the latest in an escalation of nocturnal activities below. At odd hours during the night, the repetitive rhythm of hand-operated machinery could be heard. He was often awakened by lorries and people arriving or leaving just before dawn. He could make out the scraping sounds of heavy objects being shifted around in the basement.

"What's going on down there?" he asked Rachel in the morning. "There was an almighty racket last night."

Rachel sighed and shook her head; she looked frazzled, her normally neat hair was unkempt, and her face was grey with fatigue. "I didn't want us to get involved in this madness."

Rafe coloured. "What madness? Is something wrong? Are we in danger?"

"I suppose it's time you talked to my father."

Sometime after noon, Rafe heard heavy footsteps on the stairs. Jacob and Henk entered, stooping under the door frame; the two big men almost filled the entire room. Jacob sat down opposite Rafe on the worn chair, but Henk remained standing, his arms folded across his chest. Jacob offered Rafe a hand-rolled cigarette from a battered silver tin. Jacob's sleeves were rolled up, and his huge hands were stained with what looked like ink. They puffed away in silence for a while, Jacob regarding Rafe thoughtfully through a cloud of aromatic smoke.

"I trust you are feeling better, Mr. Rourke," Jacob began, his English only slightly accented with a Dutch flint.

"Much better, sir. Thank you."

"You should be, after gobbling up all our butter and bacon, hey," Henk grunted in agreement. Rafe blushed slightly.

"We have had rationing now for a year; you would be familiar with that, hey?"

"Of course, sir."

Jacob dug into his pocket and pulled out a postcard-sized booklet. Inside was a photograph of a young man alongside his address and date of birth, a stamp with the swastika franked over the top. "This was new this year, an identity card issued by the Nazi Party. All Dutch men between eighteen and forty-five must carry it at all times." Henk made a derisive hissing sound.

"Just this month it was announced that all able men not volunteering in the armed forces must report for work at German factories and building sites, *Arbeitseinsatz* they call it." Jacob's mouth grimaced around the German word. He handed the card to Henk, who ignited it with the end of his cigarette. He turned it this way and that until it was fully aflame, and dumped it in the wash basin.

"Earlier this year many of my friends were deported to a work camp in Austria; Gusen camp, it is called. There are many like it all around the place now; they arrest you, you are put on a train, and nobody ever sees or hears from you again."

"We had a strike to protest," said Henk. He continued ruefully, "When all the trains stopped running, the docks closed."

Jacob frowned. "What would you say if I told you that there are camps in the east that are designed for the purpose of collecting all the Jews of Europe together? And not just Jews, but communists, Slavs, Gypsies, Blacks, too. "

"Put to work building tanks, I expect—slave labour," said Rafe.

"Oh, no, my dear boy. It's much worse than that." Jacob's face darkened. "These are death camps; there is no labour, these people are stripped and murdered. We have witnesses, thousands of corpses, heaps of bodies ten-feet high. Our people are being exterminated like rats, like vermin."

Rafe felt chilled. Jacob's stare was intensely unnerving. *Could it really be true? The Nazis were certainly ruthless, but were they capable of mass murder?*

Jacob took off his spectacles and began cleaning them. "You see, Mr. Rourke, my friends here and I have the unfortunate distinction of being twice-enemies of our new masters. We are Jews, and we are also communists. If we were captured, our fate would be sealed."

"What about Rachel and Anna? They are innocent children."

Jacob spread his hands in defeat. "There is no such distinction; the young die alongside the old, the infirm, the sick; they all are put down without mercy."

Jacob paused. Rafe could feel the intense scrutiny as they searched his face for a reaction.

"What I am trying to say to you, Mr. Rourke, is that you have found yourself right in the middle of a very volatile situation. Some of us here in Holland are quite happy to cooperate with the authorities, some of us are not, and some of us have no choice. We either escape, or we stay and fight." Jacob's chest swelled, and he drew his head back slightly.

"As Jews, and communists, we want to fight."

"I should think so, damned good show," Rafe replied sincerely.

"What is it that you want?"

Although Rafe was expecting the question, he found himself at a loss. The only sane course of action would be to follow his orders, burn the Mosquito, destroy the radar device, and find a way back home. It was difficult, but not impossible. Many downed airmen had returned with the help of resistance networks.

But he dearly wanted to make amends; his reckless actions had cost the life of a young man, and nearly put crucial allied technology into the hands of the enemy. Something useful had to come of it. The only redemption would be to return the aircraft and its device to England intact, and in doing so provide a means of escape for

Rachel and her sister Anne. His mind raced; he was sure that with Erik's help he could repair the damage and modify the aft fuselage to accommodate a handful of passengers. The risks were high. Even if he could somehow find the fuel, there was no guarantee that the engines would even start, let alone make the run across the Channel.

But he had to try; there was a chance, a fine chance he could make good his escape and save Rachel from this nightmarish fate.

"I want you to help me get that plane over the Channel, and I want to take Rachel and Anne with me."

Jacob and Henk shared a sagacious look. "We thought you might say that," said Henk smiling.

"Rachel spoke of this; she seems to have it in her mind that you can work miracles," Jacob sighed.

Rafe's heart swelled into his throat. "I know I can do it. The damage the plane suffered is minimal, we can patch up the tanks and wing skins and we can be in England in a matter of hours..."

"It's risky, the only way to get fuel for those things is to steal it from the Germans." Jacob seemed doubtful

"Luckily, we have friends who steal from the Germans professionally," Henk retorted.

"And the Germans, they will attack anything in the air; half the *Luftwaffe* is stationed right on the coast."

Jacob shook his head.

"This is no ordinary kite. It can outrun any fighter the bastards put up. I was personally involved in its design; it's the fastest thing in the sky. By the time they get airborne, we'll be too far ahead for them to catch us...."

Jacob held up a long finger, stopping Rafe mid-stream. "*Ja*, okay, I will think about this. In the meantime, I think we need to make some introductions."

Jacob led Rafe down the staircase from the attic to the rooms below. The windows were all blown out, replaced with sturdy timber pallets nailed to the interior frames. Fingers of watery sunlight filtered through the gaps in the planks, striping the floor and walls. Other than this, it seemed a normal working-class household: there were three bedrooms, sparsely furnished; a kitchen and washroom, meagre, but clean and orderly. "This location we took over after the bombing. From the outside it appears mostly demolished." Jacob led them down another short L-shaped staircase.

Rafe was surprised to see the ground floor was once a shopfront. The large picture window was shattered and the room's contents were strewn chaotically across the tiled floor: dead flowers, thousands of them, among countless broken terracotta pots and ceramic vases. Jacob lowered his voice to almost a whisper, "We left this as we found it; it was a florist, specialising in weddings." "The looters leave us alone," added Henk.

They all stooped to fit into yet another staircase; this one tiny, almost miniature in a medieval style. Jacob turned on the yellow, fly-spotted bulb. The weak amber light revealed a heavy iron-studded door. Jacob knocked five times in a deliberate rhythm. They waited, and Rafe had the distinct feeling he was being watched from afar. After a minute's pause, the door slowly opened outwards. It was Rachel, dressed in a housecoat and apron.

"Come in," she said cheerfully. "We are about to sit down to lunch."

The windowless basement had the air of a subterranean dungeon. Heavy, rough-hewn stone lined the walls, and a multitude of various gas lamps struggled against the deep gloom. Seated around a long dining table were six people. One he recognised as Hannie, the girl with the fiery nimbus of red hair from the farmhouse. The others, all men, appeared to Rafe like a motley collection of misfits and street thugs. To Rafe's surprise, they all stood respectfully as Jacob took his place at the head of the table.

Rachel served them all steaming piles of boiled potatoes and cabbage dripping with butter. They ate quickly in awkward silence.

Rafe felt he was being carefully appraised, while he, in turn, took a few moments to ponder this odd group.

One man stood out from the others. He was handsome and well-dressed, his hair neatly barbered and pomaded. He wore a well-tailored vest that hugged his slim waist, and his shirt was crisp and starched. He seemed like he would be more comfortable loafing around a nightclub. Next to him sat a stout fellow with a thick neck and a wide back. Although he was similarly well-dressed, it was obvious that he was a brawler. His nose was flattened and scarred from being broken multiple times, and his cauliflower ears looked like they were hastily sculpted out of dough. His pinstriped shirtsleeves were rolled up, revealing the tattoos of a sailor.

Next to Jacob, hunched in whispered conversation, was a middle-aged man with thick, curly white hair. His shoulders were unusually narrow and rounded and his great hands long and dexterous. He watched Rafe through a very thick pair of bifocal spectacles, which unnaturally magnified and distorted his pale blue eyes.

The closest scrutiny of all came from the boy seated next to Rachel. He appeared no older than twelve or thirteen, very slight and pale with a soft downy moustache clinging to his upper lip. He was dressed in baggy, dirty clothes a few sizes too big and his hands were filthy with ink and grime. He had a curious expression on his grubby face, something like admiration mixed with envy. He sat so close to Rachel he was almost sitting in her lap.

The humble meal consumed, Jacob began the introductions over strong coffee in tin mugs.

"We are an independent group, and we operate as part of a wider network of resistance. Most of us were members of the *Communistische Partij Nederland* before it was outlawed by the Nazis." Jacob's tone turned solemn. "The people at this table risk their lives everyday to defy the authorities. To protect ourselves and our families we use a *nom de guerre.*

"Hannie, you have met before, I believe." She smiled sweetly. Rafe shivered slightly as he recalled how this small shrew-like woman knifed the fat man in Erik's root cellar. "She speaks excellent German and can be very charming." Rafe had to agree. Though not especially pretty in the classical sense, Hannie had a naughty impish face and a nice rounded stern that soldiers appreciate.

"This handsome gentleman is Marcus, with the help of his companion Jan he 'finds' things for our cause; actually, before the war, Marcus could 'find' just about anything for you." Marcus looked somewhat sheepish, but he stood up and shook Rafe's hand graciously. Jan's grip was vice-like, his huge fist gnarled and hard as stone.

"I am Gerrit," the older man introduced himself curtly. He didn't offer up any further information about his role, but Rafe figured he was involved in some type of forgery; he had an oversized pocket protector stuffed with many kinds of different pens, brushes, and styluses.

"Finally, we have Anton, our junior partner." The boy clearly blanched at the insult.

He stood up and saluted stiffly like a soldier. Rafe smiled indulgently and saluted back. "Anton may look harmless," said Hannie, "but he can make himself so small he can hide almost anywhere, he can also climb like a monkey and is utterly fearless of heights and barbed wire."

"He should be in school," scolded Jacob.

"For what, to learn how to be a shit-eating Nazi?" The boy swore in high, piping French.

Everybody except Rachel laughed heartily. Anton blushed in indignation; he plainly wanted to be taken seriously.

"You must forgive Anton, Rafe ; he grew up on the streets of Brussels and Amsterdam and he picked up some bad habits."

"How many Nazis have you killed?" Anton asked suddenly. Taken aback, Rafe looked about the faces around the table, and to his chagrin they all waited expectantly for an answer.

"Well, er, let me see now." Rafe put on an air of calculation, but in truth he had his total score fully worked out already, as every young airman in the RAF had.

"I got three Heinkels last summer, two burned all the way down and the other smashed into the Channel, so that's two crews each. I also shot up a 109 on my way home—he blew up—so that's seven, and those two Stukas on my way over here, so that's a total of eleven so far confirmed for sure. I have damaged many others; sometimes you have to share kills, since we would take turns at them. Oh, also that Dutch SS chap at the farm. I'd say a good round thirteen would be a fair number for me."

The faces around the table ranged from impressed to horrified: Anton's face glowed with adoration, Jan nodded sagely, Hannie twirled her hair around her finger and looked coyly at her shoes. Rachel held her hand across her mouth in consternation.

"How many have you lot disposed of?" asked Rafe casually.

"None!" replied Marcus. "We want to change that," Hannie interrupted, "but we lack the means."

"We only lack the will!" Henk shot back. An argument ensued ; a heady mix of Dutch, French, and what sounded like Yiddish. After a few moments, Jacob stood and banged his fist on the table, calling order The protagonists quickly shrunk into a sulk like a class of errant schoolchildren.

"Okay, Rafe, please forgive this rude behaviour; we sometimes forget our manners." He sat down and took a moment to collect his thoughts. His fingers formed a steeple that touched his lips. Finally, he spoke in an even-measured tone.

"Our activities so far have been restricted. The work we do is important!" He jabbed his finger down on the tabletop to emphasise the point. "We print and distribute our socialist newspaper *De Waarheid*. It is banned, but we take great risks to keep it in print; our press here next door is the largest free machine in the Netherlands. Gerrit and I are very proud of that fact." Gerrit raised his chin and grunted with satisfaction. Jacob went on, "We also forge identification papers and ration cards; we have surely saved many lives this way, and many lives to come." Gerrit clapped his hands loudly, once.

Henk sighed "Yes, but other groups are doing more. CS 6, they have taken out three collaborating traitors this month already."

"CS 6 have proper weapons," Gerrit growled, "and trained people."

"We have weapon stores available to us!" Henk retorted. Another heated debate began. It seemed to Rafe that the younger members of the group wanted to start offensive action, while Jacob and Gerrit advised caution. It took a full minute for Jacob to regain control again.

"Rafe, we have a list of people, a blacklist. These are dangerous, evil people working with the enemy to find our agents and have them murdered. They condemn whole families to death by having them deported to camps; they are traitors and informers. Some are Dutch collaborating for money or position, some are German army personnel or staff. We know how to find them when they are vulnerable, but we don't have the means to silence them."

"*We* are not killers or soldiers, we don't know how to use weapons effectively," Hannie broke in. Rafe looked Jan and Henk over doubtfully; they both looked capable enough. Marcus noticed Rafe's appraisal, "We can handle ourselves in a scrap, but killing someone quickly and cleanly is not as easy as cracking a few heads, eh, tough guy?" He flicked his cigarillo butt at Jan's head, it bounced off in a puff of orange sparks. Jan snorted but didn't move an inch.

Jacob turned to Rafe, "You mentioned you grew up in a military family—your father, he was a career soldier?"

"Yes, still is, in fact."

"You must have had some experience with firearms, marksmanship." Rafe saw where this was going. "Of course," he replied.

"Then you will help us, and we will help you. Marcus believes he can arrange for a fuel truck to be stolen.."

"Found," Marcus corrected.

"..From a *Luftwaffe* aerodrome over in Arnhem, about three hours east of here." Rafe's heart hopped like a rabbit.

"He is confident that he can get it up to Erik's farm if he has the right documents. Gerrit will take care of those." Gerrit grunted in agreement.

"It's a dangerous game, if we are discovered we will be shot as enemy agents," Marcus said gravely. "They take you out to the dunes and put a bullet in your spine, there are many of our friends buried out there."

"What do you want from me?" Rafe blurted out. "I'll do whatever is required."

Jacob glanced at Gerrit, who nodded almost imperceptibly. Jacob took a deep breath. "It's quite simple. We want you to help us kill a high-ranking party member in Amsterdam."

#

Rafe followed Jacob, Gerrit, and Henk through a narrow shaft into a sub-basement. The stone walls seeped damp, silty canal water, and their breath fogged in the frigid air. After a few steps, they emerged into the neighbouring building's cellar. "The building above collapsed in the bombing; this whole basement was buried, and this is the only access now." Gerrit threw a switch and an odd assortment of light bulbs strung in the ceiling stuttered into life with pops and clicks. It felt like he was being admitted into an inner *sanctum sanctorum.*

The flickering light revealed a cavernous subterranean workshop filled with all manners of curious objects. The space was dominated by a huge vintage printing press. Its bulky wrought-iron frame held dozens of brass wheels and cogs, and an earthy smell of grease and ink permeated the room. "We were lucky to save this press. I restored it myself, it's fully functional," Gerrit said proudly.

Sandwiched between stacks of paper was a strange contraption consisting of two bicycles bolted to the floor that somehow connected to what looked like a jumble of old car parts, cables snaking across the room to a wall stacked with a series of motor car batteries. The whole machine emitted a low, ominous hum. Jacob whispered, "We call this Gerrit's gorgon. I wouldn't get too close to it if I were you."

"You may scoff, but this provides reliable electricity for the whole building."

They weaved through piles of junk until they came to a little office partition that Gerrit used as a workshop. A draughtsman's table was set out with the tools of a master forger: boxes of cast type blocks, ink rollers, and scalpel blades. There was even a painter's palette with a full spectrum of shades of blue, red, and black ink.

On the naked brick wall, a portrait of Karl Marx stared down at Rafe disapprovingly.

Gerrit cleared off the table and opened a manila envelope sealed with string. Jacob spoke *sotto voce*, "We have a network of people who give us information on collaborators. Gerrit and I collect evidence against them in the hope we can use it at a later date."

Gerrit spread half-a-dozen newspaper clippings on the table, along with typed notes and some official-looking mimeographs. One clipping had a large photograph under the headline *Happy Birthday!* in gothic German script. It showed Half-a-dozen *Wehrmacht* officers posed around a beautiful white horse looking very pleased with themselves. "This is the lowest publication in Holland, a local version of *Der Stürmer*, foisted upon us by the Dutch Nazi party."

Gerrit pointed out an odd-looking man in a tailored dinner suit. There was something unnatural about his facial features, like a waxen figure. "This...creature.. is called Kurt Schroeder, a financier and industrialist from Munich. This is the only decent image we have been able to find of him. He is very secretive, and avoids being photographed."

"He's the target?" Asked Rafe. "A civilian dandy?"

Jacob replied, "He is a prime mover in the upper layers of the Nazi Party; his holdings finance *Wehrmacht* purchases of petrol and coal, making him a good deal of money in the process. He has connections with Hitler's thugs in government, paying bribes and buying gifts, throwing decadent parties, that sort of thing."

Henk spat, "Capitalist swine! But that's not the worst of it."

"Indeed, this odious reptile has recently made his nest in Amsterdam, and he is wasting no time in gorging himself on our blood."

"Schroeder first came to our attention when we caught him buying information on property-owning Jews in the city. he was offering expedited sales and help with moving equity around and out of Holland after the capitulation, a kind of insurance against Nazi seizures of Jew-owned property that happened in Germany. We warned people about him and people, for the most part, stayed away. But recently these people have started to vanish without trace, and their assets somehow find their way into the ownership of his finance group."

Gerrit bit his knuckle and shook his grey head. "We couldn't figure out how he was doing it, until we discovered his little arrangement with one of our very own." Gerrit produced an identity picture of a pale, doughy, middle-aged fellow. Henk hissed at the sight of it.

"Wilhelm de Jong, a traitor and a pederast, among other things," said Jacob. "It seems they both share a taste for Pederasty "

Rafe flushed pink and felt his gorge rise; he had never heard of such a thing before.

"I think we better get Rafe a drink," said Jacob.

"It's not that unusual among capitalist elites," remarked Gerrit. "Limitless wealth breeds perversion of all kinds.

"That's how we found him. He was renting orphans from a children's home in Haarlem, they would come back stupefied and sodomized."

Rafe gratefully took a pull from a bottle of gin Jacob handed him.

"De Jong happens to be a real estate attorney of some note; he represents many of the city's largest stakeholders in apartment blocks, a good number of these are Jews who are looking for a way out.

"We think Schroeder is likely bribing or blackmailing Jong into giving up his clients, they sign over their assets to Schroeder for guardianship and he arranges for them to escape.

"But, of course, there is no escape," said Jacob gravely. "He simply murders them and keeps the properties for himself."

"Monstrous," Rafe uttered softly. "Perfectly beastly." Rafe looked more closely at the strange man in the newspaper clipping; his face was very small and rendered in the half-tone pattern of the newspaper screen print, but even so Rafe felt he saw something of the devil in him. Despite his sophisticated surroundings, he had the chilling aspect of a predatory animal.

Jacob lit a cigarette and went on, "Which brings us to the third member of this cabal, and by far the most dangerous. We have no pictures of this man, only basic descriptions from Marcus. *Obersturmbannführer* Leo Detzner. Schroeder's attack dog. SS officer and trigger man, together with Schroeder and his driver they lure these unfortunate people into a rendezvous outside the city where Detzner is waiting. They are never heard of again."

"Most likely shot and buried somewhere close by," sighed Gerrit, "Detzner then presumably gets his share of the valuables, these people come prepared for a long stay abroad and would be carrying considerable amounts of ready cash on their person."

For a moment they all stood mute, smoking. Rafe could scant believe what he had got himself into. it seemed like a scene from an American melodrama.

Rafe finally broke the silence. "So you want to get all three men?"

Jacob glanced at Gerrit. "We think we can bring de Jong to justice later, he's not likely to go anywhere after the war and he's not hard to get hold of, but Detzner and Schroeder need to be dealt with right away before they can do any more harm."

"So what's to be done? I presume you have come up with a plan of action?"

"Well, we have a....proposal," said Gerrit meekly.

"There is an opportunity coming up soon, but we need time to prepare. It's probably too late." Jacob sounded despondent. Henk was more convinced. "If we miss this chance, how many will be murdered while we wait for the next?" He hammered his great fist onto the table. Rafe winced as it nearly collapsed "We must strike this time! "

Gerrit coloured. "But we risk everything; we could all be exposed and arrested, then we all die and accomplish nothing!"

Something of a shouting match began in Dutch. Rafe took another slug of gin. Henk's brio was infectious, and the strong liquor started to work its old magic. He stepped into the fray.

"Gentlemen, please, let's try to be professional and keep a cool head about all this. Gerrit, can you please elaborate on this proposal?

Gerrit took a brief moment to compose himself; he smoothed back his shock of feathery white hair and lit yet another cigarette. "Four days from now, it is Father's Day, which also happens to be Ascension Day, the twenty-fifth. This is a public feast day in Germany. The company commander in Amsterdam, von Leeb, is here." He took a pencil and circled the mounted officer in the newspaper picture. "He has insisted on parading the whole Garrison around Dam Square. In honour of the *Führer*, he has invited all the great and the good of the NSB and SS, including many of his personal friends, to join the procession. We have good information that Schroeder and Detzner will take part. Both of our game birds will be in the same motorcar in the same place at the same time exposed, almost guaranteed..."

Jacob broke in, "In the middle of the day, surrounded by armed SS.."

Henk answered, "That's why we wait until the column breaks up, after the show is over the soldiers will go south back to the barracks in Kerkstraat. Leeb and his *makkers* will head east to the park for the beer and sausages." Henk pulled a tatty map of the city out of his pants pocket. He had drawn a crude tactical layout with a grease pencil. "We follow Schroeder's car and attack when they are out of sight of the formation, here, at the gate of the park."

"What happens then? The city will be crowded with party traitors, do we just shoot them up too? How can we escape?" Jacob bowed his head and squeezed the bridge of his nose between his thumb and forefinger.

"This is our problem, Rafe," said Gerrit. "We can't grow wings and fly away; sure, we could probably get guns or bombs on them, but we would be pursued. Even if we escaped the city they would hunt us down eventually."

Rafe thought for a bit, contemplating the map and stroking his moustache. The centre of Amsterdam looked like a giant thumb print: the square in the middle, and loops of narrow streets and canals in concentric rings radiating out like the ridges of a thumb. The vestiges of an idea nested in his head like a bird.

"Righto—firstly, may I take this map, please?"

"Take it. Anything you need, take it," said Henk.

"Secondly, what kind of weapons do we have?"

Gerrit led them to a corner that had been sectioned off with pallets of timber. He grabbed a large cylindrical object from beneath and dragged it out into the light. Rafe recognised it immediately as a SOE drop canister, it was covered in filth and corrosion. "We had this handed in to us by a friendly Belgian boson who fished it out of the Rupel."

Wrapped in oily canvas were three Sten guns, a simple weapon of pressed steel; ugly but crudely effective up close. They looked to be in fair condition. "Have these been test-fired?" asked Rafe. "No, they had been soaking in the river for God knows how long. I took them apart and cleaned them as best I could, though I don't know much about guns," said Gerrit.

There were five boxes of ammunition sealed in wax, along with the candy-bar-shaped magazines. A dozen rusty hand grenades, a box of twenty tire bombs, small shoe polish tin-shaped magnetic charges designed to disable truck wheels.

"Not exactly the subtle tools of an assassin," sighed Rafe as he picked up a Sten and felt the weight: it was fairly light with a skeleton stock. A side-projecting magazine doubled as the fore-grip. It was not an accurate weapon, it didn't even have iron sights on the barrel, they would have to rely on volume of fire to do the job. "It's an awkward shape, hard to conceal," said Rafe. "Do you have metal files and welding equipment? We could modify it, cut down the stock and barrel."

"Yes, of course, but what about these little bombs? Could we put them together, make a big bomb? We can throw it in the car and blow them up," suggested Gerrit.

Rafe shook his head. "Not likely; these have very limited punch, enough to bust a tyre and little else. These hand grenades would be more effective. I would suggest hitting them with gunfire first and then tossing a couple of those in the motorcar, then making a run for it." Henk looked delighted, and he clapped his hands. "That's what we need! Some aggressive action."

Rafe realised the three men were beaming. He felt for the first time that they were really looking to him, not only for leadership, but for inspiration, a figure of defiance to rally around. "We need to test these. Is there somewhere we can go? It will make a hell of a bloody racket, I'm afraid "

"I know just the place!" said Henk.

The sun was low in the west when they emerged out onto the darkening street. Most of the buildings were ruins; a few stone facades still stood, surrounded by high piles of smashed brick and splintered beams. Although the street itself had been cleared and swept of debris. There was no traffic, the only sign of life was a scrawny cur sniffing for rats.

Anton went ahead, running with a curious loping gait. He vanished behind a high wall across the carriageway and re-appeared a few moments later, signalling the all-clear. They hurried along as a group with Henk in the lead. Despite Rafe's misgivings, they all insisted on coming along for the show.

After about two hundred yards, they ducked into an alley and down a flight of iron stairs. Once again they were underground, this time in what looked like a dry dock, the high sawtooth roof was glazed on one side - although most of the glass was now on the floor crunching beneath their feet. The space was long and narrow, ending in a massive set of double doors. Above them in large iron letters was *BOLTJALK WIDE BEAM BARGE CO.*

"This survived the bombing, owing to its steel frame and reinforced concrete walls it should keep things quiet; this part of town is mostly deserted anyway," said Marcus. He walked all the way down to the back, where a large irregular-shaped object hid under a blue tarpaulin. When he turned and shouted back, his voice echoed down to them. "This is something we could use as target practice." With a flourish, Marcus tore down the cover, and in a cloud of sawdust was revealed a pretty little sloop, gleaming with fresh varnish and polished brass. Her mast was collapsed and she was rigged with what looked like brand new canvas and hemp. "Oh good Lord, no, we can't shoot this lovely thing up," Rafe called back.

Marcus sneered, "It belongs to a notorious NSB traitor, *Herr* Frenneicke."

"Death to traitors!" cried Henk and Hannie in unison. Marcus spat, "He is well-known around town for blackmailing young women into his bed with threats of arrest or deportation."

"Frenneicke the Frick, they call him," said Hannie. "A filthy animal, he's tried it on with almost every girl in the city."

"It's about the same size and shape as the Bugatti Tourer Schroeder drives." Gerrit shrugged. "Let's get on with it before the light goes."

Rafe carefully loaded three magazines with the little 9mm rounds; he chose the most sorry-looking gun and clicked the mag in place. His audience had gathered in close, watching him avidly.

"I suggest you all move back a bit, I'm not sure how safe these are after such a long time in the drink."

Rafe flicked the safety and worked the big brass bolt, leaning forward and locking the stock in hard to the shoulder; he took aim and pulled the trigger. One round fired with a loud pop that echoed back as a whooshing report, then the bolt jammed with a crunch. He cleared the breach and tried again, same result. "Feed is bent; this one's probably scrap."

"That was the first one I stripped; it didn't quite go back together straight—try this one."

This time, Rafe bent his knees and fired a burst from the hip in full auto. The gun jumped in staccato rhythm, emitting puffs of smoke and a deafening crack with each round. Most of the shots went wild, smashing into the cement wall behind the boat.

With a cigarette clenched rakishly between his teeth, Rafe walked forward, closing the distance and firing more eight- and ten-round bursts. Finally, he stopped about ten paces from the boat and emptied the magazine, sending dust, splinters, and sparks flying in all directions.

Rafe turned and saw everyone crouched with hands over their ears. Rachel hid behind Jan, coughing in a cloud of drifting gun smoke. Anton grinned like a loon.

"This one fires smoothly. Let's try those grenades."

This time, everybody crowded at the far end of the room behind a sturdy wall of pine planking. Rafe pulled the pin on two of the grenades with his teeth and dropped them into the cabin hatch then turned and made for a nearby pit that made for a handy slit trench.

Two heavy thumps shook the ground and made the little sloop jump an inch off the stand, listing over and toppling to the ground with a cacophonous crash. There was a moment of stunned silence before Rafe popped his head out of the trench. "Is everybody alright? That was a slightly bigger crack than expected."

They stood about, inspecting the damage in the fading light. Rafe shook his head sadly. "Waste of a good boat, but at least we know it will do the job, I don't see anybody walking away from that lot."

"All well and good," said Jacob, his ears ringing. "But how do we get clean away after this performance?"

"I have some ideas on that," Rafe replied confidently. "Let me think on it tonight. Tomorrow morning we'll discuss our plan of action.

That night at supper Rachel sat next to Rafe at the table, he noticed she put her hand on his shoulder briefly while she served his coffee. She had never done that before. Anton barely took his eyes off Rafe, insisting on lighting his every cigarette and constantly prodding him for tales of battle in the skies. Rafe wanted to oblige the lad, but found his mind wandering to the task ahead and what might happen if he was captured, or if Rachel were arrested. The thought of her at the mercy of the enemy made his guts squirm.

Late into the night Rafe lay awake, unable to sleep. His mind raced with possibilities; he took up ideas and discarded them, only to return and discard again. He knew the decisions he made in the coming days could seal his fate forever, and many good people had put their faith in his judgement. Rafe tried to foster a confident state of mind, but self-doubt always stalked in the background. He saw his father's face before him, and his bitter voice rung in his ears: *"Foolhardy, careless". From* Beckett, his CO, the words stung, but they had been proved correct: *"You're an awful shit, if it wasn't for your Father..."* His father's money and influence counted for nothing here, and there could be no excuses or arrangements made. The gravity of his position felt like a physical thing, a stone on his breast, squeezing, crushing.

Suddenly, he heard light footsteps on the stairs. Someone was creeping up, taking great pains to be as stealthy as possible. Rafe glanced at his wristwatch; it was just past three in the morning.

Rachel slowly opened the door and peeked in; she saw Rafe was awake and quickly shuffled inside, closing the door gingerly. She was wearing a light cotton nightgown and carried a bottle of brandy. Rafe felt like he had never been this happy to see somebody in his whole life.

She shushed him harshly as he began a heartfelt greeting. "We must be absolutely silent. Father would throttle us if he found out!" She came up close to him and sat on the bed, wincing as it creaked. She smelt faintly of soap and talcum powder, and when she leaned forward to whisper in his ear, Rafe caught the slightest sweet whiff of brandy on her breath.

"My dear Rachel, have you been having a late night tipple?" She frowned a little.

"Just a tiny bit, I sometimes sneak a drop or two when I can't sleep." She proffered the bottle. "I thought you might like some." She leaned over and poured some into his mug. Rafe caught a glimpse of her breasts moving freely under her nightdress, full and milky white in the moonlight. Rafe sat up and moved closer; he savoured the feel of her warm thigh against his.

"I can't stop thinking about this lunatic plan. I can't see it ending in anything but tragedy," Rachel sighed.

"Do you think your father will allow you to come back with me to England?" Rafe changed the subject.

"I don't know, he thinks your plane will crash, or be shot down; he says it's too dangerous," she replied, laying back on the bed, propped up on her elbows.

Rafe felt a surge of desire looking at the swells and curves of her body, it was cool in the room, and her nipples stood up proud under the thin fabric. She seemed completely oblivious to her exposure to him.

The brandy slid down into his core, warm and soothing. He started to relax, languidly aroused. Gently, Rafe laid his hand on her knee. "I won't leave here without you, Rachel. I mean it."

A sensual wave of lust broke over him; unable to stop himself, he turned and lay across her, kissing her hard on the mouth.

She stiffened, frozen at first, then slowly she relaxed and became soft and yielding; her lips parted and admitted him, she embraced him and drew closer still. Her warm skin was silky smooth as cream, compliant yet firm. Ravenously he tasted her flesh with his hands and lips, and he was suddenly aware of a deep ache inside him that had been too long denied, the sweet honey of ecstasy flooding his every cell.

Soon their bodies were merging in rhythm. Rafe found his hand had wandered between her thighs, she made no protest as his fingers probed; gently but insistently, she responded to his touch, opening like the petals of a rose, rolling her hips in cadence. Rachel broke off the kiss and whispered in his ear, "You must be quiet... make no sound." Her entreaty seemed to drive Rafe's ardour even higher. Rafe's engorgement found its way out of his pyjamas, some animal instinct took control of his body and he began grinding himself against her soft rump, to his surprise Rachel reached down and closed a tender hand around his glands; her movements were small and inexperienced, but that only made Rafe more aroused. Despite himself, he felt his passion rising to a premature crescendo; once started there was no stopping it, and his wave crashed against her, a convulsive eruption pulsing forth over her hand as Rafe let out an involuntary cry. Rachel pulled his head down to her bosom to smother his sobs.

For a time they held each other tightly, panting. Rafe's head cradled in her chest, listening to her heartbeat slowly settle, Rafe felt his whole being glowing incandescent like the embers of a fire. Gradually the heat ebbed, replaced by a comforting warmth. Finally he whispered hoarsely, "Sorry about that, it's never happened to me like that before."

"Shhh, don't fret," she soothed. "I just hope nobody heard us."

They climbed under the bed covers together. Rafe nestled his head in her hair and squeezed her hands; his head spun with what just happened. He was revelling in every sensation: the fragrance of her hair; the heat of her body; her delicate, tapered fingers. No words were exchanged, for none seemed necessary. She was now his and he was hers. The first pale blush of dawn played through the window by the time Rafe finally drifted off to a contented sleep, like slipping into a warm bath.

The next morning Rafe felt like he had been hooked up to a galvanic battery; he all but leapt out of bed, surging with renewed energy and drive. His head was clear and sharp as a razor, and he knew exactly what he had to do and how to do it.

"First of all," he told Jacob, "I need to get out and reconnoitre the parade route and the surrounding streets."

"It will be awfully hazardous; most men your age are now conscripted to work. The police are stopping at random to check papers."

"It's worth the risk. Gerrit will have to cook up some fake documents for me." Rafe was adamant.

The morning was spent with Rachel setting up Rafe as a young Dutchman, with some borrowed clothes and a bicycle. "You'll have to shave this ridiculous thing off." She yanked at his moustache. "You will stick out like a sore thumb; nobody here wears these around town."

Rafe was horrified. "But I have only just got it back to full strength." He began strapping on his webbing and pistol. "No guns either," Gerrit interjected.

"How do we defend ourselves?" protested Rafe.

"We don't. If it comes to that, there is no chance for us, you might as well shoot us both now."

By noon, Rafe, clean shaven, had his official identification card and work exclusion certificate.

"You are Mr. Henri Bakker and you suffer from pulmonary stenosis, which prevents you from working hard labour." Rafe baulked at the unflattering photograph. "You be with me," said Gerrit. "If we are stopped let me do all the talking, I will say you are hard of hearing and soft in the head."

"So I am an invalid and a simpleton?"

"Yes, don't talk to anybody but me under any circumstances. Keep your eyes down, don't make eye contact with anyone for any length of time. Anton will drive us to the Hague, and from there we take the train to Amsterdam; there will be *Wehrmacht* onboard, some in uniform, some not, so try not to stare or get flustered."

"Understood," said Rafe.

"And for God's sake don't start speaking English! if you really must talk to me, use your French."

Gerrit had a road atlas of the inner city; he drew a path with his finger. "We ride to the square from the train station; we can make a couple of laps and move on to the side streets. We don't want to hang around too long and arouse suspicion; half an hour at most, then we abandon the bicycles and board the four o'clock train back to Rotterdam. Marcus will pick us up from the station in his motorcar." Gerrit made Rafe run through the details three times over before he was satisfied.

Finally, all was ready. They moved downstairs and waited for Anton. Suddenly Rafe had an attack of nerves; his hands trembled slightly as he lit a cigarette, and his mouth felt dry as a desert. Gerrit eyed him suspiciously. "I'll be fine once we get moving," Rafe assured him.

Three cigarettes later, Anton appeared in a rattling, stinky lorry of last century vintage. Painted on the doors was *Heinz Floral Arrangements and Delivery.* They all crowded into the tiny cab.

"Please forgive the truck," Anton said apologetically as they jerked away in a cloud of diesel smoke. "Transport is getting hard to find around here."

A frigid squall drifted in from the sea as they made their way north out of the shattered city, carefully negotiating around mountains of rubble and deep craters. At the edges of the city centre, work parties of demobilised Dutch soldiers mournfully worked to clear the streets of debris. In places the air was thick with nauseating smoke as they burned piles of timber and decaying corpses of dead horses. Some of the city's less fortunate denizens picked through the detritus, scavenging metals and anything of value. Rafe felt a creep of despair at the thought of seeing the cities of his own country brought so low, as they drove on in funereal silence. *This will never happen to us*, he thought to himself. *We can't let it happen, we will prevail in the end.*

A miraculous transformation occurred as they left the city and headed north. The clouds broke and the sun shone down on a green and verdant pastoral scene. The passing rain shower produced a fresh scent of grasses and spring wild flowers. Neat rows of trees lined the arrow-straight road, and ordered rows of colourful tulips striped the meadows. Rafe wound down the window and drank in the clean air. It seemed everybody's spirits were lifted. "As you can see, not all of Holland is ruined," said Gerrit with a hint of a smile. "This is why we fight," said Anton. "This is our land, we will fight for it."

Just outside the Hague city limits, they encountered the first checkpoint. Rafe stiffened in his seat as they joined the short queue of vehicles. "Who are you?" asked Gerrit.

"Henri Bakker," replied Rafe smoothly.

"Good—look at your shoes, try to look bored." Rafe found it hard to not stare at the small group of young soldiers as they pulled up to the barrier; they lazed about smoking and chatting with a haughty air of indifference that made Rafe's skin crawl. A sleepy-looking sergeant gave the truck a quick once-over and waved them through. When they were a half-mile down the road, Rafe realised he was holding his breath. Gerrit gave him a fatherly pat on the shoulder. "See? Not so bad after all; it gets easier each time, trust me."

The two men sat side-by-side on the crowded train to Amsterdam. It was a normal Tuesday morning for those aboard: workers commuting into the city from the suburbs, women in pairs or small groups on shopping trips. They rocked gently in their seats, some reading the morning papers, some dozing in the warm sunlight. Rafe alternated from idly watching the scenery go past the window and looking intently at his hands or shoes. After what seemed like a very short ride, the train came to a halt in Haarlem station - a good deal of the passengers quickly alighted, leaving the carriage nearly empty. The train began to move and Rafe breathed a sigh of relief, until a rowdy shout struck him in the chest like a jolt of electric current.

A group of German officers shambled drunkenly through the carriage door. Four men, each about Rafe's age, were in full dress uniform and stinking drunk, obviously returning from a night's debauch at one of the many all-night gentlemen clubs in Haarlem's seedier districts. In some act of providence, they tumbled into the seats directly across from Rafe and Gerrit.

They were singing some German drinking ballad, one of them so worse for wear that he hung his head down to his chest and mumbled the words incoherently, occasionally jerking his head up and shouting on the obscene refrain. Rafe glanced at Gerrit; he was stiff and his face coloured pink. Rafe found something interesting to study on the back wall of the carriage.

There was suddenly a sound like somebody emptying a bucket of liquid on the floor, and the car was quickly filled with the sharp smell of vomit and schnapps. The other officers found this to be amusing and fell about in hysterical laughter, shouting, "*FRAU* HERMAN, *FRAU* HERMAN CAN'T TAKE HIS DRINK!"

A middle-aged Dutch couple quietly stood and left the carriage. Some of the others followed. Rafe looked at Gerrit and pointed with his chin at the door. Gerrit shook his head anxiously.

The boisterous singing continued - they began shouting and stamping their feet in some form of battle hymn. A bottle was tossed and smashed close to Gerrit's head, spraying them with beer and slivers of glass. Rafe felt his anger rise hot in his cheeks. A meek female conductor arrived and almost apologetically asked for tickets.

"Herman! Present tickets!" shouted the senior officer. Herman was bent almost double in his seat, completely comatose. The others sniggered and guffawed; one of them stood up unsteadily and dug his penis out of his pants, waving it to and fro in front of her.

"Here's mine!" This action threw the men into renewed hysterics until they gasped for breath. The conductor meekly turned and left the carriage, flushed red in indignation. Rafe almost stood to intervene, but he had to check himself as she hurried by.

The train came to a stop in Plantation. Gerrit slapped Rafe across the knees with his folded paper and they quickly alighted. Gerrit strode off angrily into a deserted side street. "We will have to circle back," he growled at Rafe when he caught up.

"That was not prudent what you did back there."

"I didn't do anything!" protested Rafe. "I could see it on your face, 'don't give them an excuse. If you even look like you might cause trouble, they will stop and search you'.

"I don't know how you stand it," said Rafe. Gerrit stopped suddenly and turned to face him; his eyes were pink and glassy with emotion, and he trembled with anger: "You think we don't feel it when they do this! We have to stand it! We stand it every day, you don't know what it's like..." Gerrit caught himself, turned, and continued walking. After a minute, he resumed in a calm and cool manner, "Just keep your mind on the purpose, don't lose focus, we have much to do."

They got off before the main central station and mounted a pair of bicycles left for them outside the station. Rafe took a while to get used to peddling again; he hadn't ridden one since his public school days. Gerrit led the way through a warren of side streets until they came out on a wide boulevard with modern electric trams running on a central light railway. The neighbourhood was prettily landscaped with stands of trees and box gardens. Busy market stalls lined the roadway, selling everything from vegetables to junk and bric-a-brac. It was mid-morning, and the many cafes and small bistros were preparing for lunch. The strong aroma of coffee competed with the mouldy funk of the canal water. The presence of oppressive authority was pervasive; Dutch police and German soldiers patrolled the streets with steel helmets and rifles. Off-duty personnel strolled around superciliously with the covetous air of the conqueror. Official notices and warnings were posted on every available wall regarding public policy changes, identity cards, ration books, and banned organisations. Many shops and cinemas had erected hastily-painted signs: *Joden Verboden.* "You see?" whispered Gerrit as he drew alongside. "It's starting! they promised not to impose their prejudices on us, but they lied." Rafe had the distinct impression of a population divided. Many went about their business seemingly indifferent, while others wore stony masks of tension and fear, presumably of Jewish ancestry or otherwise at odds with the occupation.

Rafe had to force himself to concentrate among the menace, making mental notes of the route from the train station to the square. They crossed five canals on narrow, almost toy-like hump bridges. The surfaces ranged from cement to worn cobbles, and he tested the grip of each with his foot as they stopped. Eventually they came to the square itself, which was in fact two polygonal shapes bisected by the tram line. It was very large. Rafe estimated it to be almost four football pitches; it was also cobblestone in a fish-scale pattern. The western side was dominated by the Royal Palace building, an imposing baroque relic of the city's seventeenth-century golden age. They rode four slow circuits around the perimeter. Rafe had Henk's sketch in his mind as he took note of the various potential entrance and exit points.

The afternoon passed rapidly, and the sun dropped behind the clock tower The sky darkened and a light drizzle descended. Rafe noticed how the rain and grime made the ancient cobbles slick; They would be slippery as eels until they dried – a treacherous surface to ride on in the best of times. They headed north to the Centraal station with their collars up, shivering against the cold gusts that blew off the waterfront. As they queued for the train, a girl caught Rafe's attention; she was being escorted by a uniformed German staff sergeant and another man in plain clothes away from the just-arrived carriages. Gerrit pointed with his chin to a newly-posted notice on the ticket booth.

*Jews forbidden from all public transport except by special order.*

She was young, about Rachel's age. As she passed close to Rafe, their eyes met for a brief second Her dark liquid brown eyes burned with something Rafe had never seen before, so profound that he caught his breath.

It was as if those eyes didn't belong in her youthful face. They wore the burden of a much older, wiser woman. They spoke of resignation, defiance, and pain. In that brief glimpse, they pleaded to him and the rest of them, "*Why are you allowing this to happen?*" In a moment she had passed and was swallowed up by the crowd.

The encounter left Rafe shaken; he felt in that instant the reality of the whole situation was made clear. Rafe realised that up until this point the persecution Rachel and the others had warned of was remote to him. If he was honest with himself, he truly hadn't fully believed what they were telling him, it seemed too far-fetched, like a kind of paranoia. Now, as he sat watching the quickly darkening city pass by the windows of the car, Rafe saw the truth. Something evil was happening here, a great human catastrophe was approaching, and when it was over the world would never be the same again.

#

De Jong sat and watched the child sleep. It was not a restful, natural slumber. The boy was heavily sedated, and even through this artificial, almost coma-like state, his face showed signs of stress. Perhaps somewhere deep in his unconscious he did feel what de Jong had been doing to him for the last hour or so. The thought made de Jong feel strangely morose.

He always felt rather melancholy after he had indulged himself, and he had been doing so more often recently, much too often.

*It's that damned German bastard Schroeder,* he cursed inwardly. Before he met him, he only used to indulge himself occasionally, once or twice a year at the most, only when the urge became unbearable, like a seething ache. He could get it out of his system quickly and carry on his normal, salubrious existence.

He had led a good, wholesome life for the most part. He didn't drink too much or smoke excessively. He seldom cursed or raised his voice at his wife. De Jong was a respected name: his business was prosperous, and he gave generously to his church, which he attended every Sunday.

*It was Schroeder who led me down this path of gluttony and lust,* he thought bitterly. He had been corrupted, polluted against his will by the man's influence. De Jong drained his glass and stood up slightly unsteadily. He dressed himself without care, leaving his shirt untucked and his tie crooked. As he left, he turned and took one last look at the sleeping boy, peering out of one eye, then the other, trying to resolve the swimming dual images. De Jong weaved down the long passageway to the foyer, and on the way he passed the dining table where the evening's work was done: some neat stacks of documents and legal pads, an adding machine, and a typewriter. Another family sent on their way, accounts settled, funds transferred, property deeds signed and sealed. Schroeder must have owned most of the prime realty in Holland by now. Schroeder was nowhere to be seen, probably retired hours ago; he didn't bother to see de Jong out any more. Schroeder's ubiquitous henchman Gunther was waiting for him in the kitchen. *Did this man ever sleep?*

"Ready to return home, *Herr* de Jong? I have the car ready for you."

"No, I'll walk tonight."

Gunther looked nonplussed. "Are you sure, sir? It is wet and woolly out this evening." De Jong didn't answer, he just clumsily pushed through the door and staggered out into the street.

The driving rain and chilling wind had a sobering effect: within a couple of blocks he was wet through and thinking clearly. He thought about the people he had sent to Schroeder, people who had trusted him. Schroeder's thin veil of deceit had not lasted long, and both men had long since given up the charade between them. There had never been any safe and discreet escort out, nor any protection for property from the Nazis. Whatever else he may be, de Jong was no fool - he had made some quiet inquiries of his own, none of these people were ever heard from again. Wherever they were now they never left Holland, and the property they signed over to Schroeder sometimes popped up on the open market the day after they left.

The thought of what Schroeder had probably done with them made him feel ill. All the rich food and liquor he had shared at Schroeder's table made him feel ill, too. De Jong lurched over to the side rail of the canal just in time to empty his guts into the water.

Again and again he heaved and choked, until there was nothing but bile, still it went on and on for what seemed like hours; he gasped for breath and his eyes stung with tears, and the tears became sobs.

In his jacket pocket was the manilla envelope with the cashier's cheques from Schroeder, his part of tonight's deal. Still sobbing and choking, de Jong tore them up and tossed the pieces fluttering into the canal. He watched them float away on the outgoing tide and thought about the old couple he had told not to worry. How he had smiled at them and sent them on their way, how they held hands like young sweethearts as they hobbled out the door of his office.

On he walked through the sodden, deserted streets. There was no moon, but de Jong knew this city so well he didn't need to see where he was going; his feet seemed to know the way. After an hour, maybe two, he found himself at his front door.

He let himself in; the house was empty, silent. As was usual on the first Saturday of every month, his wife was in Utrecht with her mother. The kitchen clock ticked; there was a note on the counter top under a glass of buttermilk. His wife's neat handwriting:

*Drink this for your stomach before bed. Morning Mass at 8am.*
*Love,*
*Femke*

De Jong went down into the washhouse and undressed; he hung his wet suit jacket and put his shirt and slacks into the washing machine. It was a new Westinghouse, American, expensive.

Naked, he went upstairs to the ensuite bathroom; he felt quite sober now, strangely calm and serene, and his movements were methodical, deliberate. He opened the cabinet and retrieved his shaving kit. The straight razor was English, Wilkinson Sword. He tested the edge with his thumb; he always kept it keen and polished.

Padding across the marble tiles, he stepped into the large bathtub and sat down. Outside, the sky had cleared completely, and since there was a blackout, there was no light from the city to pollute the icy-cold silver starlight that fell on him through the window.

De Jong took one deep breath, and in a quick, even stroke, he opened his throat from ear to ear.

They all sat crowded into Rafe's room around the strange device Gerrit had made. Half hanging out the window, it looked to Rafe like a diamond-shaped kite made of copper wire and balsa wood.

A 'Kraut Sieve," Gerrit had called it. Designed to filter out the high-power jamming the Germans were using to drown unauthorised broadcasts in static. After a lengthy search, the foot of Rafe's bed seemed to be the only spot in the whole building where it would work. Gerrit turned the gain right up, and the four of them: Rafe, Jacob, Henk, and Hannie, all bent over the little ear piece that issued the familiar six-tone introduction of the BBC news.

And the news wasn't good. Through the static, Rafe could barely make out the newsreader's thin, reedy voice. The Allies had completed the withdrawal from Crete, which was a polite way of saying that the defending British forces had been completely routed and forced to evacuate. Now all of Greece, as well as Crete, was in Axis hands. In Africa, Tobruk was still under siege by Rommel, the defending Australians on the verge of starvation. Meanwhile, Hitler's 8th Army continued its astonishingly rapid destruction of the Soviets, pushing ever further east - the estimate was that the Panzers would be at the gates of Moscow by September.

Rafe looked about at the glum faces. "Well, I rather hoped the Russians would have put up a tougher fight than this," he said sadly. "It sounds like they are getting a ruddy good whipping."

"They were stabbed in the back," Hannie sneered defiantly. "Betrayed and caught off-guard by a cowardly surprise attack."

"Stalin was a fool to trust Hitler," Jacob said sternly. "He made a deal with the devil and now he will pay the fee." None of the others seemed to have the energy to argue the point. Dejected, they all shuffled down the stairs into the crypt-like cool of the stone cellar.

"Well, after that disappointment, we do have some good news," rumbled Henk. "Hannie believes she has found a young *Luftwaffe* cadet that could provide you with your gasoline."

Rafe immediately perked up.

Hannie smiled sweetly. "He's one of us, recruited by the party from Rees. He is young but very clever; he knows where the gas for the fighters is stored." Rafe stood up and paced about anxiously. "Damn good stroke of luck. Now listen carefully: this isn't just any old petrol, it's absolutely crucial that we get hold of the right stuff or we will never get those engines started. In the RAF, we call it aviation spirit, but I have no idea what the Jerry's call it. One thing I do know is it's very dangerous, explosive, and highly toxic, and it's always stored in a pressurised steel tank, there will be all sorts of warnings and labels on it. *Achtung,* that sort of thing."

"And what of your side of the bargain, Mr. O'Rourke," said Gerrit. "You said you needed a day to think about it, but that was thirty-two hours ago. The parade is two days from now."

Rafe sat down and lit a cigarette; he took a long drag and sighed heavily on the exhale. This was it, he had a plan of action, but even in his own head it sounded like the ridiculous script of a Hollywood action play. "Okay—let's get everybody together tonight after supper. I'll set out my plan for you."

Rafe sat and watched the expectant faces of everybody gathered around him; they were hopeful and anxious. Jacob especially looked tired, his face grey and his eyes rimmed with red. Gerrit himself looked even more sceptical than usual; he was obviously a practical man, and not given to flights of fancy. Henk was eager, focused, and, as was his custom at this hour, a little bacchic. Rachel was here, too. She was hard to read, concerned and slightly dubious Her expression seemed to mirror Rafe's own; somewhere deep within Rafe he felt like a child role-playing soldiers, or a character in the theatre. Subterfuge and deception were not Rafe's forte.

"I'm here to tell you that I believe we have a solid chance of pulling this off, and getting away without being shot or captured. But only if we can get into the square undetected, and out and away so rapidly that they won't have time to put up an effective response." Rafe unfolded a tourist map of Amsterdam; he had carefully drawn the expected parade route in blue and his planned escape path in red. "One man, in disguise, will move in and join the procession for one loop, making his way to the target car - as they slow down to move over the street car track, we attack. Firstly by tossing a grenade into the back seat, and then in the confusion we open fire with the Sten, the actual attack should only last about five seconds, once the gun is empty we make a break for the railway line, here." Rafe pointed to a cul-de-sac about two miles north of the Centraal station. "Anton will be waiting with his truck, I ride up the ramp into the covered bed and the truck drives us west to the Haarlem station, and we vanish without a trace."

Everybody looked stunned and perplexed. Rachel looked ill. "You say I, you mean you, yourself, will do this?" said Jacob.

"We will work as a team, but yes, I think it's best that I myself pull the trigger." Rafe could see he had some convincing to do. "I have given this a lot of thought, and it makes sense. Firstly, I am the only man here with weapons and combat experience. Secondly, and perhaps most importantly, if things go foul and I'm captured, I can claim to be acting as a soldier on behalf of the British government; that way I can demand that they treat me as a prisoner of war according to the Geneva Convention. It's a long shot, but it's better than the alternative. If you're captured, they will most likely torture you until you give up your comrades and then shoot you."

Gerrit held his head in his hands, talking to the floor. "How will you outrun an armoured unit on a bicycle for two miles? You're not exactly Sylvere Maes, you know."

Rafe realised his error. "Who? Oh yes, I won't be on a bicycle, I will be riding a motorcycle. In SS uniform."

Stunned silence. Jacob finally spoke up. "Where are we going to get this motorcycle and fancy dress for you by Saturday?"

More silence, until there was a sudden ear-splitting crack as Henk clapped his giant hands together, and everybody jumped. "Of course!" He laughed. "You are a clever bastard." Rafe and Henk beamed at each other like a couple of smug schoolboys.

"Erik's place," said Rachel "Jaap's motorcycle sidecar and the uniforms."

"Exactly, we will need to smuggle it here somehow and make some modifications, I have a plan for that also, and all the equipment we need is down here in Gerrit's cave."

"We'll have to dig up those two bodies and strip them; that won't be very pleasant," Jacob said warily.

"And the SS uniforms have been buried for a month; surely they will be rotten," added Rachel.

Rafe shrugged. "I was rather hoping we could wash them in lye soap or something."

"What about the Sten gun? You can't swan up to the parade carrying a British weapon."

"I have a plan for that, too; we can paint it black and fudge it to make it look like a MP 40. It doesn't have to be perfect, just good enough to fool a casual glance."

The debate began in rapid-fire Dutch that Rafe couldn't follow, he decided to leave them to it and walked out to the kitchen to think.

After a few minutes, Rachel followed. She sat opposite Rafe and held his hands, looking him square in the eye she said sadly; "Father won't let us go with you back to England." Rafe was suddenly overcome with indignation; he felt his face redden as he turned away. "Why the bloody hell not?"

"He thinks it's too risky."

"Too risky? Has he been out recently? He must know what's happening out there; they are stopping Jews at the borders now, and it's only a matter of time before the hunt begins in earnest."

Rachel's dark brown eyes filled with tears. "I tried to convince him, but he won't listen to me."

"I'll talk to him."

"No, don't, please."

"I have a proposal for him, and you—" Rafe stopped himself, he cleared his throat, and smoothed back his hair nervously, then he dug deep in his jacket pocket, searching for something.

"Rachel....I....ah, just...!.."

Henk's giant head appeared in the doorway. "We have come to an arrangement."

Jacob spoke gravely, "Tomorrow morning, first thing, Rafe, Henk, and Gerrit will drive up to Erik's in the truck, the story being they are delivering bulbs and picking up cut flowers for the market." Gerrit took over. "We will work through the night to exhume the bodies and break down the sidecar to be concealed under boxes of tulips. We will return after curfew is lifted the following morning."

"That will give us the whole of Saturday to work on the bike and prepare the weapons," agreed Rafe. "It will be a scramble, but with a bit of luck we will be ready for Saturday."

In the frosty darkness they set off, stopping to pick up a load of bulbs from a nearby abandoned shed. "These are all dead, but the Germans don't know the difference," said Henk.

As they reached the main road, the sun rose, struggling to cast even a weak watery light through the heavy overcast. Henk turned off and began a labyrinthine series of turns through rural backroads to avoid any trouble. The roads were unsealed and rough. The old truck with worn saggy leaf springs lurched and bounced. By the time they arrived at the farmhouse in the early afternoon, all three men were already sore, tired, and covered with dust.

There was little time to rest. Rafe made straight for the field where the Mosquito was parked. Erik had made a fine job of concealing it under canvas and turf. Rafe spent a panicked few minutes looking for it until Erik emerged from his workshop to help.

Under the camouflage, she was clean and dry. Erik had followed Rafe's instructions with care, building a set of trusses and joists to keep her off the damp earth. Oil cloth was bundled into her exhaust pipes, cannon barrels, and every other orifice that might make a tempting nest for vermin. Rafe saw with satisfaction that Erik had almost completed the repairs to her wing and tanks. Beautifully hand-crafted spruce laminate panels had been grafted onto the damaged sections, the shredded aileron had been replaced with an entirely new section of lacquered spruce; Erik was a true artist with wood.

Satisfied the Mosquito was in order, Rafe and Gerrit immediately began work on the bike. Erik had buried it deep under a huge stack of dried peat logs and firewood in the adjacent shed. After an hour's toil, it was uncovered and pushed out into the sunlight.

Rafe had once owned a similar civilian Zundapp motorcycle and was familiar with the big, powerful flat twin motor. This model was a military version designed and built specifically for the *Wehrmacht*, and as such was built like a battle tank. Not suited to the job Rafe had in mind for it.

"First thing, let's get it running, then we uncouple the sidecar and try to get it in the truck."

The tank was almost full. Rafe tickled the single carburettor and it started on the second kick. "Say what you want about the Krauts," said Rafe over the steady throb of the motor, "but they know how to make reliable machinery."

Henk and Gerrit were posted lookout at opposite ends on the half-mile approach road while Rafe rode some test passes, sending geese and chickens to flight in a cloud of dust. The motor was strong, but she was very heavy and turned ponderously. Rafe needed speed and agility to out fox whoever might be pursuing him in the narrow lanes and alleys.

Rafe soon found the motor was running rough and misfiring under throttle. The bike had been using poor-quality petrol that had left silt in the fuel lines and carburettor, somebody had turned the mixture up to full rich to compensate. "There's nothing to be done about that here; we will have to strip it down and clean it up back at the workshop. Let's get that sidecar off, for a start."

With Gerrit's tools they set to work, it was late afternoon by the time they had the sidecar drive shaft unbolted and the subframe dismantled. With the extra weight removed she was transformed; Rafe hit a top speed of fifty miles an hour on the straight, and

although she was no lightweight racer, he found that with some practice he could lean into the turns and manoeuvre with confidence. In the meantime, Erik had constructed a ramp that fitted within the confines of the truck-bed. It was cleverly sectioned and hinged so that it could be quickly deployed and recovered, even while the truck was moving.

Rafe's first attempts to mount the ramp into the truck ended up with hurt pride and gravel rash. After much cursing and repeated tumbles, Rafe had more or less mastered the technique needed on throttle and brakes to enter and exit cleanly. Rafe was determined, and only the bad light stopped them from drilling further.

At sunset, they fell exhausted on a quick supper of farm-fresh eggs and ham hocks. They had only a brief hour sleep before the moon rose, and they set to work on the grisly task ahead.

The two bodies were buried down the back of a tulip field on a neighbouring farm. It was a surreal sight as Rafe and Henk made their way through the rows of vibrant blooms - the silvery moonlight seemed to lend a phosphorescent glow to the blue and violet flower heads nodding gently in the sea breeze. Henk had prepared masks for them to wear over their nose and mouth, gauze cloth soaked in an eye-watering mix of paraffin and menthol. After a month in the damp earth, the unembalmed corpses would be utterly rank.

The grave site was unmarked and half the night was wasted staggering around in the darkness searching for the oak tree both Rafe and Henk seemed to recall differently. The moon was high by the time they found it and began digging. It wasn't long before the sickly sweet stench of decaying flesh rose up from the sodden soil. It was hard work. Henk and Rafe stripped down to the waist and soon built up a sweat shovelling the thick heavy mud.

The two men were buried on top of each other. Unfortunately the smaller man, who was closer to Rafe's size, was on the bottom, where Jaap's corpulence had collected in a pool of sludge. It soon became clear that the cotton shirt and woollen jacket were beyond recovery, coming apart easily in Henk's hands. They retrieved the leather greatcoat, Stahlhelm, and belt with a pistol holster. Further excavation revealed riding boots, gauntlets, and goggles. Although everything was caked in foul-smelling muck, the steel and leather had survived more or less intact.

After covering the bodies with a sack of lime and back filling in the graves, Rafe was completely spent. They trudged silently back to the farmhouse in a haze of fatigue, collapsing and sleeping where they fell.

Rafe awoke before dawn, stiff, sore, and filthy. He crept past the other sleeping forms and went out in the darkness to the Mosquito He clambered in the cockpit and felt around under the co-pilot's seat until he found what he was thinking about all night: a heavy magnesium cube about the size of a hat box. It was a specially designed incendiary demolition charge. All Rafe had to do was pull a plug on a cylinder-shaped fuse inside and ten seconds later it would detonate, casting white-hot phosphorus and thermite pellets in a radius of twenty feet that would stick to and incinerate anything, even steel. Within a few moments, this aircraft, and the equipment within, would be a heap of smouldering embers.

It was his duty to King and country to do as he was ordered and destroy this machine to keep it out of enemy hands. He sat there thinking, his mind at war with itself. Slowly, the pale dawn light grew stronger and Rafe opened the box; the small lead acid battery was still charged, the fuse still intact. He could now see the familiar mosaic of instruments before him. Rafe put his feet on the rudder pedals and took hold of the stick. It felt good in his hands. Rafe had always grown fond of his aircraft; he often felt they were his personal possessions, not just appliances assigned to him temporarily. He simply could not bring himself to destroy this beautiful bird, and with it his chance to redeem himself, complete his operational objectives, bring the Mosquito home safe and sound, and even do more: save the girl he loved from persecution and death.

"Sod it! Sorry, Beckett, old boy, I can think of a much better use for this thing." He closed and sealed the box.

In an old tin bathtub, Gerrit went to work on the helmet, greatcoat, and boots with a bar of carbolic soap and a stiff brush. When he had finished, they took turns giving them a sniff test. It was agreed that they were forever ruined by putrefaction, but they were just good enough for the mission at hand. They were packed into a wooden crate with the motorcycle in the back of the truck and concealed behind a wall of empty tulip containers. Erik stacked a layer of flower boxes filled with blooms on the outer layer so that from the back, the truck-bed appeared loaded with fresh-cut flowers ready for market.

They all squeezed into the tiny cab again and headed back to Rotterdam. Rafe's thoughts jumped around between the task at hand and his feelings for Rachel; he had left her standing there in the cold dawn, sleepy-eyed and shivering in her housecoat. He thought about what he could offer her back home. He could keep her safe - warm and clean, they could set up home in the south, maybe a cottage in Devon, away from the cities and the bombs. He pictured her and Anne walking in the rolling emerald hills, picking strawberries and picnicking on the beach.

"Henri Bakker!" Gerrit was shouting at him. Rafe realised he had been daydreaming like a silly girl. "Who?"

"Wake up, man!" Henk growled, he pointed with his chin; ahead was a German roadblock and a queue of farm vehicles. It seemed the road was now closed and traffic was being turned around. "This is new," said Henk, shaking his head. "They are blocking off access to the coast, opening the dams, and flooding the fields."

"The salt water—the soil will be ruined for generations."

A realisation suddenly hit Rafe like a slap in the face; he quickly fumbled in his pockets and broke out in an abrupt cold sweat. He had left his identification card behind in his coat. "Jesus Christ ....no."

"What?" snapped Gerrit.

"My cards."

"You have them, of course."

"My other coat. I changed just before we left. Bastard. Cunt!" Rafe slammed his fist into the dashboard.

"Keep calm," said Henk. Despite himself, Rafe felt the panic creep in; his face tingled and his pulse thudded in his ears. "It's not really a checkpoint, they're just turning back traffic. I don't think they're checking documents."

There were three vehicles back in the queue; in front was an ancient iron-wheeled tractor, followed by a Citroen van, and a one-horse muck cart. Rafe strained his neck to see ahead. There was a simple barbed-wire barrier between two ten-gallon drums propped up with sandbags. Two I regulars with MP 40 submachine guns were talking to the driver of the tractor, and one more was facing away from them urinating into the roadside ditch, his Mauser rifle slung over his shoulder. There was a Kübelwagen parked about thirty yards further down the road.

Rafe had his .45 wrapped in cloth under his seat. Henk and Gerrit were unarmed. The tractor turned around and headed back in a cloud of diesel smoke; the driver, a broad-faced farmer type, was puce with rage. "Why don't we just turn around and get out of here now?" said Rafe. "It's clearly just a roadblock, not a checkpoint."

"It will look suspect, we can't risk it," said Gerrit through gritted teeth. Rafe reached down under his seat and unwrapped his pistol. "What the fuck are you doing with that?" Gerrit hissed hoarsely.

Rafe half-smiled and half-grimaced. "Just a sporting option."

"You're mad," said Gerrit. Henk     went white as a sheet. Rafe slid the weapon carefully down the side of his seat. "I'm not being captured without a fight," he said with more confidence than he felt.

The van performed a three-point turn and rattled off; the soldiers hadn't inspected it or asked the driver for papers. The muck cart driver turned and followed without a word.

"Look," said Rafe. "Just turn and leave." Henk and Gerrit hesitated, exchanging furtive glances; they seemed conflicted for a moment.

"Have either of you two chaps played poker before?" said Rafe.

"What?"

"Henk, you need to bluff these bastards; we look as guilty as a bloody whore in church. I want you to drive forward and give this chap a rocket."

"What the hell are you talking about?"

"Give him an earful, be really angry—this is your route to town and now it's cut off, it's costing you time and money." Henk took a deep breath and put the truck into gear. He stopped short of the barrier and wound down the window.

The Corporal in charge was little more than a boy; he looked fresh out of boot camp, his coat was two sizes too big and his helmet hung back on its strap, revealing an apprehensive pimply face.

Henk began a tirade in Dutch mixed with German He gesticulated wildly, jabbing an accusing finger in the boy's chest and pulling his own hair; the cab rocked around on its springs as he raged, mentioning, among other things, his querulous wife and the obscene price of fuel. The young man went bright pink and looked around at his companions, who were at first confused, and then began sniggering behind their fists at his obvious discomfort.

Henk put the truck into gear and peeled away, spinning the rear wheels and leaving the gormless boy soldier in a cloud of dust. Rafe looked in the rearview mirror and saw the other German soldiers bent double in hysterical, derisive laughter.

"I really must protest," said von Leeb from behind his hand of Skat cards. He was barely visible in the thick nimbus of tobacco smoke emanating from his enormous *Gesteckpfeife* pipe.

"All the party boys will be there! some of my dear friends from Neustadt are making the journey up here especially."

"I am sorry, *Herr* von Leeb."

"Kurt, please, call me Gus after hours. All my friends do."

Schroeder smiled effusively, his silver dental work sparkling in the candle light. "Gus, I would love to come join the fun, but alas, duty and business beckon." Truth was, Schroeder was beginning to tire of von Leeb and his crowd. Martial men had never really made good company for him, as he found all the posturing and stuffed uniforms faintly ridiculous.

Von Leeb snorted. "What business? Surely you have made enough money this year; you just bought this place." Von Leeb waved his pipe around. The Mermaid Palace Casino and Hotel was a lavish two-hundred-room resort right on the beach. Craps tables, roulette, three bars, and two cocktail lounges—with all the personnel on leave or headed to the Eastern Front this summer, it was almost a licence to print money.

"One of my close business partners has, sadly, passed away, and there are many loose ends to tie up." The last thing Schroeder wanted to do on Saturday was parade around Amsterdam in von Leeb's circus act. Schroeder liked to keep a low profile among the plebeians, and he had already exposed himself too often of late. He had heard talk that his name was getting around, and that was not a good thing. In fact, Schroeder was so concerned he had made arrangements to leave Holland for the summer and let some grass grow over things for a bit.

De Jong's death had also caused Schroeder trouble - not so much the manner of his suicide, which was unusually brutal, but the risk of him leaving behind evidence of their mutual affairs. Schroeder had to send Gunther to the man's house to look for anything that could implicate him, and despite turning the entire household upside down, he had found nothing. Thankfully, it seemed that de Jong took his crisis of conscience with him to the grave.

"Well, that is a shame," said von Leeb, his handsome brow wrinkled up in concentration at his cards. "The new *General Kommissar* for security, what's his name... Rauter... was looking forward to meeting you, he did mention you by name."

Schroeder was taken somewhat by surprise. "You are leaving us so soon?"

"Why yes, I thought you'd heard the good news. Things are hotting up on the Eastern Front and my battle group's deployment has been expedited." Only a fanatical glory seeker like Leeb would consider that good news. "Rauter is coming in early to fill the gap."

Schroeder had to think fast; he knew Hanns Rauter was an entirely different breed of man than von Leeb. Von Leeb was a soldier first and foremost; civilian administration and all its bureaucracy bored him stiff. He was more than happy to let subordinates take care of the details while he went off horse riding, hunting, and carousing. This was perfect for Schroeder, for all he had to do to keep things running smoothly was pay a few low-level bribes to his staff. Von Leeb wasn't at all interested in financial reports or ledger balances.

Rauter, on the other hand, was a notorious pendant. A former chartered accountant, he would keep a close eye on every aspect of the party's expenditure, and even a superficial audit would reveal that Schroeder himself had taken ownership of most of the public assets designated for confiscation by the party.

It's not to say that Rauter couldn't be dealt with; every man had his price, but Schroeder must appear from the outset to be an insider. Rauter must get the impression that Kurt Schroeder was a permanent fixture in the occupation regime. He would have to attend on Saturday.

"Well, of course, this changes things." Schroeder intentionally played a lower-hand trick card, allowing von Leeb to win again. "Ha! Poor choice of suit, Kurt! I have outfoxed you again!" said von Leeb triumphantly as he slammed his hand down.

Schroeder spread his gloved hands in mock supplication. "Well, my friend, you are just too good for me."

"So you will be joining us tomorrow after all?" said von Leeb languidly.

Schroeder smiled. "In fact, I insist on escorting *Herr* Rauter in my own personal vehicle."

There was no time to rest on the return to Rotterdam. They manhandled the Zundapp down a coal shoot into Gerrit's basement workshop and began work on the engine. Rafe and Henk dismantled the tank, fuel lines, and carburettor to be cleaned in baking soda. With Rachel's help, Gerrit drained and filtered the gasoline through her last pair of nylon stockings. Every unnecessary part was removed to save weight: the mud guards, fairings, and mufflers were all discarded.

After a few hours of reconstruction and fiddling with the carburettor, tuning, and timing, they had the motor running crisp and lean again. With the silencers off, the twin cylinder engine was deafeningly loud in the confines of the workshop; red flames shot out of the open pipes as Rafe gleefully gunned the throttle.

Rafe checked his watch; it was just past midnight.

"I suggest we all get some rest before tomorrow," said Gerrit, his face grey with fatigue. "We will be up at dawn to be ready to drive into Amsterdam.

"Just one more thing," said Rafe, producing the demolition box. "This device was in the Mosquito, it's an incendiary demolition package." He opened it, revealing the lethal contents.

"A fire bomb?" asked Gerrit.

"Basically yes, it has a short, ten-second fuse with a pull string." Gerrit was intrigued; he carefully cleaned his spectacles and began inspecting the bundles of wires and battery cells. Rachel instinctively backed up two steps. "It's a bomb. Why on earth did you bring it down here?"

"It's much more powerful than those dodgy grenades. If I could get this inside the motorcar, there would be absolutely no doubt that everybody inside would be killed outright."

"Burned to death," said Henk, his eyes twinkling with malice.

"It's very large and heavy," said Gerrit. "Not suited to be tossed through a window."

"I was hoping you might have some ideas about how to use it."

Gerrit nodded thoughtfully. "Let me think about it."

Rachel insisted on Rafe taking a bath. He nodded off and woke up chilled to the bone in the cold, soapy water. He towelled off quickly and jumped into bed, falling back asleep as soon as his head hit the pillow.

#

"It's your turn," said the corpse. It had once been a man, an anonymous *Luftwaffe* bomber pilot, now it was smashed, twisted, and burned black. It looked expectantly at Rafe with waxen, sightless eyes. Rafe stared at the five cards in his hand; the deck was unfamiliar, alien. Foreign suits he couldn't place. "I'm not sure how this game is played," he heard himself reply. "I don't know what to do with these." The other players sighed in exasperation. Rafe realised they were all dead. They were all sitting around the card table in the officer's mess at the old airfield. Rafe had the feeling that it was daytime, but it was dark, like a solar eclipse. It was also extremely cold. Rafe was dressed in his full flight kit; merino, wool-lined jacket and boots; and his lambskin gloves, but he was still freezing.

"But you brought us all down here to play this game; it's your game," said Billy. Poor Billy—his glasses were broken, they balanced precariously on his rotting nose. Sitting next to Billy was Rafe's wife Caroline, her nightdress soaked up to the waist in blood. She was busy sorting through her cards confidently with dainty, marble-white fingers. She had her tongue out, like she always did when she was concentrating on something. Jaap's bully boy partner was there too, when he looked down at his cards some of his brain slipped out onto the table. There were a handful of *Luftwaffe* pilots, in various degrees of incineration.

They were all staring at him now, and everybody was waiting. One of the burned pilots drummed his blackened bony fingers on the table impatiently. "So typical of you, bringing us all down here and you can't even play," said Caroline, shaking her head.

"It's so cold," said Rafe, his breath a cloud of steam. "Why is it so bloody cold in here?" There was a polite, timid knock at the

175

door. Rafe could see blurry silhouettes of people through the foggy glass. Nobody moved.

"We should let them in, maybe they have wood for the stove," said Rafe. Billy carefully put his cards face-down on the table and slowly, stiffly ambled to the door; it seemed to take him forever to reach it. The door had a bolt and a chain. He slid the bolt back and opened the door until it caught on the safety chain. Warm air and sunlight rushed through the gap. His body was blocking Rafe's view. He was talking to somebody quietly.

*I need to get out of this place*, Rafe thought. *I don't belong down here in the cold with these dead things, it's warm outside.*

Billy turned around. "She says she is a friend of yours; her name is Rachel, she wants to come in." With his body turned, Rafe could catch a glimpse of her. She was bathed in warm, golden sunlight, dressed in a pretty floral-print summer dress.

"No! Don't let her in." Rafe stood to leave. One of the pilots grabbed his wrist; its skeletal grip was hard as iron and ice cold. "But it's your turn," it said bitterly. "Can't you see? We are all here because of you."

"Don't come in here, Rachel!" Rafe tried to shout, but his voice came out as a pathetic wheeze. It seemed the icy air in the room held no oxygen, he sucked it down but it would never fill his lungs enough to scream. Rachel hesitated on the threshold, Billy grabbed hold of her hand.

Rachel awoke him about an hour before dawn, climbing into his bed. At first he thought he was still dreaming; he was shivering violently. "You're frozen," she whispered. Rafe clung to her warm, feminine softness, and slowly her body heat restored his life, the shivering stopped.

They kissed, and soon their passion became more urgent, almost desperate. Rafe felt the elemental urge rise inside him; this time he feared he wouldn't be able to stop himself. As he crushed her soft, warm body into his, he almost felt like he needed to merge atoms with her, make her part of himself.   Rachel put up no resistance; in fact she paused only to peel off her underpants and crawl on top, straddling him.

With great effort, Rafe broke the spell, and he whispered "Wait, Rachel....I don't want it to be like this, we should wait."

"I don't care about all that, you could be killed tomorrow, this could be our only chance."

She shifted her hips and took him slowly in, gasping at the small sting of pain. Rafe was patient, letting her take the lead; she soon gained confidence, the tension melted from her body, and she eased into a gentle rhythm.

Despite his best mental efforts, it wasn't long before the point of no return was upon him, at the last moment he tried to withdraw, but Rachel sensed it and sat down on him, gripping him with her thighs. In a convulsion of sublime physical ecstasy, Rafe pulsed deep into her. She smothered his cry with her kiss.

Afterwards, Rafe held her tightly to him; her body curved neatly into his like a spoon. Rafe was far from a virgin, and he had had his fair share of lovers, but he never had an experience like that before. It was genuine love, he thought. Pure and mystical. All too soon, the sallow dawn light crept in through the window. She rose to leave, and Rafe clung to her; every cell in his body cried out for her to stay. "Stop it! Father will be up soon, and if he finds me up here with you..."

"Rachel. I love you."

"I know," she whispered, breaking free and gathering up her undergarments. "I love you, too." She kissed him once and lithely skipped out the door.

#

Schroeder spent more time than usual dressing this morning; he tried on and dismissed several jacket and trouser combinations before deciding on a basic worsted woollen single-breasted jacket in charcoal grey. He didn't want to give people the impression that he was ostentatious. Schroeder also chose a slightly fairer-coloured hairpiece than was his normal tone, with corresponding adjustments to the shades of his powder and rouge.

While assessing his final look in the wall-to-ceiling mirror, Schroeder rehearsed some salutations and phrases of welcome for Rauter, even practising his, by now, well-accomplished hand salute. His personal preference was more on the civilian side, with less emphasis on the heel click and stiff arm chop of the military style, more of an upwards-facing palm with bent elbow fashion, like the man himself. The final touch was his gold Nazi party pin. Schroeder very seldom bothered to wear it, as the crooked black stamp held no real meaning for him. He carefully pinned it to his left breast lapel.

Finally satisfied, Schroeder sent for Gunther. "Bring the 320 around, we will leave in five minutes."

"Sir, beg your pardon, it is drizzling outside; nothing too heavy, but it may get worse later in the day, so may I suggest taking the Maybach? It would be more comfortable for our guests this afternoon."

Schroeder had intended to take the usual open-top Mercedes 320, but perhaps Gunther had a point; the steel-roofed Maybach limousine would keep the elements off, and offer some better security. Schroeder had ordered it from the factory with armoured doors and ballistic glass.

"Very well, bring the Maybach, but hurry up about it, will you? We are running late as it is."

#

When Rafe got down to the workshop, Gerrit was already there, hard at work. Bent over something with a soldering iron, dressed in his pyjamas and slippers. The place smelled strongly of sweat and electrical ozone.

"Bring me that box of screws, will you?" he said without looking up.

"Did you get any sleep?" asked Rafe, handing over the box of assorted nuts, screws, and tacks.

"Not much, I couldn't get this thing out of my head." Rafe was horrified to see he had taken apart the demo box. "Good God, man, are you sure that's safe?"

"Without the battery it's completely inert," said Gerrit calmly. He pointed a screwdriver at the battery pack. "That's the main problem, the heavy acid battery and magnesium casing make up most of the bulk of the thing. If I could put a number of smaller dry cell batteries in series and produce the same charge, it could be half the mass."

Gerrit had apparently been up half the night testing every battery he could get his hands on; strewn across his workbench was a jumble of every conceivable portable electric device in various states of disassembly. "Any luck?" asked Rafe.

"I'm testing it now." Half-a-dozen mismatched batteries were wired up in what looked like a rat's nest of wires. He applied a voltmeter probe to a terminal and fingered a switch. "You might want to take a step back."

Gerrit hit the switch; there was a loud snap and a puff of smoke. "That's it, twelve-and-a-half volts, two volts more than your existing one."

"Now what?"

"See this?" Gerrit held up an empty ten-ounce Home and Colonial coffee tin. Gerrit was not a big man, but he could easily hold it in one hand.

"You can fit all that in there?"

"Most of it - we would have to drop about twenty percent of the thermite."

"It should still be more than enough to do the job. If it works."

Gerrit made a dismissive gesture. "It will work! Go, you need to help Henk with loading the truck."

In the semi-darkness, Henk and Rafe prepared the truck, winching the bike out of the coal chute and into the truck bed, reversed so it could be ridden out at speed. Next came the familiar facade of flower boxes, leaving a space for Rafe to crawl into behind the bike. When they had finished, the rain began.

Henk shook his head and sucked his teeth. "Not good."

"Will it come in hard, you think?"

Henk gazed out to sea with a practised eye. "Hard to say, this time of year."

Rafe decided to put a brave face on it. "Don't worry, old chap, I'm British—we are used to riding in the shit."

Down in the workshop everyone was assembled: Rachel, Jacob, Anton, and Gerrit had his device ready. To Rafe, it looked incredibly dangerous, packed inside the tin was a Frankenstein's creature of hurriedly-cobbled components together with powerful explosives.

"I have made some changes to the detonator. Ten seconds is too short a fuse; you can't be seen fiddling with one, anyway." He moved a bunch of frayed wires to one side to reveal the guts of an electric alarm clock of the rotating barrel type.

"This can be set to any time; when the alarm is triggered by the wheel, it closes this circuit, which will connect the battery to the detonator, and it will activate."

"I won't be able to see this when it's closed."

"No, but you can give yourself a chance to get away with this, if you use grenades and a gun the bastards will be on you like a pack of jackals right away; this is a safer bet."

Rafe looked at Rachel; her pretty face was twisted with conflicting emotions. Rafe was similarly torn—his direct assault was more surfeit of success, but it was tacitly understood by everybody that his chances of getting away were slim to none. This thing Gerrit had made looked like it had just as good a chance of killing him as the enemy - he had no control over it; once it was set in motion, it was unstoppable, no safety checks or abort switch.

"How will I get this in the motorcar? I can't just toss a can of ticking bloody coffee in the back seat, can I."

"I have thought of that, too," said Gerrit, motioning to Rachel. She held up a roll of gaily-coloured gift-wrapping paper and a bright red ribbon.

"Traitors and collaborating pigs will be offering up garlands and bouquets of flowers to our mighty conquerors, so attached to a bundle of fine tulips, this small gift might not look so dubious."

Rafe nodded thoughtfully. "The ruse will only allow me to get close. I'll need to time it just right so that the thing goes off a few seconds after I dump it in the car."

Rachel smiled sardonically. "You have to admit this has a certain poetry to it."


Gunther pulled up smoothly to the lobby of the Amstel Hotel. The car park was occupied by the *Musikkorps* brass band noisily tuning for the parade. A smiling porter dressed in coattails with an umbrella opened the door for Schroeder as he stepped out. "This way if you please, sir. Breakfast is served in the ground floor dining room."

The baroque-style dining hall was already crowded with party officials, officers, and NSB notaries enjoying a light breakfast buffet and champagne. Tables had been set out on the promenade by the river; a small army of hotel staff were dashing about in the drizzle, packing them up.

Detzner appeared holding a glass of champagne in each hand; his dress uniform shirt was already damp with perspiration, despite the cool morning.

"Not a nice day for it," he spoke around a mouthful of smoked salmon and cream cheese. He looked quite awful, like he had been up all night. He had lost a lot of weight in the past weeks, his glaring eyes sunk into deep sockets and his cheek bones jutted from his wide sweat-greased face. Schroeder watched him pull out a large white tablet and chew it down with a gulp of booze.

Schroeder took a glass from a passing tray. "Von Leeb won't let a little spring shower stop him from having his moment."

Schroeder spied von Leeb and Rauter holding court across the room with a group of *Luftwaffe* officers and their female companions.

"Look, change of plan; you'll have to find another seat if you feel you must join in. I'm having Rauter in the car with me." Schroeder stalked off in their direction without waiting for a reply.

Rauter was a short bird-like man in his fifties with obviously dyed black hair and beetling eyebrows. He looked every inch the Nazi Party desk commander. Schroeder had met him once before briefly and took an instant dislike to him. He was one of the numerous party men who rose up the ranks, not by special merit or competence, but solely on his blind obedience and studious attention to detail.

Right now he was gazing up at von Leeb over his champagne glass with a look of hero worship as he recounted one of his many amusing combat stories. Von Leeb finished with an obscene gesture that elicited raucous laughter from the men and hands before mouths of the women.

Schroeder timed his arrival with precision. He caught the group's attention with a perfectly executed Seig Heil.

"Ah, here he is, *Herr* Schroeder, *Herr* Rauter and *Frau* Rauter, you will be riding with Schroeder in his auto this morning." Von Leeb was resplendent in his full parade dress, draped with aiguillette, battle ribbons, and medals. He even wore a jewelled cavalry sabre and glittering spurs on his boots.

"And where will you be?" asked Rauter. Like von Leeb, he had a strong Austrian accent.

"I will be mounted on a very fine Polish Arabian, a birthday gift from this fine fellow." Von Leeb put a chummy arm around Schroeder's shoulders. He was pleased to see Rauter was suitably impressed, and a little envious.

"Yes, we saw him out in the garden, a beautiful animal. My wife Ella was enchanted." Rauter playfully patted her bottom. She blushed pink.

*Frau* Rauter was a surprise: tall, slim, and elegantly beautiful. She must be a new acquisition. Schroeder guessed her to be at least ten years his junior. The other surprise was the burgeoning mound beneath her lacy frock.

"After the baby comes, Hanns has promised me stables of my very own," she beamed, her credulous face radiating a childlike innocence.

"I am sure *Herr* Schroeder here will be pleased to arrange that for you. He has an eye for quality horseflesh," observed von Leeb.

"The policies of the Reich must favour an astute businessman like yourself," said Rauter.

"The stream flows both ways," Schroeder replied graciously. "Equity has amassed in the hands of a certain people whose days are numbered. Somebody has to manage the administration of these assets."

Rauter seemed enthused. "Indeed, as the new *General Kommissar* for security, I have a new directive from Berchtesgaden, we will be making changes! There will be nowhere to hide from now on."

Schroeder raised his glass. "I'll drink to that."

"Oh, I do hope you both won't be prattling on about business all day long; you will bore poor Ella half to death," said one of von Leeb's girlfriends. "Why don't you stay with us here at the hotel, leave these boys to their silly parade."

Rauter put a protective hand on her belly. "Maybe you should stay, my dear, it will be a long ride and rather noisy."

Ella screwed up her little pixie nose at her husband. "Nonsense! I love a good parade, and I'm sure *Herr* Schroeder's auto is very comfortable."

Schroeder gave her a warm paternal smile. "Of course, my dear, we would be delighted to have you with us."

"Right, let's go through this one more time." Rafe cut a menacing figure, draped head-to-toe in black leather. The jack boots and Stahlhelm made him a good three inches taller. The wide lapels of the greatcoat concealed the plain civilian shirt beneath, and with trousers tucked into the knee-length boots, it would be difficult for the casual observer to see he was not in full dress uniform. Everybody stood off a few feet, since despite concerted effort and liberal amounts of cologne, the leather still reeked of mud and rot.

"We all meet at the staging post on Vinken Street at eight, Gerrit and Henk up front in the Citroen, me in the back. The procession should reach Dam Square by nine; Hannie will be our eyes on the mark, and she will reconnoitre on bicycle and report back on the target. If everything is correct, I will ride to the square with the package and join the parade for the second loop to make the drop-off. If the package fails to activate, I return to Vinken and pick up the Sten and grenades for a second attempt. In the meantime, Henk will loiter on the corner of Binnen and Vinken and cover me with the Sten if I get followed."

"You won't carry the Sten on the first round?" said Gerrit

"It's too awkward to deal with the Sten and the package, so I'll take my .45 instead. Henk, you think you can handle the Sten?"

"No problem."

"The key is to take this narrow route away from the square where vehicles cannot follow." Rafe's finger traced the series of right-angle twists and turns that squeezed through laneways and foot bridges that lead north-west, parallel to the rail line.

"Any more questions?" Rafe was eager to get moving, inactivity giving his common sense time to take hold. Everyone was highly agitated; Rachel clung to her father, and was close to tears. Henk was pacing back and forth, cracking his knuckles loudly. Gerrit looked like he wanted to back out of the whole thing.

"Good, let's get this over with."

Just as Rafe moved to leave, Jacob pulled him aside, well out of earshot of the others, and he lowered his voice to a near whisper.

"Listen, son, if you find the explosive fails, don't go back with the guns; don't try to be a hero, you hear me? You'll only get us all killed."

"But what about our arrangement?"

"We can discuss that when you get back."

Rafe felt something was off; he glanced to his left and caught Gerrit watching them intently. Whatever was afoot, it would have to wait until this was over.

"Swear to me, man—get that thing in the car and get out, no shootouts." Jacob offered his hand. Rafe searched Jacob's face for signs of deceit. There was something behind his eyes that Rafe couldn't quite read.

Rafe took the hand in a firm grip. "I swear, no second round."

The ride in the truck was long and uncomfortable. Rafe had to hold the heavy motorcycle upright in the turns, something they hadn't anticipated. Little light or fresh air reached the rear of the lorry; it soon became very hot and stuffy. Petrol fumes from the bike and the reek exuding from Rafe's clothes combined to make a nauseating miasma in the small space. Rafe had time to reflect on the last-minute conversation with Jacob; it seemed like a stay of execution. If Rafe was totally honest with himself, it was a great relief; taking on a whole Nazi parade with a paltry machine pistol would be a hazardous sport, even for him.

After what seemed like hours, the truck came to a halt, and there were three knocks in quick succession on the cab wall, the signal for 'arrived safe."

Gerrit and Hannie squeezed into the back through the access gap with electric torches, bringing with them a welcome gush of fresh cool air.

"We have the road closed off on both ends, all is clear," said Hannie. Rafe checked his wristwatch; they were dead on time. "Get down there and take a look. Remember, we need a positive visual identification of these two characters and an exact description of the motorcar, the one behind it, and the one in front. Take note of the armed forces surrounding and any extra security around the square."

Rafe watched her fiery mop of red hair as she charged off on her bicycle. She was fearless, but he worried that he should have sent Henk instead. Hannie was five-foot-nothing and would have trouble getting a good look in the crowd, another oversight.

Hannie peddled as hard as she could down the Prince Canal; she soon worked up a sweat under her heavy wool pea coat. Nestled in the pocket was her newly-acquired FN 9mm pistol; the heavy little gun bounced around dangerously, and every minute or so she had to put her hand on it to assure herself it was still there. The rain had eased to a light sprinkle and she passed groups of people on their way to the square. She ruminated on why good Dutch people would want to see these Nazi pricks strut around like peacocks on a wet Saturday morning. Apathy? Curiosity?.....

Hannie dismounted at Palace Street and proceeded on foot. There was surprisingly little security around the square: people walked around freely, children played amongst the legs of mothers, men stood around smoking and talking. Some of the more entrepreneurial folk had set up carts selling hot waffles, herring, and bitterballen. Despite this, the atmosphere was anything but festive.

Stony-faced NSB volunteers marched around handing out leaflets and Nazi propaganda publications, mostly begrudgingly accepted by reluctant hands. It seemed there were two factions attending: die-hard NSB supporters wearing uniforms and waving flags, and a minority who had a morbid curiosity or were simply bored and had little else to do. Hannie caught the eye of a pretty young girl in an NSB uniform passing out little paper swastika flags; she took one and smiled. "Heil Hitler."

"Enjoy the parade," said the girl, beaming with enthusiasm.

The distant beat of martial music began to build steadily. Hannie made her way through the crowd, following the sound. When she reached the west side of the square, it was clear the procession would come through Rokin Street. Two police cars were parked on either side and Dutch officers began clearing a passage through the mob.

The music grew louder still. Despite herself, Hannie felt a small thrill of excitement as she watched the column round the corner into view on Rokin Street. When the cavalry appeared, the crowd around her surged forward, blocking her view. She only caught a fleeting glimpse of a man on a tall, powerful white horse.

Hannie was jostled and pushed back further; she tried to see between the jackets and coats but they formed a solid wall around her as the head of the procession passed by. She heard the throb of motors and felt the rumbling of heavy vehicles, seeing only the tops of fluttering pennants and standards carried by the vanguard. Frustrated, she broke free and dashed eastward, where the crowd had suddenly thickened, and she found that even right up against the shopfronts she had to push and shove to make any headway. Instinctively, Hannie thrust her hand into her coat pocket and clutched the pistol, the cool, hard steel giving her courage. She picked up her pace. No longer caring about niceties, she cursed and elbowed her way through the throng; she had only a few precious moments left to confirm the targets were here.

Thinking fast, Hannie found a metal garbage bin; she up-ended it and climbed on top, waving her two flags furiously. Up front were three officers side-by-side, walking slowly in an exaggerated goose step. The man in the centre held a huge swastika flag; they were closely followed by the man on the horse, whose chest was covered in medals and colourful tassels, his steel helmet polished to a high shine, as were his long riding boots and glittering spurs. He turned towards her for a split-second and they made eye contact.

Her heart sank. It was von Leeb; he was supposed to be in the car with Kurt Schroeder. Hannie watched anxiously as a group of vehicles approached two by two, Kübelwagens carrying soldiers, half-tracks with more soldiers, some motorcycle sidecars like the one Rafe had. Hannie noted with dismay that the riders wore fancy, long woollen coats with decorations, not the plain leather type that Rafe was wearing.

The musicians were next, ranks of drummers all stepping high and rolling in perfect unison, the band with burnished brass instruments stomping in time with the rhythm. Finally, a pair of normal cars came into view; they were BMW cabriolets with older officers. Suddenly, Hannie recognised the shiny, nut brown bald head of Detzner; he was sitting in the front passenger seat of a BMW with another anonymous soldier driving.

Hannie flushed with anger; everything was falling apart, the men were not together in the same car as they had been told to expect. She would have to go back and tell them to call off the attack, as it would simply not be worth the risk to get just one.

Seething with hatred, she watched the rest of the parade go by, clutching her pistol in her pocket. Detzner had passed within mere feet of where she was standing—even she could have easily made that shot, put a bullet into that fat, sweaty head, watched his brains ooze out. She had killed before; it was easy, a pop and a puff of smoke, all over in a few moments, if you knew where to shoot.

But what then? In broad daylight in the middle of the city, there was nowhere to run, and even if she could get away someone would recognise her, someone would talk. She could never show her face again. And when they got her there would be no mercy; everybody she knew would be arrested, tortured, and murdered.

*No, better that the crazy Englishman take the chance, at least if he was captured he couldn't be linked to us.* A sleek, modern limousine caught Hannie's eye. Its glossy obsidian paintwork was flawless, polished to a high sheen. Unlike the other cars, this had a closed roof; whoever was inside must have been shy, since the windows were firmly shut. With the glare from the overcast sky, and the dark interior, it was hard to make out the facial features of the occupants, but something about the car made Hannie sure this must be Kurt Schroeder.

He was an enormously wealthy man, and this was by far the most ostentatious motorcar Hannie had ever seen. She had to be sure, though. Somehow, she would have to get a good look inside. Climbing down from the garbage can, she pushed her way to the front, slowly creeping, keeping pace with the march. She could see dark silhouettes through the back window; it looked like two men in the back, facing each other. Who was the other man? It certainly wasn't Detzner or von Leeb, but it must be somebody very important indeed to be sharing a limousine with Schroeder on an occasion such as this.

In her mind's eye, she pictured Kurt Schroeder's face. The photograph they had of him was grainy and out of focus, but there was a distinctive weirdness to his features that was unmistakable, and just one glimpse would be enough. On she went, past the Royal Palace, and still the glare and reflection of the cloudy sky confounded her. Time was running out. She gave herself until the right turn on Dam Street to make the sighting, after which she would have to leave it. Hannie clenched her little fists and uttered a silent prayer, *Please, God, please help me send this evil man to Hell where he belongs.*

Just as she finished, the car made the slow ninety-degree turn onto Dam Street. The sun was now in front of them, and for a few seconds shined bright and strong through the glass to perfectly illuminate the occupants. Time seemed to slow down, and Hannie felt she could make out every tiny detail of the men's faces. Schroeder was indeed an odd one: he was once heavily scarred by acne, and he attempted to conceal the damage with pancake makeup; in fact he wore more rouge than most of the painted whores in De Pijp. The other man she didn't recognise. Middle-aged, he wore a swastika pendant and ribbon around his neck and he had the arrogant mien of a high-level official. Just as suddenly, the angle changed and the light was gone.

Hannie stopped and watched the car move slowly off down the street; her heart thundered and her head swam. This was it - Detzner and von Leeb would have to wait, but they could still get Schroeder.

The Maybach was a palace on wheels, custom-made to Schroeder's exacting specifications by the Zeppelin coach company in Stuttgart. Schroeder opened a bottle of Dom Perignon from the cabinet and they all sipped from crystal tulips. "Things are going well out east?" asked Schroeder as he gazed thoughtfully out at the band.

"So I hear." Rauter shrugged as he lit a long, thin cigarette. "I'm no parlour room general, but it seems Stalin can't hold the Caucasus, and we should have control before winter."

Schroeder nodded sagely. "Good, good. And what is the mood in Berlin? It's been a while since I've been in the old shark tank."

Rauter chuckled at the affectionate name for the *Reichstag*. "Well, I can tell you there is a strong feeling that we need to do more about the Jewish question here in the west."

Schroeder's left eyebrow rose quizzically. "Is that really a priority? Considering all the heavy fighting still going on?"

"Oh yes, indeed, this comes right from the top." Rauter pointed skyward with his cigarette.

"We can't have the little rats running about over here stirring up trouble, they will be put to work! Labour camps are being built out east, and a rail network is being prepared to ship them out in force."

Schroeder's mind began calculating; there must be countless Jews still in the Low Countries, a lot of people to be rounded up, and presumably when they realised what was happening, many would go into hiding. The logistics of such an endeavour was daunting.

Rauter smiled and nodded knowingly. "Yes, it's going to be a big job, and that's why they sent me." He pointed out the window with his thumb at von Leeb as he majestically rode by the opposite side of the square. "A man like von Leeb, he is a soldier, not an administrator, he is not suited to this work; better for him to be at the front, on the battlefield, where he belongs." Rauter knocked back his drink and proffered the empty tulip. Schroeder refilled it. "People like you and me, *Herr* Schroeder, from finance and management backgrounds, we can take better care of things here."

Schroeder could barely credit his good fortune—tens of thousands, nay, hundreds of thousands of people will have their hoarded wealth confiscated. That meant real estate, artwork, businesses, inventory, stocks and bonds, bullion. It would be the largest-scale robbery of all time, and Schroeder himself was poised to take command of the entire operation.

They stood hunched over the can in the cold shadows of a narrow byway. Rafe had stripped off his SS gear; Gerrit was winding the mechanism inside with a screwdriver.

"Five minutes, that should give you enough time to get down there. Let's say another five to get in circulation, allow fifteen to get the can in the car, twenty-five minutes total."

"Better give another five just for a safety buffer," said Rafe. "What if I have to call it off? Can I bring it back to you to disarm?"

Gerrit winced. "I wouldn't risk messing with the detonator once it's on."

"So it will explode in thirty minutes no matter what."

"Yes, you will have to ditch it if we abort. I would throw it in the canal."

"Maybe I should just toss it into a random staff car; at least it won't be wasted."

Gerrit was horrified. "Absolutely not, that will expose us to too much risk! it's not worth the possible reprisals just to burn up a couple of army regulars."

They were interrupted by a short, sharp whistle. Henk stood with Hannie at the entrance to the street beckoning them over. Hannie was flushed scarlet and breathing hard, sweat glistening on her forehead.

"Kurt Schroeder is there, but there's trouble." She gasped for air; the words were coming out in a torrent, and she looked like she might pass out.

"Take your time," said Rafe calmly. "Breathe, try to relax." Rafe sat her down on the curb, squatting down next to her.

"Detzner and von Leeb are not in the Mercedes car with him; von Leeb is riding a horse, Detzner is in another car....and there's more...the car is not the one we expected, it's a big limousine with a roof.... "

Gerrit and Henk both cursed bitterly. "That's it, then, it's fucked," said Henk.

"....Wait, let me finish. There is another man in the limousine with Schroeder, he looks like NSB or maybe Nazi Party, big cheese....he..."

"What did he look like?" Gerrit was suddenly agitated.

Hannie closed her eyes tightly, seeing the mystery man in her mind. "Civilian dress, middle-aged, dyed black hair, medium build, heavy eyebrows, big swastika medal around his neck....."

"Could it be..? Rauter?" said Gerrit under his breath.

"Rauter who?" Rafe was at a loss.

"Hanns Rauter, we heard a rumour that he was coming from high command to take over the security operations here, but he wasn't due until.... " He suddenly seized Rafe by the sleeve in a fit of passion. "Jesus Christ, man, we could strike a powerful blow here!" Gerrit looked up and down the street nervously; he lowered his voice almost to a whisper.

"This man, Rauter, is a high roller in the SS; he reports directly to fucking Himmler. The word is, he is being sent here to set up a policing division to wipe out subversives and organise mass deportations."

"So, this bastard is an even bigger scalp than von Leeb?" said Rafe.

Gerrit's eyes sparkled. "Much bigger. If we can eliminate him, we will be sending a message to Berlin that the Dutch resistance here means serious business, it would be a huge coup for us."

"Well, what are we waiting for? Let's go light him up." Rafe stood and headed towards the truck. Gerrit held him back, clutching his shirt in a white-knuckled fist.

"Wait! I need to talk to Jacob first."

"There's no time," said Henk. "We can't get a hold of him in Rotterdam, there's no telephone line."

Gerrit wrung his hands "Fuck, I can't make this decision alone; the backlash could be too much to handle, and we need to warn the other groups...."

Hannie shot to her feet. "We can do that after, we need to act Now!"

Rafe saw a couple of curtains twitching in high windows; they had started to attract attention.

"Hannie is right. Gerrit ; you are the leader in the field—right now, right here, you must decide."

In despair, Gerrit put his hands on his head and turned around in slow circles. Somewhere from a few blocks away, the sound of the marching band drifted over them. Precious moments ticked by. Rafe felt curious eyes burning holes on his back.

"Fuck it," said Gerrit finally, he picked up the gift-wrapped explosive and headed for the truck.

Gerrit set the timer and had one last check of the connecting circuit with a handheld voltmeter. With trembling fingers he connected the batteries to the timer. Rafe synchronized and buckled his wristwatch to the Zundapp's handlebars. Disturbingly, the electric clock did not tick; they had to wait nervously for a full minute for the minute barrel to flick over to confirm the countdown had started.

Rafe stuffed the package down the front of his coat and checked his watch. Eight-thirty right on the mark. "Henk, get outside and check for any watchers; when it's clear, get the ramp down.

Rafe mounted the bike, turned on the fuel spigot, and primed the carburettor. As usual before going into action, he felt strangely serene; all the mental anguish and graft was finished, and now it was just a matter of a few well-timed, expertly executed physical gestures, and the whole affair would be accomplished. Fear of being injured or killed simply never touched him; he had always leaped into the fight with reckless abandon.

But this time, just before he kicked the big German bike into life, an image jumped into his mind's eye: it was Rachel's face, just before he left this morning, high contrast and pin-sharp. Her eyes were pink and moist with tears, her little nose was red, and her normally tidy hair had fallen loose and misshapen. "Don't cry, I'm coming back," he said to the face. "I'm going to make sure I come back."

He kicked the motor over, once, twice, and on the third kick it coughed and growled fiercely, settling into a deep, reassuring throb. Rafe selected first gear and burst through the wall of flimsy flower boxes, sending tulips flying in all directions as he flew down the ramp and along the street.

Turning right onto Orange Street, Rafe found that the cobbles had dried out in a patchwork pattern; shadows of buildings left dangerous areas of slick, wet stone where the sunlight was blocked. It would be a problem on the way back when he might be riding hard.

Rafe let the bike settle into a relaxed cruise, adopting a confident, upright posture. What little civilian traffic there was immediately moved aside to let him pass. Rafe felt the coffee can press against his chest like a living thing; he felt it gradually getting warmer, maybe the timer had malfunctioned? Could he smell smoke? Rafe found himself checking his watch compulsively.

In a few short minutes, he arrived at the end of Raadhuisstraat and the Royal Palace. A group of Dutch police officers on bicycles barred the way to vehicles; this would be the first real test. Rafe decided not to give them time to scrutinize his appearance too closely; he would blow through without stopping. They were facing away from him, watching the parade. As he approached, the sound of his motor drew their attention; they turned, and quickly taking in his uniform closing speed, scrambled to move out of the way. Rafe nodded brusquely as he passed by.

The crowd was engrossed in the spectacle before them. The sound of Rafe's motorcycle was lost in rumbling vehicles and bombastic music. Rafe was forced to stop and sound the horn. Suddenly startled, they parted like the curtains on a stage, revealing the orderly procession of Nazi soldiers.

Rafe's blood ran cold as he saw, by fate or divine providence, that he had arrived just as the *Panzergrenadiers* were passing through. They were the feared mechanized units that smashed the French lines wide open and pushed the British expeditionary forces into a humiliating evacuation in Dunkirk just a year ago. Up front, a half-track towed a captured Royal Artillery  twenty-five-pounder gun draped with a shredded regimental flag, a sombre trophy of war. As Rafe watched it pass by, he bristled with fury. Coming up the rear of the column were a formation of Zundapp sidecars. Rafe saw his chance; he kicked the bike into gear and shot in the gap.

Thanks to the impeccable discipline of the *Wehrmacht*, all the personnel remained staring straight ahead as Rafe joined the rear of the column. As Hannie had warned, the riders were all wearing smart parade uniforms, not the usual battle dress and greatcoat. Nobody seemed to notice, however, as Rafe fell in behind the group. At first he had trouble keeping the machine steady at the slow speed of the procession, since the bike was geared to carry a heavy sidecar and did not handle well without it at walking pace. Rafe again glanced down at his wrist watch: twenty-two minutes remained.

Rafe found the limousine right away; the sleek mirror-polished body was hard to miss amongst the hard military machinery. The tinted windows were firmly shut, and the car squatted low to the ground. Rafe felt sure it was reinforced with armour plating; the glass was almost certainly tempered. If the occupants didn't open the window voluntarily, Rafe would have a hard time getting through. Among the sombre crowd, Rafe only saw a small band of half-a-dozen starry-eyed NSB members waving flags and cheering. They were grouped around a propaganda stand on the north side of the square, where the Maybach had just now passed. Rafe would have to somehow get in sequence to join the limo the next time around.

Rafe felt fairly safe for the time being with this group of riders. Accelerating past them would be too aggressive, cause alarm, and attract too much attention. The better option would be to slow down and allow Schroeder's car to catch up.

As he approached the NSB stand, Rafe saw a mounted officer at the head of a cavalry regiment stoop down to accept a garland of laurel from a pretty, young staff girl. It was an obvious bit of staged theatre; as she kissed him on the cheek, he turned and for a brief moment looked directly at Rafe. The square, handsome face was unmistakable: it was von Leeb. For a heart-stopping second, von

Leeb's face registered some slight bemusement or concern before he quickly regained his charming smile and turned to kiss the girl's lips. The man was no fool; he had spotted Rafe's tatty field uniform instantly, but his subtle reaction was either indifference or well concealed.

It was a close call, and now Rafe felt dangerously exposed; there was no time to dither, he had to strike right now.

Pulling off and stopping by the NSB stand, Rafe fixed his eyes on the Maybach. It made a long, lazy turn eastward back in his direction. At its present speed, it should reach him in no more than three or four minutes; his watch read 8:45, still a quarter of an hour to go; he would have to follow it some way.

Rafe looked about him; he had stopped right in front of an old matron and her brood. The loud, smoky exhaust directly in their faces, some in the crowd had begun to regard him with open hostility. The NSB members simply looked slightly bemused as to why he had stopped. Rafe bent over and fiddled with the gear lever, attempting to look like the bike had some mechanical problem and wouldn't go into a drive gear.

After a time, he glanced up at the Maybach - it looked as if it hadn't moved an inch. Again he checked his watch; only some twenty seconds had passed, but it felt like five or six minutes. Sweat now trickled down his flanks and off the end of his nose, dripping on his glove; his goggles had fogged up and he could barely see.

A smiling Dutch police officer with shiny buttons appeared directly beside him. He said something in German that Rafe couldn't understand. Rafe tried to ignore him and went back to adjusting the gear shift.

The man was persistent; he put a friendly hand on Rafe's shoulder, and this time he raised his voice above the throb of the motor, "*Darf ich dir mit etwas helfen?*"

Rafe struggled to come up with a likely response, but he went blank. He just shook his head and pointed to his ear as if he couldn't hear over the engine noise. Rafe went back to fussing with the gear lever. It was when he bent forward to adjust the linkage that the coffee can slipped out of his jacket.

It fell in slow motion to the ground, rolled over twice, and came to a rest against the polished shoe of the officer.

After a moment the German Officer stooped over and gently picked it up. It had been carefully wrapped in bright orange wrapping paper by Rachel, but in their haste Gerrit and Rafe had torn and wrinkled the outer layers slightly. Rafe watched in stunned disbelief as the officer turned the package over, carefully inspecting the cornflower-blue silk ribbon and dark smudges of oil. Rachel had attached a small card with the ribbon, and the man peeked inside to read the message.

Rachel had written German in neat Gothic script:

# Welkom in Amsterdam. X

#

Rafe held his breath as he searched the man's face for a reaction. He was an older fellow, in his late forties with receding blond hair; he looked like a no-nonsense school master type. For a few seconds his freckled brows furrowed as he read the message.

Desperately, Rafe searched for an avenue of escape; the crowd was dense and about five deep, and he might have to knock down a few spectators if he was to get away quickly. He glanced over his shoulder. To his surprise, the Maybach was passing him by; he saw the parade was over and the procession had sped up as it began to move out of the square.

The policeman had been joined by a colleague. Rafe shunted the bike into gear, and when it engaged with a thump, he began to turn the bike to escape. "Stop!" the officer shouted.

Rafe cringed and he turned, expecting a drawn pistol or a truncheon.

The officer slowly moved to hand it back, and when Rafe took a hold of it, he held his grip firm until Rafe made eye contact. The officer nodded slowly; he spoke in Dutch, "I hope whoever receives this gift is deserving of it." The officer abruptly turned and joined the throng as they began to drift away.

Ella yawned and stretched like a great sleepy kitten. "Well, that was lovely, even though I had to listen to you two waffle on about money all morning." She snuggled up to her husband, clutching his arm in a childlike display of affection. "How about some lunch!"

"We just had breakfast," chuckled Rauter indulgently.

Ella blushed "Champagne makes me hungry, and anyway, I'm eating for two."

"We can dine at my bistro, it's only a few blocks away." Schroeder knocked on the glass partition that separated the passengers from the driver. "We can drive through the park, give you a feel for the city. Gunther, turn off here, please; we will head for the restaurant, so go the long way around the gardens."


Rafe edged slowly through the thronging crowd. Everybody was funnelled through the narrow Prince Street, and the Maybach was quickly engulfed in the shuffle. Rafe had to stand up on the pegs periodically to keep it in sight.

The crowd was painfully slow in dispersing. Rafe checked his watch: five minutes left. The can was like a living thing against his chest; he swore he felt it stir and flutter. Once more he popped up on the bike, craning his neck to see over the multitude of hats and umbrellas.

The Maybach had vanished.

Frantically, Rafe looked left and right, his whole body burned like a furnace, and his mouth went dry. Rafe felt real panic slide its claws around his chest. *They must have turned off somewhere.* Rafe went to pound on the horn, only to realise they had removed it.

In a spasm of terror, Rafe gunned the engine and began shouting at the bustle of people blocking his path, "MAKE WAY, LOOK OUT!" the words were out of his mouth before he could think properly; to his horror he realised he was shouting in English.

Although the majority of the garrison had headed north back to barracks, von Leeb's mounted officers lingered in the square just meters away. Rafe prayed to God they wouldn't notice him.

"*ACHTUNG, ACHTUNG!*" Rafe kicked out with his boots and pushed his way forward; slowly, like the Red Sea before Moses, the mob parted. Rafe opened the throttle and charged down the narrow street to the first intersection, coming to a shuddering, sliding halt on the greasy cobbles.

Rafe just caught sight of the rear end of the limo as it disappeared around a corner towards one of the many small canals that ringed the city centre. Rafe gunned the throttle, spinning the rear tyre and swinging the bike around ninety degrees to give chase.

As he turned, he saw that further down the *straat* von Leeb's group of horsemen were now paying him close scrutiny. They still appeared puzzled and curious more than anything else, and that might just give Rafe the time he needed.

Rafe pulled alongside the immensely long Mercedes just as it stopped to allow a cart horse to pass; all the windows were closed and tinted dark green, and he could make out vague shapes of the passengers moving inside. Rafe put on his friendliest smile and knocked gently on the rear passenger window, brandishing the brightly-coloured package in his left hand, gripping his .45 in his right beneath his coat.

"Who could this be?" asked Rauter. "A friend of yours, perhaps?"

Schroeder regarded the smiling, young soldier through the glass; he was wearing goggles and a helmet that obscured his features. He seemed to be offering up a box tied up with a gay blue ribbon. Something tingled curiously at the back of his skull, like a faint protest that something was not quite right with the man.

"Never seen him before, drive on, Gunther."

"Oh, but he's got a lovely gift for us." Ella's eyes lit up. "Perhaps it's chocolates, Hanns; you *know* how I can't resist chocolates." She tugged on her husband's sleeve playfully.

Glare from the sun reflected in the window glass made the occupants all but invisible; Rafe was in fact looking at a mirror image of himself when there was a soft whir of electric motors and the inch-thick glass began to glide smoothly down into the door. Rafe stole a glance at his watch; only seconds remained.

Two things happened almost simultaneously. There was an admonitory shout from back down the lane where von Leeb and a group of policemen were approaching. Concurrently, a dainty, white-gloved female's hand emerged from the car to take hold of the gift. Behind the hand floated the pretty young face of a girl.

Rafe froze; he rapidly scanned the exterior of the vehicle, had he the wrong car? How could he have made such a mistake?

"You, there! Don't you move!" A police officer shouted out of the window of a Kübelwagen driven by a *Heer* soldier. Von Leeb dismounted and led his horse to follow close behind.

"Who the hell are you?" spoke an angry man's voice from the interior of the limousine. Rafe ducked his head and peered past the girl into the darkness within. The two men were there, Schroeder and Rauter, dressed up to the nines in dinner suits, the sweet smell of booze and expensive tobacco filling his nostrils.

The girl's powdered brow crinkled up in confusion; Rafe experienced a curious momentary flux in time as it seemed to hang suspended. He saw with incredible clarity the details of the lace on the girl's frock, and the telltale bulge beneath it. The odd texture of Schroeder's cheeks, like a waxen doll, the rose red slit of his mouth.

In that moment, Rafe and the girl both had hold of the gift. Rafe gripped it from the top, and the girl cradled it in her two small hands. They both felt it beat once, like the heart of a living animal, and then it began to fizz.

In one deft movement Rafe tossed the now smoking, hissing package into Schroeder's lap, while simultaneously reaching boldly into the window and gripping the girl's slim arms in both fists.

Her scream mingled with the unholy, banshee-like howl of the incendiary as it erupted within the confines of the vehicle. Within seconds, the car was engulfed with thick black smoke and sparks of white hot thermite. In a convulsive jerk, Rafe arched his back and pulled with all his might. The girl came halfway out the window, her knees caught on the doorframe. It took every ounce of Rafe's physical strength to twist her over so she was facing upwards; she was no mere slip of a girl, and she was fighting like a tigress.

The driver of the limousine, blinded by smoke and in an apparent fit of panic, stomped on the accelerator. The rear wheels spun and smoked as the heavy car ponderously slid sideways and then suddenly lurched forward as the tires found purchase, surging diagonally across the narrow street and crashing into a shop window in an explosion of shattering glass.

Rafe and the girl tumbled across the pavement, ending in a smouldering heap just feet from the edge of the canal. Thankfully, the girl had now fainted. Rafe quickly rolled her over and snuffed out the myriad of tiny flames and embers that glowed on her frock and stockings.

An inhuman shriek preceded Schroeder as he crawled on hands and knees out of the now-blazing wreck of the Maybach. Blinded by pain and flames, he jerked his feet and staggered down the lane towards Rafe, hands outstretched like some macabre marionette. Although he must surely be completely blind, some strange, animalistic power made him come forward directly to Rafe, threatening to fall upon him and the girl in a murderous embrace.

The men approaching in the Kübelwagen, momentarily stunned, had now regained their composure and now also advanced on Rafe; they would be upon him in seconds.

Rafe swiftly rose up on one knee and drew his .45. Aiming directly at Schroeder's glowing, flaming head, he squeezed off two rounds; the first hit him in the centre of his face just above the lip, the second penetrated his throat, exiting through his spinal column and killing him outright. He fell to his knees and arched over backwards.

Without pause, Rafe turned and emptied the clip at the approaching soldiers, who were already diving for cover. One round shattered the Kübelwagen's windscreen just as the driver ducked under the dashboard; the others flew wide, kicking up sparks and dust on the cobbles. Leeb's courser bucked and tried to bolt, pulling him around in mad circles as he fought for control.

Rafe tucked the empty pistol under his belt and heaved the fallen bike upright. Bright stars bloomed behind his eyes until finally he got his shoulder under it.

There was no chance of anybody else escaping the Maybach, which had become an inferno. A huge column of thick, black smoke drifted across the lane. Rafe opened the throttle and flew through the screening smoke just as the others began to return fire.

Rafe emerged from the black cloud and had to break hard to avoid a group of wide-eyed gawkers who broke and ran before him. He felt a couple of pistol rounds hum and buzz past his head like angry bees as he stomped on the rear brake and drifted the Zundapp into a sliding one hundred and eighty-degree turn to head westward. Just as he passed by the block of shops, he caught a glimpse of the Kübelwagen in pursuit.

Rafe charged back the way he came; he felt the power of the bike surge under him as he flew over the uneven pavement and cobbles. Although it was Sunday, the streets were still busy with traffic. Rafe weaved skilfully through cyclists and crossing pedestrians as he approached the main boulevard. He carefully controlled his speed with the throttle and gears so as to shoot through a narrow gap in the passing tramcars. Glancing back, he saw the Kübelwagen charge through the same gap; the driver was surprisingly tenacious, expertly squeezing every ounce of speed out of the little car. As he watched a German soldier balanced precariously on the backseat aimed a MP 40 machine pistol and fired a burst in his direction. Rafe turned and flattened himself over the bike's petrol tank, a smattering of bullets impacting ground around him, with one buzzing right past his ear.

Rafe had to get back on the planned escape route before he was shot to pieces. He recognised through a narrow lane the twin Gothic spires of the old post office building.

The dark medieval lane was barely wide enough to admit a horse and carriage. Piled in front of door steps on either side were the morning's delivery of coal, forming a kind of slalom; it hooked a slight right before opening out on the sunny, two-lane carriageway. Rafe down-shifted, weaving carefully through the obstacles.

The Kübelwagen's driver gamely came on without check, sweeping aside the piles of coal; he just failed to make the bend, impacting the rear quarter hard, forcing him to counter steer and regain control.

Exploding out of the lane like a shot out of a cannon, Rafe sailed over the hump of the canal bridge, landing hard and almost losing control on the other side. Rafe used the inertia of his swerve to slide the bike around and head north; the wide boulevard was clear, so Rafe slammed open the throttle. The rear tyre squirmed under his backside, found purchase, straightened up, and surged forward, lifting the front tyre inches off the ground. Two more rounds cracked the stone flags on his left-hand side, sending bystanders scurrying for cover.

Rafe now had his bearings and saw the upcoming byway he had picked out on his recce trip days before; it was a perfect escape slot between two ancient stone buildings under a Roman-style arch, barely wide enough to admit two men walking side-by-side. When he had passed through on foot he had measured the gap with his elbows outstretched, fists tucked under armpits, which he knew to be the approximate width of the Zundapp; he had a few inches to spare on either side. At the time, it seemed like ample room, but now, approaching at almost eighty miles per hour, it looked like threading the needle.

Rafe hesitated, remembering his promise to Rachel, her face filling his mind's eye for a fleeting moment like a flashbulb, then was gone, replaced by the looming stone wall that grew with astonishing speed. There was no way back now, he was fully committed—he would either shoot through the slot like a rifle bullet or be smashed into atoms in a fiery explosion.

Rafe tucked in even closer still to the bike, peeking just over the handlebars as he made tiny adjustments to the steering, shifting his weight forward at the last moment and closing the throttle to give him maximum steerage. His aim was true, and the big motorcycle sliced through the narrow gap, Rafe felt like a ball of shot in a cannon as he flew through the furlong or so length of the byway, a rush of air ear-splittingly loud in the narrow space, then suddenly, he burst free onto the sunlit boulevard.

When Rafe and Gerrit had walked here last Wednesday, *Raadhuisstraat* was notable only for its width and lack of traffic. Now, as Rafe saw to his horror, Town Hall Street on a Sunday was host to a busy market thronging with vendors and customers.

It was simply too late to take any evasive action, so Rafe ducked his head down as he smashed through a cheap furniture stall, sending splinters and broken legs of chairs and tables flying in his wake. He felt the impact of one of several soft bodies and cries of pain and outrage before he himself lost control and went down in a shower of sparks and tangled limbs.

The bike slid on for another twenty feet with Rafe tumbling after it; he rolled over twice on the hard stone cobbles, smashing his elbows and knees hard before he managed to flatten himself out and control his slide, slamming feet-first into the opposite curb, the impact knocking the wind out of his lungs with a terrific gasp.

There was a flash of white light as Rafe's helmet bounced off the stone curb. Blood filled his mouth and dribbled out his nose. For a few seconds, his consciousness receded down a grey fuzzy hole; when it emerged he found himself on his feet, staggering towards the fallen bike. The ground was strewn with splintered wooden furniture and shattered china, and an irate man was shouting at him in Dutch. Rafe ignored him and bent over to try and lift the bike; it was then that he felt the hot wetness in his boot and the weakness of his knee.

Rafe pushed his hips under the bike and heaved upwards again; this time his knee collapsed under him and he folded over, and the bike fell across his thighs, twisting his knee further and crushing him under its massive bulk.

A group of nearby boys dressed in their Sunday best rushed to his aid, it took three of them to hoist the Zundapp upright. Another strong set of arms gripped Rafe around waist and helped him to his feet. "You're hurt, you're bleeding," said the man in German. Rafe saw from his collar and cuffs he was an off-duty Staff Sergeant. "We'll have to get you to the *krankenhaus*; what's the damn hurry, anyway...?" The sergeant's words trailed off as Rafe stripped off his glove and groped over his left knee - his trouser leg was wet with blood, soaked down to the boot. There was a strange lump under his fingers, but strangely Rafe felt no pain, just a numb, tingling sensation.

Rafe mounted the Zundapp and began kicking it over. "I'm okay.. thank you.. it's really nothing," Rafe replied in halting, slurring German. The sergeant shook his head sadly. "Oh my, you have taken quite a knock to the head as well."

Rafe kicked the motor over and over; there was a strong petrol smell, and the carburettor was likely flooded. Rafe struggled to find the German word for 'push'. There came distant angry shouts from the direction of the wrecked Kübelwagen. Finally, Rafe simply made a pantomime gesture. The two Dutch boys seemed to understand and teamed up behind the rear wheel. The distant shouts drew nearer and more distinct.

"*Schnell, schnell!*" Rafe bellowed and began paddling the bike forward with his good leg; obediently, the boys put their shoulders into it and the bike began to slowly pick up speed.

"Wait." The off-duty sergeant appeared confused; he was looking around for a threat. Rafe saw the man's hand instinctively reach down to his hip for a pistol, which wasn't there. He watched them roll away, dumbstruck.

Rafe waited until he had reached a fast walking speed and kicked the Zundapp into first gear. The bike bogged down, lurched forward, and finally sputtered into life with a big cloud of blue smoke and a crackling chain of backfires.

It was immediately apparent that the Zundapp had been damaged, and most of the front brake lever had been smashed off, leaving a short stump. Rafe couldn't apply enough pressure on it to squeeze the brake closed. What was worse; the left-hand side cylinder head was cracked, oil and fuel were spraying out in a fine mist. Rafe daren't open the throttle all the way for fear of cooking off and catching fire; already his gas-soaked trousers were smouldering against the hot exhaust pipe between his legs. Rafe had to try and nurse this thing home. He slowed down and tried to blend in with the light Sunday morning traffic; his heart had just about returned to a normal pace when a shout from not far behind turned his blood into ice.

Rafe had to blink twice to focus on the distant spectacle. From the narrow byway a majestic figure emerged, like a Teutonic Knight from a Wagnerian opera mounted on a magnificent white courser. Von Leeb pulled his mount up short and danced in an elegant circle. Von Leeb's furious eyes locked on Rafe. For a profound moment, the two men exchanged glares; it seemed like von Leeb's face grew enormous and filled Rafe's field of vision. Von Leeb's eyes glowed with outrage like two smouldering black holes. Somehow, with the instincts of a hunter, von Leeb had spotted him and tracked him across the city, using the same narrow alleys and canal bridges that only a two-wheeled vehicle, or a horse, could use. In an instant, the spell was broken. Von Leeb drew his Walther from his thigh holster and drew a bead on Rafe.

Rafe had just enough time to turn and flatten himself on the tank as the round buzzed past his cheek with millimetres to spare, kicking the Zundapp down a gear and racing for cover.

Rafe mounted the pavement, sending pedestrians scrambling, and two more rounds shattered glass in front of him. Von Leeb was a good shot, leading his target; it was only a matter of seconds until one found its mark. Rafe jinked right, bunny-hopping over the curb and cutting in front of a coal truck. In his peripheral vision, Rafe sensed von Leeb whipping the courser into a full gallop; the great animal's steel-shod hooves slithered and sparked on the stone surface.

In a straight contest, the courser would be no match for Rafe's motorcycle, but with his motor burning up and in this maze of crowded streets, von Leeb had more than a fair chance.

Seeing a tight left turn into a canal side street, Rafe waited until the last moment and abruptly slammed on the rear brake, drifting the bike through an elegant arc he controlled with the throttle. Using the pendulum effect of inertia, Rafe shifted his weight and slid the bike in the opposite direction, slipping between a copse of trees into a leafy avenue heading east.

Rafe emerged into a wide four-way intersection, and a convoy of three bright red trolley buses were in his path. Rafe picked a gap between two and committed. It was finely judged, and the rearmost bus kissed his rear tyre, sending him into a fishtail. Rafe peeked under his arm to see von Leeb make the same gap, also with inches to spare.

Again, Rafe made a drifting turn across a right angle bend, this time into a narrow canal-side lane covered with a thick canopy of elm trees. A young man on a bicycle took evasive action into the water with a splash, while another shrieking woman dived into an alleyway, dragging her toy dog with her.

Rafe kept the spire of Westerkerk Cathedral as his waypoint; he knew if he kept it on his starboard side he would be heading north. Now he was heading south - he had to turn around if he was going to make it to *Oranjestraat* where Henk was waiting. The next intersection was a hump-backed canal bridge, the far side ran westwards before joining the north-south Prince Way.

Rafe mounted the arched footbridge at speed, took to the air for a heart-stopping moment, and landed hard on the other side, planting his boot down as a pivot and sliding the rear around in a one-eighty. The manoeuvre didn't fool von Leeb; he simply jumped his mount expertly around the bridge in two leaps, cutting the corner completely.

The way ahead was clear, so Rafe changed up a gear and accelerated away. Just as the engine turned over four thousand rpm, she coughed, misfired, and surged. The Zundapp was flagging, burning oil, and losing power; she wouldn't handle this punishment much longer. Rafe would have to think of something fast.

There was another distinctive whip-crack of the Walther as it zigzagged through the trees, bollards, and street lamps. As in a dogfight, Rafe needed to keep up constant manoeuvring, always presenting a moving target. Laying flat along the tank, Rafe peeked under his arm - Von Leeb was gaining. Rafe steered around low obstacles, von Leeb's mount simply leaped over them like a show jumper. Within moments, von Leeb had drawn almost alongside Rafe on his port side, so close Rafe could see the bulging blood vessels in the horse's neck and hear its snorting blow.

Rafe's tactical intuition kicked in, honed by hours spent in the seat of a Hurricane jousting with the faster-diving Messerschmitt. He snapped the throttle closed and squeezed the rear brake.

Von Leeb overshot, surging in front of Rafe. He instantly realised his mistake and pulled up, but the massive creature had too much momentum, and the courser reared up and slid on its haunches, almost sending its rider flying. Rafe pivoted and swung left into a side street.

After a few hundred yards, Rafe fishtailed to a stop and turned around. With shaking hands he retrieved his Colt .45, ejected the empty clip, and fumbled around his pockets for the spare. Von Leeb rounded the entrance to the street just as Rafe slammed the clip in and racked back the action. Rafe took careful aim directly in front of the horse's hooves and squeezed off two rounds. The ear-splitting report alone would have sent most horses into a bolt, but von Leeb's mount was clearly trained for war; it came on apace without check. Von Leeb lay flat along the animal's neck, only the top of his shiny Stahlhelm just visible above the waving mass of windblown forelock.

Rafe held his breath and waited; his hands steadied and the iron-sight locked into the rhythmic dance of the gallop. Rafe timed his shot like a musician, judging the flight time of the round in sync with the wavelike undulations of von Leeb's bouncing head. When the shiny helmet disappeared from view, Rafe squeezed a single shot.

Rafe was so intensely focused that he swore he saw the round in flight as it spiralled downrange, impacted, and flattened itself dead centre on the steel dome of von Leeb's helmet with a loud, carillon-like a church bell. The courser was at full gallop, and von Leeb must have gone limp; the horse's forelegs locked and it flew headlong into a somersault, throwing von Leeb out of the saddle and high into the air, his body making two lazy revolutions in a star pose before smashing hard into the stone road surface. Unconscious and helpless, he continued tumbling like a broken marionette helmet bouncing off the stone cobbles and sliding to a stop in a tangle of mangled limbs.

Rafe was not about to hang around to see if von Leeb survived; there was a crowd of onlookers already gathering at the end of the street. Rafe kicked the now-smoking Zundapp into gear and headed north to *Oranjestraat.*

Rafe wound his way through the city streets, giving the central area a wide berth; soon all of Amsterdam would be flooded with police and *Wehrmacht* hunting him. Now the adrenaline was tapering off, Rafe began to feel the extent of his injuries. His left leg was stiffening and beginning to throb in time with his heartbeat, and his boot was half-full of blood. One of von Leeb's shots must have grazed his flank; there was a neat hole in his greatcoat and a mixture of blood and sweat trickled down his back. By the time he pulled into *Oranjestraat,* nausea and dizziness came upon him in waves while his hands were trembling on the grips of the bars.

Rafe's heart sank into his belly when he saw the empty street; it was deserted save for a scrawny cat glaring down at him from a window ledge. He was about to leave when he saw Hannie appear at the other end of the street, gesticulating wildly.

Rafe rounded the corner and dumped the smoking Zundapp into a nearby alleyway. Henk and Gerrit helped him out of his leather coat and boots, which they piled atop the bike and doused them with kerosene; they burned readily with an acrid, smoky flame.

Without a word, they clambered into the back of the lorry and Henk drove off towards the Centraal Station.

"Sorry to scare you," said Gerrit apologetically. "We were getting too much attention from the locals back there, we had to move around and hope you..."

"..I got Schroeder," Rafe interrupted, his voice in low monotone. He seemed to be staring blankly out into space.

"Jesus, are you sure?" Gerrit whispered hoarsely. Hannie giggled gleefully and clapped her hands.

Rafe squeezed his eyes shut and shook his head "No doubt, he's gone for good."

"What about Rauter?" Hannie was glowing.

"Nobody said anything about a bloody woman being in the car," Rafe growled.

Gerrit and Hannie exchanged a furtive glance.

"Did you get Rauter or not?" Hannie hissed.

"Everyone in the Maybach got it." Rafe winced as he sat up. "I managed to get the woman out, but they nearly cooked my goose by doing so. Why the hell didn't you tell me, Hannie?"

"Would you have gone ahead if I had told you?"

"Of course not."

"Then there is your answer." Hannie sniffed. "Who cares about some Nazi dog's whore, anyway?"

"You're a mess," said Gerrit. "You can't get on the train like that. Can you walk?

Rafe felt his left leg through his trousers; It was slick with blood and his knee was twice its normal size.

"I can make it, just need a stiff drink." Gerrit handed over a hip flask of jenever. Rafe grimaced at the juniper sting. "I'd prefer scotch, but this will have to do."

Rafe wore a mask of soot and oil where his goggles covered his eyes. Hannie used her handkerchief to do her best to clean up the worst of it before Henk stopped to drop her off.

"We split up; Hannie takes her bicycle to a safehouse at the docks, Henk drives to Zandvoort, Rafe and I take the train back to Rotterdam."

They exchanged solemn embraces and went their separate ways, knowing that this could be the last time they'd see each other.

Rafe found the fortifying effect of the gin had loosened up his knee enough to limp onto the train without drawing too much attention to himself. Gerrit followed at a distance and they boarded the lunchtime train to Haarlem. Just as the train moved out of the platform, there was a flurry of frantic activity as police and *Wehrmacht* arrived in force; they began lining passengers up to be questioned and searched. The inevitable crackdown had begun, and Rafe and Gerrit had escaped the city with moments to spare.

#

Hannie mounted her bicycle at a run and pedalled like the wind; soon the whole city would be overrun with soldiers and policemen looking for so-called terrorists. Hannie's safe house was actually a boat, a twenty-meter Schuyt barge called the *Loopkat* tied up at the docklands at Houthavens.

The barge was skippered by her lover and fellow communist scholar Constantin. He wrote a column on ethics for *De Waarheid* from a tiny secret office cleverly hidden below decks. Constantin was brave but not stupid; the space was custom built by an expert shipwright to smuggle wine from Belgium before the war, and it was completely invisible inside and out. Hannie looked forward to being in Constantin's strong, warm embrace, safe and secure for a few days while the reprisals died down. She blushed a little when she pictured what they would get up to in the confined space for so long.

Hannie was rudely awakened from her daydream as a police car roared past at speed, nearly knocking her down. It was soon followed by another, and then a Kübelwagen crammed with soldiers carrying rifles; they screamed off westwards down *Haarlemmerstraat.*

Hannie felt the first twinge of fear deep in her belly. They were moving fast, and the reaction was happening quicker than expected. She turned south and made to circle around the major intersections. The sky darkened and it began to drizzle, and more *Wehrmacht* personnel flooded the streets - they seemed to appear out of nowhere. Rushing into buildings and herding the men out into the street, smashing in locked doors, shouting and screaming. Hannie saw one man cracked over the head with a rifle butt; he collapsed like a puppet with its strings cut and a woman began sobbing, another shrieking hysterically.

Up ahead, police were setting up a temporary road block. Hannie moved to turn down a side street, when she suddenly found herself caught up in a crush of terrified people; she was knocked off her bicycle and almost trampled underfoot, a tall, skinny German soldier roughly pulled her to her feet and shoved her, along with his rifle. When she resisted he pricked her with his bayonet in her kidneys, his wild eyes were bloodshot red and bulged out of his skull as he screamed at her.

They were all forced into a queue. Hannie was last, with a bayonet in her back. An officer was at the head of the line supervising the document check and body search of each in turn. It all happened so fast Hannie had no time to think; she reached into her coat pocket for her identity card and her hand closed around cold steel. Her heart stopped—she still had her pistol.

Frantic, she looked around for a place to ditch it; they were lined up in the middle of the street, well clear of any trash cans or window boxes. Even if there was something nearby, she would have to somehow toss it without drawing attention. The line moved forward; they were working fast, the soldiers were stripping people down to their underwear, hastily ripping and cutting away clothes with knives and bayonets, any protests of modesty from the woman ignored, or occasionally met with a slap or punch. The line moved forward again, like a production line in a factory; the young man in front of her began to weep softly, a dark stain spread in front of his trousers.

Hannie began to tremble, she couldn't help it. Her body betrayed her and her knees shook, she shifted her weight from leg to leg in an effort to disguise it, she tried to look annoyed and indifferent, but her muscles wouldn't comply, every cell in her body telling her to run, run and never look back. The line moved on, Hannie counted three ahead of her; her heart was a sledgehammer in her breast, she saw dark spots in front of her eyes. The line moved on, two left.

On many an evening, Hannie and her comrades had talked bravely of what they would do if captured alive, bravado fuelled by drink, mostly; the most favoured option was to take as many of the enemy with one as possible before taking one's own life, like in a dramatic, heroic fashion. Hannie looked at the soldiers around her; three of them carried black-steeled sub-machine guns, the rest had Mauser rifles, the officers wore pistols on their hips. She wondered how many shots she could get off before they cut her down. She imagined what that torrent of bullets would do to her body, would it hurt? Would she go quickly or would she linger, suffering?

As the tears welled up, she fought them down. Whatever happened, she wouldn't go blubbering like a little girl. The line moved on. Her fevered mind went to explanations and excuses:

*It's my husband's.*

*I found it and was going to sell it.*

*It's not my coat, I stole it at the train station.*

*Can't we discuss this somewhere more private?*

There was no charming or flirting herself out of it this time.

It was her turn. Her body seemed to decide what to do before her brain took action. Robotically, like an automated machine, she stepped forward and smoothly drew the pistol out of her pocket .

The whole world slurred, colours and shapes smudged as she thumbed the safety off and put the pistol into her mouth; it tasted like oil and copper pennies. There was a shout, it was long and drawn out, like a cattle's mew. Something hard struck her from behind, a flash of light, and she hit the ground sprawling, her pistol flying from her hand, skipping across the cobblestones out of reach. Strong hands gripped her arms, more shouting and yelling, she was jostled and manhandled, rolled over onto her back, a boot came down on her throat, crushing her larynx, Fists and boots rained down; with each blow she felt the light of her consciousness grow dimmer. She tried to fight back but they were too strong, too many. When it came it was a relief; Hannie surrendered to the darkness.

By the time the train pulled into Rotterdam station, Rafe felt like he had been run over by a bus, he had felt this way before and after air combat—something to do with hormones, the flight surgeon had told them, adrenaline dump. The journey on foot from the station felt like a long, torturous trip through hell; the sun was setting and the rain came down hard, every dark corner seeming to conceal an enemy, every barking dog a German hunting party, every motor lorry a Panzer battalion. They moved cautiously through the bombed-out buildings, avoiding the streets and pathways, doubling back and concealing their tracks.

It was well after dark until they felt sure enough they weren't followed and made it back to the sanctuary of the flower shop.

Rachel pounced on Rafe before he was even through the door, her embrace hot and desperate with relief.

"I'm wet," Rafe protested.

"I don't care."

"I'm dirty."

"I don't care, you're alive." Rachel finally released him and looked him over. "You're hurt, you're bleeding."

Jacob examined Rafe's bullet wound first. "The ball grazed your ribs, very lucky to be alive, but it should heal nicely."

Next, Jacob cut off Rafe's trousers with a scalpel. Rafe held back a whimper as Jacob palpitated the red, swollen flesh with his hard fingers. "It's a simple fracture of the patella; I should set it in plaster now or you could have a permanent limp."

Rafe took a long drag of his cigarette and winced. "I'd really rather not, old boy; a cast will slow me down."

Jacob shrugged. "A long soak in a cold bath might help with the swelling, but I'd say by tomorrow morning that knee will be the size of a football."

"I'll manage. Where is Henk?"

Jacob looked gloomy. "He hasn't come in yet."

"He should be back by now."

Gerrit had gone upstairs to set up the wireless - now he came pounding down the stairway, his face white as a sheet.

"The whole city is being torn apart, the bastards are arresting everybody in sight."

Between them, Gerrit and Jacob helped Rafe up the staircase, and they all crowded around the crystal set. The faint, ghostly voices hissed and crackled in the static. They were broadcasting in cipher, sweeping up and down the frequencies to avoid jamming. Gerrit scribbled down notes while Rachel used a one-time book key to decode the messages.

She read them out as they came in, her voice increasingly tremulous. "*C S 6 all members get out of Amsterdam immediately. Death squads and Gestapo systematic search and interrogation throughout city west of dockyards. Abandon all pending ops and disperse. Burn all hard comms.*"

Gerrit peeled his spectacles off and knuckled his forehead. "We expected some reprisals, but this is unprecedented."

"There is no way they could have mounted this kind of response so quickly." Jacob shook his head. "They must have had this in the works regardless; we just set it in motion."

Rafe held Rachel's hand; it was hot and damp with sweat. "So what now?"

Jacob glanced at his watch on the inside of his wrist. "We give Henk one more hour, then we get out of Rotterdam; we will split up and make contact again after the worst is over, in a week or two."

Rafe pulled Rachel closer. "We will wait for Henk, then we make for the farmhouse and take off right after dawn."

Jacob's eyes hardened. "Rachel and Anne will come with me; you can take your chances by yourself." Rafe felt Rachel stiffen in his arms.

"We had an agreement."

"Forget it, there's no way I'm letting my children go up across the sea in that contraption with half the German army after us." Jacob stood and left the room as if the debate was over. Rachel burst into tears.

"Look here.." said Rafe, following as Jacob pounded down the staircase. "Can't you see what's happening? You said it yourself, it's genocide!"

Jacob ignored Rafe and began stacking and packing his things into an old, brown leather doctor's bag.

"We can bury the equipment here and return later in the summer to regroup."

Rafe grabbed Jacob by the shoulder and spun him around. "Good God, man, won't you listen to reason!"

Jacob spoke calmly and quietly down his nose at Rafe, "We will not flee like cowards, we can go to ground and wait this out. "

"But you can't hide forever; they will get to you eventually. How long do you think the girls can survive in a camp like the ones you described to me?"

Rachel and Anne appeared in the doorway. They had their meagre possessions packed and were ready to leave. As Rafe had instructed, they wore all the winter woollens they owned, hats, gloves, and scarves for the frigid temperatures at altitude. Both looked so small and fragile.

"Look at them, Jacob, they've had enough, it's no life for them, running, hiding in the shadows, hunted like criminals."

Jacob rounded on Rafe and he jabbed his finger in his chest. "And where will they go, eh? In England, in some filthy workhouse or worse? I have been to London, I know what happens to...."

"We are getting married," said Rachel suddenly; her eyes were wet with tears but she held her head high in defiance.

There was a stunned silence and her words hung in the air like a rung bell.

Rafe was just as astonished as everyone else, but his mind worked fast and he soon regained his composure; he strode confidently over and put a protective arm around her. "That's right, I have asked Rachel to be my wife and she accepted, and we will be married as soon as we land in Sussex; she and Anne will live with me as their legal guardian."

Jacob was in some kind of shock; he sat down heavily and put his hands in his lap. He shook his head sadly. "Why must you always defy me, Rachel? You are just like your mother, she would never listen to me either, always running off on some foolish flight of fantasy."

Rachel opened her mouth to speak but was silenced by a shuffling, thumping sound from the outer stairwell; they rushed to extinguish the oil lamps and find hiding places. Rafe drew his .45 and got in front of Rachel, and he could feel her heart pounding even through her thick coat.

There was a long pause that felt like hours; they all gasped with relief when they heard the familiar coded knock on the steel door.

Henk was covered head-to-toe in coal dust, and everything but his eyes and lips were pitch black, giving him the appearance of a ghostly minstrel. He took a swig of beer and went into a coughing fit that lasted a good five minutes. "Had to hide in a damned coal chute most of the night." He coughed up a wad of tarry black phlegm and spat. "They got Hannie," he croaked.

Jacob's face crumpled "Who has her?"

"The police, Gestapo, she's at the theatre." Jacob and Gerrit hissed.

"What's the theatre?"

"It's where they question enemies of the Reich," Gerrit spat. "Nobody leaves there alive."

"She will give us up," said Jacob

"Fuck off, she won't talk," Henk rumbled. "She's tougher than all of you put together."

Jacob lit a cigarette; he took a deep drag and exhaled a great cloud of smoke as he spoke. "She's strong, but everybody has their limits; let's be realistic, how long can she hold out? A day, a week?"

Gerrit stamped his feet in frustration. "It doesn't matter—in the end, we are finished here for good, we may as ...."

"..Henk do you still have the Citroen?" Rafe butted in.

"Yes."

"Can you get us all to Erik's cottage?"

Henk rubbed his chin thoughtfully. "With all the fuel cans, it will be a close-run thing, but I think so."

"Right!" Rafe checked his wristwatch. "We have a couple of hours before dawn; if we leave right now we can be well north of Amsterdam before the sun rises."


When Hannie woke, she was shackled to a bench in the back of a truck, face-down in a puddle of filth - choking on something stuck in her throat. She sat up and coughed out broken teeth and clots of blood until she could breathe again Every breath was agony, she could feel fractured ribs grind in her chest when she tried to lay back and rest, and her only bearable position was sitting straight up. Her left eye was swollen completely shut. The tall, skinny private sat on the bench opposite; he had his rifle aimed at her heart. They sat in resolute silence as they bounced along.

It wasn't long before they reached their destination; the truck backed up into some sort of covered courtyard and the back gate was flung open. Hannie was unshackled and kicked to her feet, and she was forced to jog with half-a-dozen other prisoners down a ramp into a concrete bunker where they were all lined up against a wall at rifle-point.

Hannie took note of the others arrested; all were young men, and she recognised three of them: two petty local criminals and one unfortunate old drunk touched in the head. None of them were in the Communist Party or were part of her resistance unit. For hours they waited, no talking, no sitting, no water. Just as Hannie thought she might collapse, a group of officers appeared, pushing a young boy tied to an invalid's chair; he had a blood-stained flour sack over his head.

They wheeled the boy past, stopping at each person and lifting the sack so he could get a good look at their faces. Hannie stared straight ahead, focusing at a spot on the far wall; nausea hit her in waves, and out of the corner of her eye she saw the prisoners escorted out of the room one by one. Then it was her turn. The sack was pulled up, it took Hannie a moment to recognize Anton, but when she did, a physical shock ran down her entire body that she could not suppress.

They must have had him for a while; he was gaunt and grey, all of his apple-cheeked youthfulness gone. Anton looked like a man ten or twenty years older—sunken features, hard lines on his bruised and battered face. His eyes were cold and black as the grave as he looked her over.

The German intelligence officer leaned close and whispered something in his ear; Anton simply nodded. They turned and wheeled him out, and the door was bolted shut.

Seconds later there came heavy boots and the door was again unbolted. A big man flanked by two burly sergeants strode into the centre of the room. It was Detzner; he looked odd, somehow cadaverous, his shirt was soaked with sweat and it clung to gaunt shoulders, and his eyes were bloody globes burning deep in bruised sockets.

The sergeants began roughly cutting Hannie's clothes off with sharp bayonets; they carefully sliced open every seam and stitch in the lining of her coat, even crushing the buttons underfoot and cracking open the heels of her shoes. When they were done, Hannie stood nude, shivering in a cloud of shredded cotton down and wool.

Hannie felt Detzner's piggy little eyes run slowly over her body. They all stood in silence while he paced back and forth, regarding Hannie thoughtfully as one would a potential purchase. He pursed his lips, sucked his teeth, and shook his head. After a few paces, he stopped, and with sudden violence, punched Hannie full in the stomach. Hannie had no time to brace for the blow; his huge bony fist plunged deep into the soft flesh of her abdomen, she doubled over and sank to her knees; retching and gasping for air.

One of the sergeants produced a long iron chain; he tossed it up across one of the thick timber beams of the roof while the other man dragged Hannie across the floor like a sack of coal. They threaded the thick links through Hannie's shackles and hoisted her upright. She was pulled off her feet, suspended by her arms behind her back, with her feet just half an inch off the floor.

Hannie swung there for a few minutes while she coughed and gasped, the muscles in her shoulders and arms held rigid in fear and pain. They strained against her bodyweight, keeping her torso flexed and her shoulders firmly in their sockets. It wasn't long before the sinews shuddered and slowly gave up the fight. With horror Hannie realised that both of her shoulder joints were about to dislocate The man holding the chain must have been watching her body closely, and with practised timing he eased her down just in time. A chair had been placed under her and she sank into it.

Detzner lit a thin, brown cigarillo, held it in the flame until it was burning evenly, and regarded the end thoughtfully as he spoke.

"I am going to ask you some questions, and you will answer them to the best of your knowledge. Does that sound fair?"

Hannie declined to reply; she watched the drops of blood drip slowly from her nose and form perfectly round, red dots on the floor.

"Who was the man with the fire bomb today? He wore a German uniform, where did he get it?"

Hannie was silent; her breath came in rattling, sawing spasms.

Detzner fished in the pocket of his greatcoat and pulled out Hannie's pistol.

"A nice little weapon, FN nine millimetre automatic—what is it for?"

"Rats." Hannie surprised herself with the strength of her voice.

Detzner snorted. "You must have big rats in Amsterdam, hey?"

Hannie pointedly looked Detzner up and down. "The fattest, most disgusting in Europe."

Everyone in the room laughed heartily.

Detzner himself seemed particularly amused; his great belly shook up and down as he chuckled. At a small gesture of his hand, Hannie was pulled up off the chair and suspended in the air once more This time she couldn't stop herself from letting out a shriek of anguish as her shoulders cracked and popped under her weight. The pain seared through her skull in vivid red flashes and white-hot lightning.

Hannie seemed to have lost consciousness briefly as she suddenly found herself sitting back on the chair with Detzner smiling at her beatifically.

"Interesting form of persuasion, isn't it?" He grinned, leaning back casually with his hands behind his head. "I often find the simplest methods are the most effective.

"'*Strappado,*' they call it; the Spanish came up with this one during the Inquisition. I perfected it back in Africa on the Blacks. Nobody ever lasts more than an hour; they give me what I want, or they suffocate in their own blood."

"I will die before I betray my comrades," Hannie hissed.

Detzner shrugged. "Perhaps."

He dropped his cigarillo and ground it out with his heel. "But perhaps we don't need to go that far, eh?"

Hannie heard footfalls behind her as the door was unbolted. She strained her neck around to see Anton being wheeled in by a thick-set orderly in a white uniform. He was pushed around to face her, wearing the same flour sack over his head, his hot breath steaming through the fabric in the frigid air.

Hannie winced as the strong stench of faeces wafted off his wasted body. Evidently the boy had been strapped into the chair for days, denied the simple dignity of using a bucket to relieve himself.

Detzner snatched the sack off his head and slapped his face. "Wake up, boy! A friend of yours wants to say hello!"

Anton's eyes slowly adjusted to the light and focused on Hannie; there was a stark moment of recognition and he quickly turned away, flushing pink with indignation. Although he made a valiant effort to chew it back, he began to choke and sob bitterly.

The orderly locked his muscular arm around the boy's chin and forced his head around to face her.

Hannie was hoisted up just off the ground and the chair was kicked out from under her. "Don't tell them anything!" she shrieked

"Bastard! You lied to me," Anton wept. "You promised not to touch her!"

The chain was tied off and the two sergeants took a leg each, forcing her knees apart.

Detzner giggled delightedly. "OHH, LOOK at that, boy, I bet you've always wanted to see this cunt, eh?" Detzner leered, rolling his eyes and flicking his satyr-nine tongue around Hannie's thighs.

"Leave her ALONE!" Anton squealed, his unbroken voice pitched high as a girl's.

"WHO IS THE MAN WHO ATTACKED TODAY, BOY? WHERE IS HE?"

Although it caused her agony, Hannie bravely squirmed and kicked like a tiger. "Keep your stupid mouth SHUT, Anton!"

Detzner slobbered on the barrel of Hannie's pistol until it was slick with spittle; he then roughly forced it between her legs, plunging the weapon deep into the centre of her body. She cried out in terror and shame, a dreadful, animal sound. Detzner thumbed the hammer back; he grinned at Anton. "What a mess this will make, eh, boy? Fucked by a bullet! I might even let you pull the trigger!"

"RAFE! His name is Rafe. He's a British pilot and he has a plane hidden up north.." Anton's words came as a torrent after a burst dyke. "I know everything, everything, I'll tell you everything."

#

Gerrit and Jacob scrambled about in the light of oil lamps, gathering up armfulls of forged documents and ration cards, piles of pamphlets, posters and newspapers, reams of stolen paper stock, and even tins of ink needed to be destroyed. The little household incinerator in the bunker was quickly overwhelmed. Barrels of purloined heating oil were tipped out and pressed into service as crematories. They had to work fast, as with Hannie captured, they had to assume that every location she was privy to was compromised.

It took them more than an hour to load up the Citroen; it was a three-dimensional puzzle of luggage, tins of fuel, and bodies. In the end, they had to resort to sitting on top of the hazardous-looking square cans labelled *Flugbenzin ACHTUNG! BRENNBAR*.

There were a total of twelve twenty-L jerry cans. With the leftover fuel in the plane, Rafe calculated that after takeoff it would allow him to run at half-throttle for about one hour at ten thousand feet. They would be cutting it fine, and Rafe had to admit that if they had to run from any hostile aircraft for any length of time, they would have to ditch in the Channel well short of the coast.

None of them would last long in that freezing water. Rafe had to put the thought out of his mind. He watched Anne and Rachel laughing nervously in the dark; perhaps it was the sleep deprivation, but everybody seemed giddy, almost like they were embarking on a trip to the seaside.

Finally, they all piled in; the little truck sat low on its springs, creaking and lurching over the uneven, cratered roads of Rotterdam. Rachel clung to Rafe in the cold, perched atop sloshing cans of fuel in a starless night as black as the grave.

Detzner chewed down another pervitin tablet, washing the bitter drug down with a mouthful of schnapps as he watched the men gather in the darkness. The heavy assault force he had put together was more suited to a battlefield than a police action. Twenty of his own *Panzergrenadiers* mounted on two massive armoured Sd.Kfz 251 half-tracks. Three K-9 squads with packs of specialised human-hunting dogs. He doubted the resistance group they would face could put up much of a fight, but Detzner always liked to go into a confrontation with the odds overwhelmingly in his favour.

A staff sergeant jogged up and clicked his heels in salute. "All vehicles fuelled, armed. and ready, sir."

"Thank you, Sergeant. We will leave at once, get the men aboard, and move out!"

"*Jawohl!*" He turned and blew a shrill steel whistle.

Detzner's body trembled and his heart thundered as he climbed up next to the driver, as much from the anticipation of the coming violence as the amphetamine and liquor surging in his blood. The convoy pulled out, following a local police car into the blacked-out city. Far to the east, the first faint silver light of the coming day touched the sky.


When they arrived at the cottage, they were all already exhausted. Twice in the night they were obliged to unload the truck and ford canals and portage the cargo over dykes to bypass checkpoints. It was hard going waist-deep in freezing water and scrambling up slippery clay banks in the darkness. The truck had to be hauled up the bank with hawser ropes. In the dawn light, Rafe looked like a pale ghost, haggard and covered in clay mud that had dried white as flour; his muscles ached and his hands were red raw with blisters.

There was no time to rest; the frosty grass crunched under Rafe's boots as he jogged across the field to where the Mosquito sat hidden in a copse of elm trees, and he began clearing off the canvas sheets and foliage camouflage. It took all five men to take the weight of the aircraft's wings on their backs while Rachel knocked the supporting blocks out with a mallet. Way too big and heavy for this, they settled her down on her gear, and Rafe checked each tyre with a kick of his boot.

Erik had his mighty bay mare Frieda tacked up and ready to pull the big fighter bomber out of hiding. She puffed out great clouds of steamy breath from her nostrils as she pulled on the yoke and the Mosquito made its majestic progress out into the golden morning light. The low sun played across her clean, sleek lines. Rafe's heart swelled when he saw the proud RAF roundel painted on her side.

"It's smaller than I imagined," said Rachel. "Can it really take the three of us all the way to England?" Rafe thought about the few meagre cans of fuel in the truck and put a reassuring arm around her shoulders. "Certainly!" he said cheerfully. "No problem at all."

It was peak tulip season, and the blooms had transformed the once-barren fields into a vivid patchwork of colour. The grassy green meadow where Rafe had landed weeks before was now a thick carpet of purple and pink flower heads almost knee-high. The bulbs had been planted with great care in rows straight as an arrow, providing an excellent natural runway in line with the offshore wind.

Rafe paced out a generous takeoff run of seven hundred feet, turned, and looked back at Rachel and Anne standing by the Mosquito in the distance, shielding their eyes against the sun. They spied him and began waving happily. Anne capered and danced in circles with delight. He smiled and waved back; he took a deep breath of the clean ocean air and his fatigue lifted like a heavy cloak. He was going home at last, and taking his girl with him.

Something caught his eye in the far distance; a low cloud, perhaps. It changed shape and vanished. Rafe blinked and looked again, using the old fighter pilot's trick of focusing his eye slightly off-centre. The cloud returned, except Rafe knew it wasn't a cloud. A gust of wind brought the faint but unmistakable sound of diesel motors and whining tracks. Rafe's heart sank into the earth, the icy hand of fear gripping his bowels. It was an armoured column, a large one, making its way up the main road and heading straight for them.

Rafe tossed his cigarette and broke into a sprint; his swollen knee screamed out in agony, but he ignored the pain. He shed his jacket and spun it above his head, wildly gesturing with his other hand. At first Rachel and Anne thought he was playing around; Anne even began to copy him until he got close enough for Rachel to see the expression on his face, and she blanched white as a ghost. "We are in trouble," gasped Rafe.

"What is it?"

"Hannie..must have broken.. They're coming down the main road in force—get everybody together now."

Rafe scrambled up the short ladder into the cabin. His exhausted brain struggled to recall the emergency start procedure for the Merlin engines. There was no time to hook up the batteries, they would have to hand-crank them over. Rafe crawled down into the dark fuselage to hunt for the emergency crank lever. Henk's head appeared in the hatchway.

"Are you sure? Could just be tractors, trucks, anything."

"I know the sound of those bloody Hanomags." Rafe found the crank and dropped down out of the hatch. They both ran to the end of the drive and listened intently. Rafe's blood was thudding so loudly in his ears, he had to concentrate to block it out. As the breeze moved in from the east, the sound of birds and trees yielded to the whistle and rattle of revving motors. They both felt the unmistakable swell and shiver under their feet; something colossal was heaving over the earth.

Henk cursed. "How long do we have?"

"Less than twenty minutes. I'd say they are rolling over that last canal bridge now."

Henk loaded and cocked his Sten.

"You won't hold them off with that."

"What then? There's nowhere to hide around here, at least we can die fighting like men."

Rafe gripped Henk's collar. "If I can get in the air now, there is hope—come on!."

When they got back to the plane, Gerrit and Jacob were standing by with the charged batteries.

"No time for that," panted Rafe. "Help me with the fuel."

Try as he might, Rafe couldn't stop his hands shaking as he poured the fuel; a good portion of the precious spirit slopped over the wing, powerful fumes stinging his eyes and nostrils. The German fuel was potent stuff. Within five minutes, the last tin was drained into the aircraft. Rafe tossed it aside and sprang into the cockpit.

Rachel and Anne were crammed into the observer's compartment in the nose; they huddled together, eyes wide as saucepans as they followed Rafe's every movement.

"Whatever you do, don't touch any of the equipment unless I ask you to, understand?" said Rafe as he flipped the booster pumps on. Two small, pale faces nodded in unison; the former levity was gone, both girls absolutely terrified. Rafe took a moment to grasp and kiss Rachel's hand; it was corpse cold. "Don't worry, we will make it out of here, trust me."

Rachel swallowed a sob. "What about father...Erik...?"

Rafe squeezed her hand but looked away; he couldn't save everybody. As he dropped out of the cabin, he could hear them choking on sobs.

There was no time for platitudes. Rafe had to get the two giant Merlin engines running with no power. On a typical airfield, there were ground crew with heavy equipment to generate the electricity needed to crank over the massive V12 motors. Here, Rafe had to fall back on human muscle power. Each engine had a hand-operated fuel primer pump in the nacelles. Rafe quickly showed Gerrit how to operate the portside pump. "Pull this lever up and down slowly, stick your nose up against this hole; as soon as you smell petrol, stop and close it up."

Rafe clambered up into the cabin and went through a mental checklist: he flicked on the booster coil and magneto switches, unlocked the valves for the pneumatic lines, and set the throttles for start-up. There was a reassuring whine as he powered up the instrument panel - there was still just enough charge in the system to spin up the gyroscopes.

The earth was shaking now, and the enemy was closing in. Frieda whickered and stomped; Erik had a hard time restraining her bridle.

"Henk, I need you to follow my hand signals from the cockpit, when I do this..." Rafe made a circular motion with his index finger pointing up. " ..you will need to turn this crank clockwise with all your might." Rafe handed him the S-shaped steel tool; it looked like a toy in Henk's massive fist. "Once the motor spools up, I'll hit the starter switch in there, and the whole show will start, there will be a colossal noise and a huge cloud of smoke—don't pull the crank out until I give you the thumbs up, got it?"

Henk nodded solemnly; he unbuttoned his shirt and stripped down to his waist. Years of rationing had taken its toll on what must have once been a Herculean physique, but he was still lean and taut as a lion, his flanks rippling with sinewy muscle.

Now was the moment of truth. Rafe had to be honest with himself and admit the chances of both engines starting were now quixotic to say the least.

The Rolls Royce twelve-cylinder supercharged engine produced an incredible amount of horsepower on the absolute leading edge of current technology. Even with full battery power in ideal conditions, it often took a team of specialist ground technicians several attempts to get them running right.

The battle-damaged plane had been sitting in a damp tulip field for almost a month; the fuel tanks were barely half-full with who-knows-what German cocktail of synthetic petrol. Even if they had the whole day to work on it, there were about fifty-fifty odds on both engines running up to takeoff power.

Panic suddenly gripped Rafe's guts. Had he led them all on a fool's errand? Had his reckless hubris once again put innocent lives at stake? Ghosts from the past surged up to accuse him: his wife Caroline, her young life ended prematurely in childbirth; Billy, the American boy whose shot-up body mouldered nearby; Hannie, who surely was even now being hanged or worse. Were they all victims of circumstance? Casualties of war?

Rafe turned and looked at Rachel and Anne huddled in terror. Despite her obvious dread, she caught Rafe's eye and smiled, a fragile, fleeting expression of trust.

Immediately, a new resolve lent Rafe renewed courage. He couldn't let self-doubt drag him down now; he had to believe in himself and follow through. With a carefree brio he didn't really feel, Rafe gave Rachel a cheeky wink as he pushed the throttles up and set the mixture to full rich.

Rafe gave Henk the sign and the colossus went to work. The whole aircraft rocked as Henk's powerful body forced the engine into motion, slowly at first, then progressively faster it revolved; the supercharger spun and began its shrill whistle, forcing compressed air into the cylinders.

The pressure built until Rafe saw the fuel begin to mist out of the exhaust ports.

Rafe muttered a silent prayer and pressed the starter button, engaging the magnetos; a series of pops and crackles followed by high-pitched falling whine as the clutches wound down. Rafe frantically gestured to Henk to keep cranking. Again, Rafe engaged the spark, there was a loud, barking cough, and the entire aircraft shuddered. The nine-foot-high propeller began a long, lazy revolution. Rafe held his breath. There was another piercing whine, and abruptly the cylinders fired in sequence, the motor chugging asthmatically and turning over slowly, popping and puffing. The

Mosquito danced left and right on her legs and suddenly exploded into life.

A gigantic cloud of smoke engulfed the field as the mighty Merlin engine cleared her throat. The crank leapt out of his hands and knocked Henk off his perch, two-metre long blue flames shot out of the exhaust ports, and the massive prop vanished into a blur. Gerrit and Jacob turned and ran for their lives as the wind blasted like a force ten hurricane, scattering geese, leaves, and anything not tied down within one hundred feet.

For a heart-stopping moment, the fireworks ended and the motor seemed to die; it spun, misfired, then came back on song with twice the ferocity, pushing the Mosquito dangerously around to port. Rafe eased the throttle down and adjusted the fuel mixture; after a few indecisive moments, the monstrous engine settled into a steady, thunderous pulse.

Rafe was jubilant; he punched the air and whooped, all his fatigue and pain forgotten, his heart soaring.

He had forgotten about the girls; he found them both cowering in the nose with their ears covered The poor dears had never been near a large aircraft and must have thought the apocalypse had come. Rafe gathered them up in his arms.

"Is it supposed to do that?" shouted Rachel over the din of rushing air and hammering machinery.

Rafe laughed with relief, crushing them both in a bear hug. "Yes, my love, it's very much supposed to do that."

The convoy had stopped again. Detzner was apoplectic with rage. The local potato farmer they had collared as a guide was taking them around in circles. He was sure he had seen this rotten old canal bridge before; the old bastard obviously thought he could play them all for fools.

Detzner climbed down out of the half-track and strode over to where his sergeant was stabbing an accusatory finger at the Dutchman. The elderly farmer stood up straight with his chin defiantly raised; he cut a pitiful figure standing there shivering in his pyjamas and muddy bare feet—they hadn't let him dress after he had been kicked from his bed.

Detzner had played enough games with these people; as he approached he casually drew his nine-mm automatic from his holster and lashed the old Boer across the face. The frail old man crumpled to the ground. Detzner kicked him over on his back and put his heavy jackboot on his throat; he racked the slide on the pistol and fired a round into the damp earth an inch from the old man's ear.

"I am going to count to ten; in that time, you will decide whether or not you want to cooperate with us, and a simple nod or shake of the head will do."

The old man drew his knees up to his chest and rolled into the fetal position, pulling his nightshirt over his face. A dark patch of piss spread out from his crotch as he moaned in indignation.

As Detzner drew breath to begin counting, there was a chain of concussive reports in the distance; some of the riflemen instinctively dropped to the ground or dove for cover. It was followed by the distinctive and unmistakable sound of a large aircraft engine starting.

Rafe climbed down out of the cabin and called the men together; in the roaring din and turbulent air, he searched their haunted faces. They all had the hunted look of the condemned. Erik had his ancient bird gun, Gerrit had produced a nine-mm pistol from somewhere. Only Jacob was unarmed, and he refused Rafe's proffered .45. Over the cacophony, he leaned in with a raised voice in Rafe's ear. "I'm no soldier; when the time comes, Gerrit has agreed to do what must be done."

"We can't let them do to us what they did with Hannie; we know too many secrets." shouted Gerrit, face set like concrete. Rafe knew they wouldn't be persuaded otherwise.

Rafe pointed with his chin to the ruin of an old stone *grondzeiler* by some woodland. "That's a decent enough spot with good cover, a good place to make a last stand, and from there you can escape into the woods." They shook hands awkwardly. "Good luck, old boy."

Rafe felt his heart wrench as the doomed trio set off at a trot. There was little doubt that they would all be killed or captured by sunset.

Rafe secured the hatch and made sure Rachel and Anne were securely strapped into the co-pilot harness before hastily running through the pre-flight checklist. Both engines now showed just enough oil pressure for a takeoff run. The pneumatic brake system hissed and they were tossed around in the harnesses as he manoeuvred the plane over the sod field to the tulip rows and aligned himself to the takeoff point; he had chosen a distant windmill as his reference point, which he would keep in the nose pointed.

Once he was lined up, he held the brakes on and took one last look around the cabin. He reached over and squeezed Rachel's trembling hand. He leaned in close and spoke in her ear with as much confidence as he could muster. "In an hour, we will be across the sea and safe in England."

She nodded and squeezed her eyes shut, two fat tears rolling down her cheeks. "Just tell me when we are in the air and I can open my eyes." Anne buried her face into Rachel's blouse and clutched her in a fearful death grip.

Rafe set the prop pitch and supercharger boost for takeoff power. With his left hand, he slowly pushed the throttles forward; the twin Merlin engines' awesome power pulled the aircraft slightly to the left. Rafe corrected the plane's yaw with deft movements on the rudder pedals. Once he saw sixty inches of manifold pressure on the dial, he thrust the throttles all the way to the stop.

He heard Rachel's terrified yelp as the plane suddenly surged forward and bounced down the runway. The ground was not as even as Rafe had hoped, and he fought for control as they rapidly accelerated.

At sixty knots, Rafe eased the stick forward to lower the nose. As the rear wheel lifted off the ground, the lurching and bumping eased, and he had a much clearer view of the ground ahead.

The propeller tips now reached the top edges of the young tulip blooms, shredding twin rooster tails of gaudily-coloured confetti high into the air behind them.

A familiar sound, not unlike a handful of rocks on the roof of a tin shed, caught Rafe's attention. At the same moment, a spiderweb of cracks appeared across the aft of the cockpit glass.

Rafe ducked his head down, grabbing Rachel in a half headlock, and he shouted in her ear.

"Get your harness off and get on the floor, we're taking fire!"

Rafe craned his head around and saw, through the rain of tattered tulips, a company of riflemen in a massive, open-topped half-track advancing across the drainage ditches towards them. For now, the uneven ground fouled their aim, but soon they would reach the flat expanse of the field. A big officer with a bald brown head was struggling to mount a heavy machine gun. Rafe knew that once they had that gun sighted on them, the Mosquito could be torn to shreds in seconds.

Suddenly, one of the riflemen flung his arms up and collapsed over the edge of the vehicle, another's helmet flew off his head and tumbled high in the air, and every man in the vehicle ducked down for cover as sparks of bullet impacts danced off the machine's side armour.

Rafe turned around in his seat and saw a sight that brought tears to his eyes and put a heavy stone in his heart. Henk, Gerrit, and Erik, two middle-aged men and a giant, were charging down the hill, spraying pistol bullets and bird shot at a fifty-ton troop carrier.

Rafe turned back the aircraft controls; the end of the tulip field was fast approaching, and beyond that, the old earthwork dyke and high sand dunes. A glance at the airspeed indicator told him he was about twenty knots shy of normal takeoff speed; his frantic work on the rudder pedals had kept them straight but cost them drag. With an experienced calm, Rafe fought his instinctive reaction to yank back on the stick; he kept the nose pointed down until the last possible second, easing the stick back in a firm, progressive movement just as the main gear cleared the very last row of flowers.

The aircraft shuddered reluctantly into the air. Rafe had to use all his skill to keep the wings level, pumping the rudder pedals and wrestling with the stick. For a moment he felt the sickening, gut-churning, sinking sensation every pilot dreads as the wings began to stall. Ahead a mountainous sand dune loomed, and it seemed hopeless. In desperate frustration, Rafe punched the canopy with his fist and swore. "GET.. UP.. YOU.. BITCH!"

Just as all seemed lost, the machine caught a stiff sea breeze off the beach, the wings seemed to suddenly grip the air and gain lift, she levelled out, and Rafe felt himself pushed down in the seat. He reached down and pulled the landing gear lever. "YES, YES COME ON, COME ON YOU BIG.. BEAUTIFUL.. BITCH!"

As if the machine could hear him, she buoyed up; like a racing yacht catching a swell, she soared up into the air, the tyres of the gear just grazing the very top of the dune as they pulled up into the wings, tucked in like the taloned feet of a great bird of prey.

As Rafe watched the waves recede beneath him and they climbed up into the low cloud base, his elation turned to a withering grief; behind him, three of the bravest men he had ever known were surely suffering; they had sacrificed their lives for their escape, and now would face torture and a lonely death. The cruel injustice of it gnawed at Rafe's bones. Could he live the rest of his life in peace knowing he had flown clear away and left them to that fate?

Rafe reached down to pull Rachel and Anne off the cabin floor. "We are up, we got away."

Rachel was frozen with fear and wouldn't move.

"I heard shooting!" she shouted. "The soldiers found us!"

"They did but we got out." Rafe twisted around in his seat looking for damage; there was no visible oil smoke or leaking fuel, and the small arms fire seemed to have missed its mark. Rafe reached down and rubbed her back, she began to sob.

"Papa," she wept bitterly. "They got Papa." She rocked Anne in her arms, her little body shaking with spasms of grief. Rafe felt his own outrage rise up and threaten to unman him. The instruments blurred as his own tears came. Rafe forced them back.

Detzner watched the dark plane climb up into the clouds; he had been outplayed. The boiling rage and fury at this humiliation had passed on, and it was now strangely serene and quiet, cold and hard as a diamond, a level of vitriolic hatred seldom reached before. He actually felt an icy smile crawl across his face like a spider.

The three assailants had surrendered, they had thrown down their weapons and knelt with hands laced on heads as soon as the aircraft was clear. Detzner had them bound and stood up, and he considered them calmly. They were a motley bunch, two old men and a skinny circus-freak giant.

The giant especially drew Detzner's eye, for he had a self-satisfied twinkle in his eye, a smug smirk on his face. These terrorists most likely had value to the police and Gestapo, but Detzner was in no mood to take prisoners - they would have to pay a higher price for making Detzner look the fool in front of his men.

At bayonet point, he had them blindfolded and lined up in a single- file line. "Everybody mount up, we move out now." Detzner himself took control of the foremost Hanomag, and he carefully manoeuvred it into position. Some of the men realised what was happening and began to look away squeamishly. He ordered the second machine to pull in line behind him. One of the NCOs asked sheepishly.

"Shouldn't these men be interrogated? I mean, we have to write a report and..."

"Shut the fuck up, you fool, they were killed trying to escape... do you have a problem with that, sergeant?" The other man glanced around for some support; none of the other officers would make eye contact, as they all quickly found something important to do.

Detzner leaned in close. "Well, sergeant, do we have a problem?" His breath made the other man's eyes water. The sergeant took a step back, clicked his heels, and saluted. "No problem, Colonel. *Sieg Heil!*" He pushed his way to the back of the cab and sat down.

Detzner lined up the massive front tyre to the giant's turned back. Hopefully by the time they figured out what was happening it would be too late; even if they fled on foot, he could easily run them down, and it would be some good sport.

Detzner drained the last of his schnapps bottle and tossed it over the side He then calmly lit one of his good Davidoff cigarillos, puffing contentedly and savouring the rich, aromatic flavour.

An annoying buzzing sensation disturbed his indulgence; it seemed to be getting stronger, like the air was singing, a deep bass thrumming sensation he felt in his chest and his bowels. Some of the men behind him began shouting and pointing at the sky. Drunkenly, Detzner slowly turned around.

The thing suddenly burst out of the clouds like an enormous black crow. Detzner watched in stunned disbelief as it speared down directly at him; he found he was quite paralysed with fear, his feet felt nailed to the floor. Some of the men crowded into the vehicles, ducked down, and covered their heads; some attempted to vault over the high armoured sides; one or two even tried to work the bolts of their rifles and take aim at the thing. The three men, blindfolded and hands bound, stood and bolted in all directions; instinct told them to head for some sort of cover, and they were the only ones able to do so, since the rest were packed into the open-topped half-tracks and weighed down with weapons and equipment.

The high explosive-filled twenty-mm cannon shells came rippling down like a leaden hail storm, ploughing a deep furrow in the ground and kicking up geysers of earth ten-feet high. When the stream of tracers reached the steel armour and soft flesh of men and machine, they shredded both with equal effectiveness. Pink mist, glittering sparks, splinters of bone, and molten metal mixed with cartwheeling rags of cloth filled the air. Every third shell from the Hispano cannon had a chromium moly armour piercing tip;

these punched right through the steel plating and penetrated the fuel tanks, adding a fire-ball cloud of burning fuel to the conflagration.

It was all complete in a few seconds of ferocious violence; the few soldiers that escaped the storm of steel crawled on hands and knees, burning like human torches before they were finally overcome and collapsed.

Triumphantly, the Mosquito pulled up and banked away west, leaving twin whirling vortices in the black smoke. Rafe dipped a wing to see Henk, Gerrit, and Erik take to the woods; there seemed nobody else was left to give chase.

The low-level strafing attack had cost them, though Rafe had to climb again to cruising altitude; there was now no contingency for evasive manoeuvres should they come across any enemy aircraft. Rafe had to fly straight as an arrow at fifteen-thousand feet to have a chance of making it.

Rafe trimmed the plane up on the best heading, riding a slight northeast.

Rafe managed to get Rachel up in her seat and strapped in, and he made sure they both wore the two remaining yellow "Mae West" life vests and inflated them.

For about half an hour, they flew on in silence. Rachel seemed numb; she had stopped crying and stared out the window at the sky and the ocean below, Anne had fallen into an exhausted sleep.

Finally she spoke. "It's so beautiful, isn't it?" She was gazing dreamily at the high, mountainous peaks of cumulonimbus as they drifted by.

"It's the most beautiful place on earth, the sky." Rafe put his hand on her knee. "I can't wait to show you everything..."

"..Are they all dead?" Abruptly, she turned and looked right into his eyes. Her face was empty, her eyes dull and out of focus.

Rafe took a deep breath, he gripped her by the shoulder, and shook her hard.

"I saw Henk, Erik, and Gerrit run into the woods; they escaped. I hit that formation hard, none of those soldiers could have survived; I saw them all burn.

"And my father, Jacob, you saw him?"

Rafe looked away, he shook his head. "I didn't see Jacob."

"Maybe he burned, too, then?"

"No, no, I didn't see him at all; he wasn't with them...he.."


"..It doesn't matter, anyway." She returned to gazing out at the sky. "There will be more soldiers, always more will come."

Rafe tried to think of something comforting to say. The unfortunate reality was that Jacob probably chose to take his own life rather than be captured alive; he was the head of the operation in Rotterdam and had the most to give up under torture. The others decided on a suicidal charge.

Rachel was right about one thing: none of it would matter if they didn't make it over the Channel, so he had to focus on making that happen.

Rafe did some running arithmetic with a grease pencil on a cigarette packet. He calculated the ground speed, factoring in a guess on the wind to get the distance travelled; he compared that to how many approximate minutes of flight time per gallon of fuel.

He was exhausted, and his mind kept wandering away from the task at hand; his eyes wouldn't focus on the numbers he was scribbling down. He kept seeing the burning soldiers on their hands and knees, the glowing gunsight in his eyes; however he tried, the numbers wouldn't add up.

All the time he had to scan the sky for other aircraft, friend or foe; they could easily get shot at or collide with RAF flights in this busy wartime airspace.

He checked the fuel levels and pumped what remained in the fuselage tank into the starboard wing tank. All the time he wavered between the outcome, they would make it with fuel to spare, or they would pull up ten miles short of the coast, back and forth.

It was actually Rachel who spotted it first. The blue haze on the horizon changed shape and darkened; it could have been a bank of rain clouds, the seconds ticked by, the engines droned on.

It grew, and suddenly it was unmistakable: it was land. Rafe's spirits lifted; it could only be the eastern coast of the British Isles, they were in sight. He saw his dead-reckoning navigation had been accurate enough, and he recognized the beaches of Norwich County, the sandy bulge of coastline he had been aiming for.

It was almost simultaneous with the first sputter of the port engine. Rafe pulled the throttle back, the starboard engine soon following; it surged and coughed, belching oily smoke.

The coast drew closer. Rafe cut both throttles to almost idle and they began to sink.

Rafe's exhausted brain was playing tricks on him; at first he thought they would sail right over the coast and make it halfway to London, then he thought they would drop straight down into the Channel like a stone. They dropped down and down, and Rafe watched the vertical speed needle begin its spiral. Rachel seemed oblivious to it at first, then she seemed to awaken from her dreamy stupor and sense the danger.

"You have to wake up Anne; we could end up in the drink, make sure you have her vest secure."

"Where is yours?"

"There are no more; just please do as I say, I have to concentrate."

Both wing fuel gauges read dead-empty now; they were running on fumes and sinking fast. The beaches still looked unreachable. Rafe cursed himself bitterly; if it wasn't for his foolhardy decision to turn back and play the hero, they would have made it—he should have just followed the plan and they would have survived.

Rafe spotted a Royal Navy Destroyer turning below about five miles out; they had seen him and were coming in to investigate. That was a chance, at least; he had to turn into them and pray the lookout didn't mistake them for a *Luftwaffe* bomber coming in to attack and open fire.

He made a slight banking turn on an intercept course and both engines sputtered and went dead; he feathered the propellers and shut them down. Now they were gliding.

With the engines dead, Rafe could speak normally. "Rachel, we are going into the water, do you understand?" She nodded. "Are we going to die now?"

Rafe smiled sadly; he stroked her face and kissed her forehead. He lied, "Good Lord, no, we are just going for a bit of an unplanned swim."

He glanced over at the destroyer; it was moving fast, plunging gamely over the swells; they must have recognised them or they would have fired on them by now—there was a chance, a small one. If the crew of that destroyer were good, Rachel and Anne could be rescued.

"You must stay strapped in until we hit the water, and we will hit it very hard—hold tight to Anne. I'm going to release you from the harness and you are going to swim for that big boat over there that's coming to get us, okay?"

"What about you?"

"Don't worry about me, I'll be right behind you. Take your shoes off." Rachel did as he said.

Rafe felt the stick go limp in his hand; the sea raced up to meet him, and he artfully used the last of his airspeed to pull the nose up. The tail wheel kissed the top of the waves just as both wings stalled, a perfect sea ditching. Even so, the impact was violent; Rafe's arm smashed into the instrument panel, he felt his collar bone snap on his harness, and his head slammed into the canopy. A bright flash of white light. When he regained his senses, they were afloat; he leaned over and detached Rachel from her harness—she had fared better than him, but a thin trickle of blood ran down her scalp into her eye.

Freezing cold sea water rushed into the cabin. Rafe pulled the emergency canopy release lanyard and smashed it off with his good elbow; more sea water rushed in, the shock of the cold water numbing. Rafe fumbled with his harness. Rachel was free and floating upwards; she grabbed the collar of his flying jacket and tried to pull him up, but he managed to break her grip and push her away. The freezing water quickly sucked him down, and it was salty in his mouth.

Suddenly, he was submerged; he saw Rachel's pale little feet kicking in front of his face. He felt  cold. Tired and cold.

# Acre, Israel 1956

Rachel looked out to the sea; she shaded her eyes from the low morning sun, relishing the salt-scented breeze. She recalled a beach not unlike this one, many years ago, it seemed. The memory brought a stirring from her belly. She stroked the developing bulge; it was heavy now, growing fast.

The tinkling sound of laughing children behind her made her smile; she had three now. She never imagined herself as a mother, never imagined she would be raising her family in this place, so far away from home.

There was a little tug on her skirt. She looked down and saw a mischievous little boy's face; he smiled and spoke in a plumb English schoolboy accent.

"Grandpapa Jacob said we can have ice cream for breakfast." He screwed up his little freckled nose.

"That sounds about right," Rachel replied indulgently. He put both fists on his hips and tilted his head, and when he did that, he looked just like his dad.

"He also said that when he met Father, he tried to kill him in the war."

Rachel chuckled and patted his head. "Oh, now that sounds wrong."

"How did Father die in the war?"

Rachel picked him up and settled him on her hip. "I'll tell you the whole story one day."